THE ACADEMY OF THE FAE

A CONTEMPORARY SCIENCE FANTASY

RETURN OF THE FAE

BOOK THREE

MARTY C. LEE

Bookaholics Press

Book design, cover, and publication by Bookaholics Press LLC
Edited by Martha Rasmussen
Author photograph by Melissa C. Baxter

ISBN-13: 978-1-950230-41-9 (epub)
978-1-950230-42-6 (paperback)
978-1-950230-43-3 (large print)
978-1-950230-44-0 (hardback)
978-1-950230-67-9 (audio)

Published by Bookaholics Press LLC
Provo, Utah bookaholicspress@gmail.com

Contact the author at MCLeeBooks.com

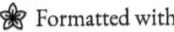 Formatted with Vellum

For Virginia, my favorite teacher,
and for my James, who brings the stars to my eyes.

CONTENTS

Academy Maps

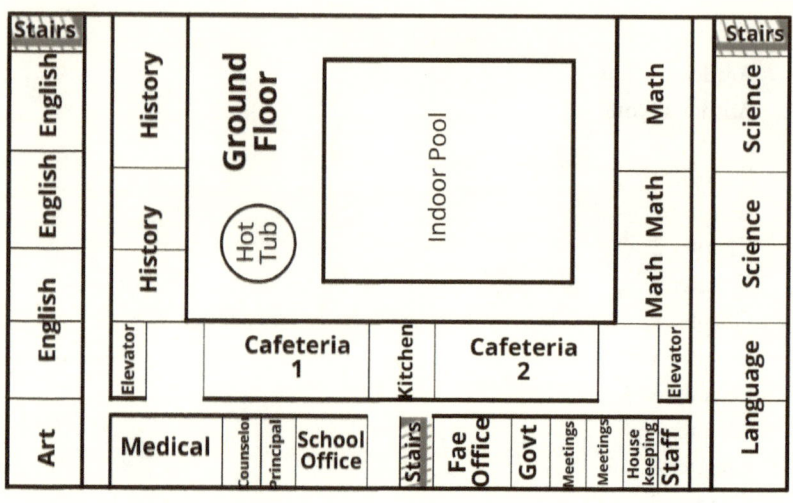

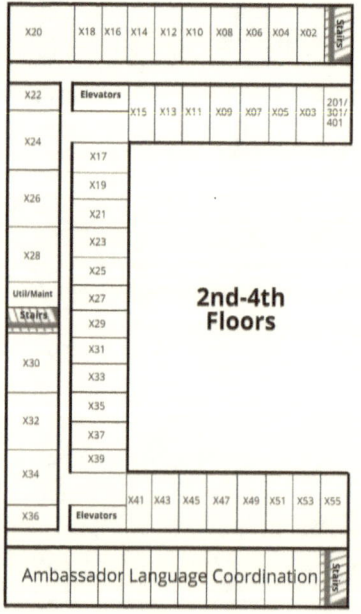

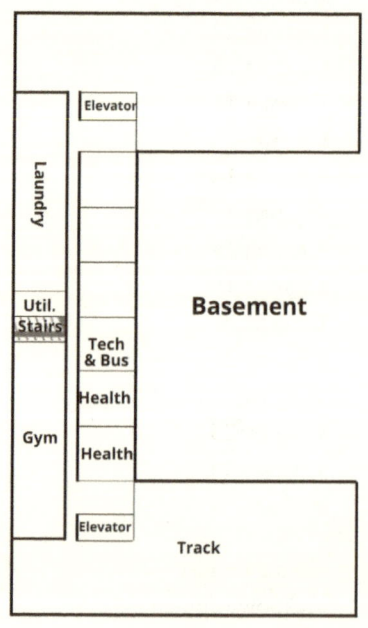

Author's Note

While I have been meticulous to real life detail and science in some places, in others I could not find information, or changed things for the sake of the story or to protect real people, or simply made mistakes. Most of all, please remember this is a work of fiction. The characters are completely imaginary.

PROLOGUE

FIRST DAY

August 29, 2022, Allentown, Pennsylvania, United States of America, Earth

The alarm rang shrilly, and Ian Fitch stuffed his pillow over his head to block the sound. Five a.m. was way too early.

"Woof," Gil said. The massive wolf stuck his nose under the pillow and licked Ian's cheek.

"Okay, okay." Ian flipped the pillow onto the wolf and crawled out of bed.

On the other side of the room, his new oldest brother Nikos was already heading out the door, clothes piled neatly in his arms. The private shower in the girls' room came on, followed by the one in the hall.

Ian sighed. "Not fair. By the time I get to shower, the water will be cold."

Gil shook his black fur, jingling the silver crest and the gold ring he wore on a fine chain around his neck. He shifted to boy and laughed. "Too slow."

He dressed quickly in his usual knee-length skirt and colorful t-shirt, merely finger-combing his straight black hair to cover his noticeably pointed ears. Getting him a proper haircut to fix the mess Nikos had made was still on the list of things to do, but the school barber had been busy with all the new students who needed trims even worse. After all, they couldn't take aliens to a hair salon without blowing the secret of their existence.

Once shod in sandals, since Mom refused to let Gil go barefoot, he grabbed his pink backpack and bounded carefully out of the room. Ever since his broken leg had healed and his bones had strengthened enough to lose the crutches a few days ago, he walked more like a rabbit than a wolf. Ian wasn't sure if that was sheer bouncy personality or the remnant habit of half-G.

Ian made a face and gathered his own clothes. He *could* bathe at night like Alexandria, Miknon, and Gil did, but then he'd have to stop reading earlier. But... now that school was starting, Ian had swim class right after seminary. He had to shower after that anyway, so why bother now? And tomorrow he could sleep in another fifteen minutes. Perfect.

Grinning, he threw off his pajamas and pulled on shorts and a plain t-shirt. In this heat, there was no way he'd wear pants, and his new school didn't have stupid uniforms. He dragged a comb through his hair, then tossed his bangs out of his eyes. Good enough. He threw his swimsuit, comb, and notebook of alien vocabulary into his backpack, then hunted for his school ID.

He still hadn't found it by the time the water turned off in both bathrooms. Argh! Good thing he didn't need to shower after all. His ID wasn't on his dresser — where it ought to be — nor in it. Not in his yard-sale nightstand. Not on the closet floor. Nowhere in the folding bookcase Grandma had made.

Nikos came back, freshly scrubbed, hair combed into orderly curls, and wearing long pants and a shirt pressed last night. The overachiever grabbed his already packed bag and walked out.

Ian crawled under the bunkbed.

"Ian," Mom called.

"Yeah, yeah," he grumbled.

Ah ha, there it was! He wiggled farther under the bed, stretching his arm to the max, but could barely touch the stupid badge.

"Ian!" Alexandria bellowed.

"Coming," he yelled. He stretched another inch and grabbed his ID, then wiggled backward.

The whole family was crowded in the doorway, watching him. Alexandria, also headed to early morning seminary, had a half-eaten bagel sandwich in one hand. The others would eat at school with all the students, to translate and explain things.

Ian waved the badge. "Found it."

Mom sighed. "Okay, are you ready now?" She offered a granola bar and a banana.

He grabbed his backpack and the food. "Of course."

Nikos jingled the keys and tossed them to Alexandria. "Your turn."

"Ugh." Ian's sister shrugged her backpack higher on her uninjured shoulder and strode for the door, long legs outpacing everyone.

She also wore shorts, but with a pretty blouse that made her look too grown-up. Since she normally wore t-shirts with astronomical jokes, Ian wondered if she was nervous about their first day. What did she have to be nervous about? She was smart, athletic, and *tall*. Even the slash across her back barely slowed her.

It wasn't fair that Ian got three new siblings this year but was still the youngest. And the only one who was shorter hardly counted in the height department, all things considered.

Gil bounced after Alexandria, Miknon perched on his shoulder as usual. The little fairy kept her place by holding onto her adopted brother's necklace and balancing with half-spread wings. With her blue skin and his black, they looked more different than Nikos, who came from Greece. Ian rolled his eyes. As if skin color was the most shocking difference for *aliens*.

Mom followed, firmly clasping her new briefcase, one of Alexandria's thrift store finds. Her school badge was already hanging around her neck, and she wore a determined smile.

Nikos motioned for Ian to go next. "Hurry up, slow poke."

"Who's slow?" Ian dashed through the house, dodging around Mom and Gil in the kitchen and reaching the front door so close behind Alexandria that he almost crashed into her.

Now that Gil could climb into the truck himself, loading all six of them took only a couple of minutes. Gil even knew how to fasten his own seatbelt, running it through the straps of the backpack Miknon used for a safety restraint.

"I've been thinking," Nikos said.

"Uh oh," Alexandria teased.

Nikos raised an eyebrow. "We shouldn't keep calling them 'aliens.' They must have a name for themselves." He turned around in the front seat and looked at Gil. "What should we call your people?"

Aliens was perfectly accurate, since they came from somewhere in outer space, but it *was* kind of rude. Ian should have thought of that himself.

Gil rummaged in his backpack and pulled out one of the three books he always carried. He flipped through the pages, looking at the pictures of myths. "Us, yes. Your word?"

He held up the open book for everyone to see. That was typical of Gil, always wanting to know the Earth word before he offered his own. Nikos looked thoughtful.

"Elves?" Alexandria suggested.

"Werewolf," Ian said.

"That's too specific," Mom said. "We need something to describe them collectively. But calling them myths and legends seems too confusing."

"Ah, of course," Nikos said. "The fae."

"That's perfect," Mom said. "I should have thought of it earlier. Is that okay, Gil?"

Gil nodded and closed his book.

"I'll tell Ms. Maxwell and the rest of the staff," Mom said. "Are you all ready for school?"

"Orientation is the same old same old," Alexandria said, "except the last of the new students arrived over the weekend." She flexed her hands on the steering wheel and scowled.

What was her problem? Ian scowled with her. *He* wasn't even supposed to be in high school, much less a top-secret one. When the government discovered he was the best Alienglish — uh, Fae speaker, they made him skip a grade so he could translate or teach for half his day. Too bad they wouldn't let him stay in homeschool, because then he could have translated all day long. But no, he had to be an official high school student as well as a teacher.

And who would take him seriously? He was just a kid. He'd filled an entire notebook with Gil's vocabulary, but what if it wasn't enough? All the human students in the school were there to learn Fae, like the fae teens needed to learn English to start with, and other human languages if they had time. That was the whole point of the secret school, along with teaching the fae how to live on Earth.

Once all the students had enough language in common, they would be ambassadors for the rest of the fae when they landed. With that as the goal, two thirds of the human students were juniors or seniors in order to produce graduates sooner. As for the fae, Gil was the youngest and one of the few fae sophomores.

The first barge full of adults had landed only last week, and they were housed in a nearby building. More were expected every week from the spaceship parked on the moon, and in a year or so, the rest of the fleet would arrive. Then they'd have to tell the world about the fae, and the fate of Earth depended on making a treaty with them. Which needed a common language. What if he messed it all up?

A hand entered his field of vision and patted him on the knee. He looked up and met Gil's knowing blue eyes.

"Okay, Ian," Gil murmured. "Okay."

Ian took a deep breath. Gil had come to Earth to make the treaty, so if he thought they were still doing fine, then they must be. At least, Ian would go with that theory until someone told him differently.

They made the last turn, and the school came into view, lights already shining against the dark morning sky. They drove past it a few blocks to the church building where seminary was held.

"Do you remember the way to school?" Mom asked.

"We can almost see the school from here," Alexandria said. "We won't get lost."

"Does everyone know their new schedule?" Mom clenched her briefcase tighter.

Nikos grinned widely. "College after breakfast. I'll be back after work to bring everyone home."

Since Ian and Alexandria had early morning seminary, Mom and

Nikos were taking the breakfast shift for translating and orientation. Mom would spend the rest of the day teaching history.

Alexandria frowned. "I have calculus after seminary, and lifeguarding before supper. Everything else is translating."

Ah, there was the scowl again. Gil reached forward and patted her shoulder, and she sighed.

"Yes, Mom," Ian said. "I know my schedule."

During his swim class, he would also translate for the fae students in physical therapy. Then algebra and Spanish before translating for fae English classes until supper. Algebra homework would have to wait until after that, though he expected to get Spanish done during class.

Mom took a deep breath. "Okay, we'll see you in an hour."

Alexandria parked, and she and Ian headed for the church while Nikos hopped into the driver's seat. Ian stared at his ID badge. "Student-Faculty." Like that was a real thing. He stuffed it back into his pocket. At least Alexandria and Nikos looked like adults. He didn't even look like he belonged in high school.

Clutching his backpack strap, he tried to stand taller. He knew more of the fae language than any other human. That had to count for something.

Didn't it?

Chapter 1

In Which the Fae Start School

Zakiti sat in front of the mirror and tried not to gag on the fear rising in her throat. The magic glass reflected her image perfectly — too perfectly.

"You look good, Zee," Gaby said.

Her roommate smiled from her seat on Zak's neatly made bed. Her own was above Zak's, mirroring the bunks across the room.

With her greater language skills from an extra conjunction on Earth, Miknon translated that into Fae. The blue pixie had arrived a few minutes ago and was still perched on Zak's shoulders so she could reach her hair.

She pushed the last hairpin in more securely. "There, you're done."

Zak twitched her full skirt away from the wheels of the chair, tugged on the short sleeves of her bodice, and touched the single braid plaited in a crown around her head. Nearly all the fae had braided their hair on the ship to keep it from shedding all over or floating around when they were weightless, but men and women still wore different styles. And this was not her usual boy's arrangement.

"Look I girl," she mumbled in her pitiful Ki words.

At least she was covered in this outfit, unlike the embarrassing "swim-suit" they wore for therapy. Her other two roommates had already left for the first swim class before breakfast.

Miknon patted Zak's long green ear. "You are a girl."

Technically, perhaps, but Zak had spent her whole life pretending she was male, even in her own thoughts. From the time she was a baby, her father told everyone she was a boy to protect her from the lords who had murdered her grandmother just for being a female contriver. Grand-mother had invented the navigation device that led them to Ki, and they couldn't stand her having that power and influence.

But now Father was still among the stars, and Zak was here, going to school with creatures nobody had dreamed existed. Ki — Earth — was supposed to be either empty or populated with the descendants of rebel fae who had fled their home world of Kunisu tens of thousands of conjunctions earlier. Either scenario would have made it easy for the current refugees to move in. These humans complicated everything, both for the fae in general and Zak in particular.

For one thing, she no longer had a private room with Father in the navigation tower, and thus couldn't maintain her disguise. As soon as Father returned, she would leave this school to live with him, and then she could go back to pretending to be a boy.

But more importantly, the humans and fae had to find a way to get along. Everything depended on the treaty the fae hoped to make. Most of the fae. Some of them still thought that conquering Earth was a better solution. Stupid. War always had casualties, and warring against unknown capabilities was even more stupid.

"Are you ready?" Gaby asked.

"Yes," Zak lied.

Oh, she was looking forward to going to school for the first time in her life, but she only knew a few Earth words. What if they changed their mind about letting girls and commoners take classes? What if they decided they only wanted students who already spoke the language? No, that was silly; they had specifically said they wanted everyone to learn the Earth language.

But what if that was all they were willing to teach her? On the ship, she had been one of the best navigators, after Father, but here she hadn't even known how to turn on the water or lights. Every day, Gaby taught her something new. Today had been "zippers," an amazing contrivance, though simple in design. Sadly, Gaby hadn't been able to explain how the lights really worked. Someone had to understand them, though. Zak just had to discover who.

If she could learn enough about their contrivances to integrate them with fae knowledge or determine what the humans lacked, that would be a trade opportunity to offer in the treaty, as well as her abilities as a navigator. The more they could offer to the humans, the more likely they would win a peaceful home. But she was the only one who could offer those skills. None of the other navigators had landed yet, and when they did, they wouldn't know the language.

Gaby hung Zak's book bag on the handles of the wheeled chair and slipped her own onto her back. Miknon stayed on Zak's shoulder while Gaby pushed the chair to the deck-transfer, so much more convenient than the ramps on the ship.

"El-e-bay-tur," Miknon practiced as they waited for the doors to open.

"Ele-Vator," Gaby corrected.

"Vvvv," Zak droned.

The deck-transfer arrived — the elevator — and Gaby pushed the chair inside. Once on the correct deck, she maneuvered between other wheeled chairs to the large dining hall, where half the school ate breakfast at once. They found places on the left side of the room, and Gaby lifted Miknon to her miniature chair on top of the table. On the right side, the human Nik nodded at Miknon and raised his hands for silence.

The fae instantly stopped chattering, but it took the humans a few minutes to settle down. Zak shook her head at their lack of discipline.

"Good morning," Nik said in human, then "Greetings," in fae. "Welcome to the first day of school."

He continued, speaking in a mix of both languages as he explained what to expect. When he got stuck on fae vocabulary, Miknon provided the words. Nik's adopted mother and Gil would do the same for the next breakfast shift, and Nik's siblings helped at meals later in the day.

Zak listened intently, proud that by now she could understand most of Nik's admittedly simple sentences. It helped that he had said many of the same things every morning, but what was important was that she was finally remembering the words.

"Every morning, we will have translators here to help," Nik said. "For this time, Miknon and I are available." He pointed across the room, and Miknon waved. "You can ask either of us, though we are still better in our own languages."

For now, Zak preferred to ask Miknon. Though her friend knew fewer answers, she was still easier to understand. Once Zak's vocabulary was bigger, she already had a list of questions for the humans. So many questions.

Nik answered a few questions from humans who had only arrived a couple of days ago, then sat to eat. After two weeks of eating with Zak and Miknon, Gaby knew what they liked and sped up the process by fetching it for all three of them without the nuisance of Zak's wheeled chair.

Miknon named all the foods for everyone who asked, in the opposite language of the one they knew. She answered random questions from fae and humans alike until a bell rang. Unlike the musical bells on the ship, this one only bleated in one tone, no matter what time it was. Obediently, Zak and the rest of the students headed for their next location, leaving the room empty for the incoming diners.

Gaby pushed Zak's chair first to the pool, where she dropped off Miknon, then to the door outside. Before class, Zak had chores. She was nearly useless in the kitchen, but Ash had agreed to let her help in the garden. The blinding light of Earth's star stabbed Zak's eyes until she put on the dark eye shields.

"Greetings," Ash chirped.

The dryad had already crawled from his chair to sit on the ground and weed the garden. Leafy tendrils snaked from his red hair to hold a wide-brimmed hat in place. There were no trees next to the building, but he had planted vegetables and herbs that already poked up as small green leaves. His magic was also a good future trade commodity, and once the fleet landed, there would be many dryads available to grow gardens.

Other fae were scattered around the garden, carefully weeding or watering. Some leaned over from their wheeled chairs, while others had copied Ash to sit on the ground.

"Good morning, Abe," Gaby said, using his human name.

The fae generally shared their names only with close friends as security against thought-mages. The only reason Zak knew part of Ash's name was because he was Gil's friend. In fact, Gil probably knew more names than almost anyone, since he somehow made friends everywhere.

But apparently humans weren't satisfied without names to use, so Shalla and Mak-swill had assigned names to most of the fae. Gil and Miknon had already given their names to the humans, like trusting idiots.

"Okay," Gaby said, "I'll come get you for class." She patted Zak on the shoulder and hurried back inside.

Ash eyed Zak's outfit, and she held her breath, dreading his opinion of her new identity. Since they had landed and her disguise was ruined, she spent as much time as possible in her room, especially avoiding anyone who knew her on the ship. For her, that was fairly easy, since she had spent her entire life avoiding people. Even among the fae, few knew she existed. Most of those who had met her either worked in navigation or were friends with Gil.

"You'll be weeding the carrots," Ash said. "Remember that they only get feathery when they're bigger. Right now, they look like *this*." He pointed to two thin leaves.

"Okay." Zak used the Earth word for practice, thankful he said nothing about her new femininity. Maybe it wouldn't matter now that they weren't on the ship. The humans didn't seem to care.

Ash laughed. "Okay."

He bumped himself to the next row of plants and instructed another worker. Zak slid from her chair and carefully pulled everything that didn't match "baby carrot" description. The sunlight burned on her shoulders, and by the time Gaby came to collect her, she was sweating. The ship had never been this hot, and if Gaby hadn't looked totally unconcerned, Zak would have worried.

With her roommate's help, Zak got back into her chair, and Gaby pushed her into the building, winding through the crowded halls. Wheeled chairs and wagons streamed in all directions, and sometimes a tiny, noisy barge would zip between feet with a small fae perched on top.

"I hate chair," Zak said. "You hate push."

"I don't mind," Gaby said. "When you're stronger, you will get a chair you can push yourself. We don't want your bones to snap by doing too much."

Once she deciphered most of the words, Zak sighed. Gaby was right, of course. The ship had used acceleration to maintain half-weight for half the time and no weight otherwise, but that simply wasn't enough to keep their bones completely solid through such a long flight. And it was worse for most of the youngsters, who had spent little time on a planet before the journey. Gil and Ram had been born only the day before they evacuated their old world, though as shifters, they had an advantage in rehabilitating their bones. The non-shifters were stuck with time and exercise as their only solutions.

Miknon and Gil had been on the planet half a conjunction longer than any of the other fae, and Gil was gingerly walking. Zak expected some of the other shifters to start walking any day.

"Here we are." Gaby turned around and pushed the door open with her back so she could pull Zak's chair through.

At the front, Gil's friend Alex stood with Miknon. "Sit any place," Alex said in Fae.

The large room was filling with the wheelchairs streaming in. A few tables served as high podiums for the smaller fae, who were lifted up by their roommates. Gaby rolled Zak to a stop in the front row, then hurried out the door to her own class.

"Welcome to math and science class," Alex said half in Human and half in Fae. "When teacher come, we learn numbers and how world works."

Zak sat up straight. How the world works. Perfect! Once she knew where she had knowledge the humans lacked, she would know what to tell Gil to offer in the treaty. And if the humans knew anything she did not, she wanted to know it all.

"For now," Alex continued, "we learn words."

She wrote something on the front wall. The class gasped at her blatant use of magic. Alex sighed and rubbed a black block over the writing. It disappeared without a mark, and the class gasped again. Zak itched to examine the block, not that she could detect magic anyway.

Alex's mouth twitched. "I write numbers, okay? No magic in writing or taking away. We learn now."

On one side of the board, she wrote the fae numerals Zak knew. On the other side, she rewrote new characters, then said their names out loud. All the fae practiced counting until the bell rang again and their roommates arrived to collect them.

"How was class?" Gaby asked as she pushed Zak to lunch.

Zak shrugged. "Numbers good."

Gaby laughed. "I like numbers, too."

In the dining hall, Gaby and Zak joined the line for food. Someone pulled up behind them and cleared his throat. Zak looked over her shoulder and waved the highborn and his chair-pusher in front of her, then watched them progress through the line until they stopped behind someone of higher rank. Ironically, they passed Shar, who would have been at the very front if he weren't still hiding his identity as prince.

"What?" Gaby protested. "You can't do that."

Zak stared blankly at her. "But he more important."

Gaby said a word Zak didn't recognize. "No way."

Their other roommates entered, and Freya motioned for Jinyuan to push her toward the front of the line.

"Stop," Gaby said. "Jin, what are you doing?"

Jin shrugged and pushed her pink-and-blue striped hair out of her eyes. "She said someone was holding her place in line."

"Is highborn," Zak said. "Always first."

"Wait," Jin said. "Always first? That's not fair."

"Is highborn," Zak repeated.

"Highborn my eye," Gaby said. "We don't do things like that here."

She stomped over to the adults in a corner. Though she didn't yell, or even talk loud enough for Zak to hear, her waving arms expressed her frustration. The Helen-teacher frowned at the line, then rose to her feet and called for attention.

"I sorry I not notice before," she said in Fae, "but we eat by who here first, not by who we are. If you come late, you eat late."

The highborn stared blankly at her, then turned their heads away. After surprised looks at each other, the fae adults nodded.

"Move back to where you were when you entered the room," Shalla commanded. Without the lords, the king's housekeeper was one of the highest authorities they presently had.

The highborn made various expressions of disdain, but when every fae adult nodded, they groaned. The humans moved their highborn roommates backward, and the line continued.

Gaby nodded briskly at Zak. "I told you, we don't do that here." She handed a tray to Zak. "Do you want me to read the food?"

Zak nodded, though she was too stunned to listen to any of it. When it was her turn, she pointed to the first item, took a familiar blue drink box, and held both her and Gaby's trays on her lap while Gaby pushed them to a table.

The random food she had selected was as strange as usual but no worse. She ate quietly, listening to the humans talk about the situation. She didn't understand most of the words, but it was clear they thought something was wildly unfair.

Why were they upset? The highborn had always had preference, like men ranked over women. If that weren't true, she wouldn't have had to disguise her gender her whole life. But she didn't have the vocabulary to ask Gaby about it. The only surprise was that the highborn had gone along with the command to get back in line according to their time of arrival. Either they were still used to the order maintained on the ship, or they hadn't yet decided how far they wanted to goad the humans. Or both.

After lunch, Gaby left her to study before returning to push her to her next class. This one was in an equally large room, also occupied by fae. The teacher was another of Gil's human friends. Zak studied the pale-haired boy, who wasn't much taller than she was.

When the bell rang, U.N. smiled. "Welcome to English class," he said in Fae. "Our regular teacher hasn't arrived yet, so I will teach you until then. Once he comes, I'll translate for you."

A nearly inaudible hum of surprise marked the reaction to his fluent speech. Zak raised her eyebrows. Yet again, Gil was right. He said some humans were learning Fae rapidly.

"Let's start with Earth introductions," U.N. said. "The first thing you need to know is that it is considered rude not to say your name."

The class muttered.

"I know," U.N. said, "it's the opposite for you. But humans can't read your minds, and you don't have to say your *real* name. Chantelle helped us give you all human names, so let's practice with those."

Shalla was important enough that all the fae knew her name anyway, but using her alias was good practice, and of course, the humans knew only her Ki name. U.N. chose Shar from the front row and after talking quietly for a minute, the two demonstrated the introduction for the class, using the Ki words.

"Hello," U.N. said. "My name is Ian Fitch. Nice to meet you."

Zak shook her head at his slip. He should always go by his use-name, even around people who knew his real name.

"Heylo, U.N.," Shar said, compensating for the mistake. "I em Shaun Smith. Nise too meet yu."

"Some people shake hands," U.N. said, "but it's not required, so we'll skip that part."

A collective sigh of relief swept the room. Sharing their name and a touch would give any thought-mage the ability to read their minds. The fake names should prevent that, but old habits were deeply ingrained.

"Everyone pick a partner," U.N. said. "I want you to practice introducing yourself to at least three people, even if you already know each other."

Zak raised an eyebrow. Most of them were strangers, or nearly so. The ship had four living decks, and most of the fae stayed on their own deck. But when she turned to her right, the writhing hydra overflowing a little red barge was another of Gil's friends. The bouncy shifter had way too many friends, but right now, Zak was glad of it. At least she didn't have to practice first with a complete stranger.

"Heylo," Zak said. "I em Zee Brown. Nise too meet yu."

Shalla had assigned all the highborn the same second name, and all the commoners another. Even if the humans didn't care about rank, the highborn would be intolerable if they had to share a name with commoners.

"Heylo, Zee," the hydra said. "I em Nate Brown." He pronounced the Ki name carefully. "Nise meet yu."

"Nise *too* meet yu," Zak whispered.

One of Nate's heads ducked in embarrassment, but he corrected himself. Zak turned to her left and repeated the exercise.

As she spun her chair to talk to the person behind her, U.N. raised his voice. "This time, tell the other person something about yourself, like what you did on the ship or what you like about school."

"Heylo," the highborn facing her said. "I em Wes Smith. I do—" He made a face. "I have shielding magic," he said in Fae.

"Heylo, Wes," Zak said. "I em Zee." She considered saying that she liked the world and numbers class, but he had offered his job, and it would be rude not to do the same. "I—" She didn't know the words, either, and finally resorted to their native language. She would have to ask Gil about the vocabulary later. "I was a navigator."

He jerked backward. "Liar. You're a girl!"

"I'm not lying! My father was the chief navigator, and I worked with him. Chantelle or Gil will tell you so."

Wes sneered. "Gil is a Ki-lover, a child, and an idiot, and Chantelle is only a woman." He spun his chair sideways and ignored her.

Sick to her stomach, Zak turned her chair back to face U.N. She had spent her whole life hiding, both disguised as a boy and literally staying in her room as much as possible. Most of the adults who knew her were still on the ship. Shar could have told Wes the truth if he had revealed himself yet, but he was still hiding his identity.

Her experience as a navigator suddenly didn't matter, and her gender mattered too much. She shouldn't have dressed like a girl. All the humans said it made no difference, but clearly she would get no respect this way. But how could she stay a boy when she had to share a room with someone other than Father? She couldn't stay in her room anymore, so hiding was impossible. Father's lifelong efforts to disguise her were now ruined.

Worse, what if being a girl meant the humans wouldn't accept her skills any more than the fae did?

What if the highborn, common fae, and human students never learned to get along? If the school failed, so would their chance at a peaceful home on the new world. Since the fae could not leave, that would force the war they were trying to prevent.

CHAPTER 2

SCIENCE CLASS

ON MONDAY, Alexandria squeezed in bites of lunch between giving explanations. Once the fae had been convinced that questions were allowed, they asked a *lot* of them. By now, they spoke a scrambled mix of a little English and much Fae. Since the human students only knew a few Fae words so far, the answers were left to the handful of translators. Though Ian was the language expert, Alexandria knew enough to help. Since this school had been her idea in the first place, she was determined to make it work, and part of that was helping the fae learn about the ordinary things of Earth.

"Why does the barge eat the leaves?" a girl asked, waving her cow tail for emphasis.

"The truck," Alexandria emphasized the pronunciation, "sucks up the leaves to clean the street."

She had to demonstrate sucking her milk with her straw before understanding dawned on the various faces at her table.

"What does the *truck* do with the leaves?" That was Gil's red-headed friend, Abe, that had real leaves in his hair.

Alexandria shrugged. "Throw them away with the rest of the garbage."

Heads swivelled toward the trash bins. "You throw all that away?"

"Yes. You've seen the people collecting it outside."

"But it has food in it," Abe protested.

"Yes," Alexandria agreed. "There are some leftovers that get thrown away."

"I thought it went to the compost collectors," Abe said.

"Um, I don't think that's a thing," Alexandria said.

Abe's eyes grew wide, and he pressed his lips together. "I need to talk to Chantelle," he told his lunch neighbor. "Will you push me there?"

"Sure." The other boy drained his milk, crumpled the carton, and lobbed it into the trash.

The cow-tailed girl pursed her lips. "Then... are the other boxes also for garbage? The blue ones outside?"

That took a few minutes and Miknon's help to sort out. Finally, Alexandria had enough information about what the fae had seen through a window. It took even longer to explain the postal service, though. The fae didn't have mail, both because few of them could read or write and because these had all been on the same spaceship. As for the other ships in the fleet, getting mail to them was completely impossible. Wait until the fae heard about junk mail!

Alexandria checked her watch. "Sorry, I have to leave early. Miknon can answer a few more questions before the bell rings for class, okay?"

The fae students chorused, "Okay."

Dashing across the hall, Alexandria yet again cursed the chaos of her life. All she wanted was a happy family and a future as an astronomer. What she had was no father, a family with two alien additions, and a whole school riding on her shoulders. Or so it seemed. In truth, there were adults in charge, and she was only supposed to handle student cultural and social opportunities. As if that wasn't enough. *Sure, Alexandria, discover how to make humans and aliens — excuse me, fae — become friends. No pressure, just interstellar war if you fail.*

But she had the whole school year to work on that. Right now, she had a more immediate problem. Poor Mr. Riggs was still working on last-minute changes to the student schedules, including hers.

She poked her head into the principal's office. Ms. Maxwell was lounging on the visitor's couch, feet on the arm. Unlike the first few weeks after they met, she now wore a skirt and nice blouse to advertise her gender and throw the patriarchal fae off balance. Her military-short hair even had a pink bow in it.

"Hey, Raquel?" Alexandria said. "Did Mom tell you about Artemis?"

Raquel put down her clipboard and smiled at her. "Sure did. Too bad the launch was postponed for the second time, but it can't be helped."

"Three times," Alexandria said. "NASA's decided not to try for the 27th, either."

"Phooey," Raquel said. "I really want some better photos of the spaceship on the moon."

Alexandria sighed. "Don't we all?" The warning bell rang, prompting her to ask her burning question. "Hey, do you have my new class schedule yet?"

Raquel winced.

Alexandria stepped inside the office to let students move past her in the hall. "Come on, Raquel, you promised. If I don't get into my classes soon, I won't be able to catch up."

"I'm sorry, Alexandria. We simply don't have enough translators to put you in more of your own classes. Allan tried, but..." Raquel shrugged. "By next semester, we can reduce your work load."

Alexandria moaned. "I'm sunk."

"Oh, now—" Raquel started.

Alexandria leaned against the wall and closed her eyes. "We moved every single year — thanks a lot, Dad — and every state has a different curriculum. I'm always playing catch up. Next semester won't compensate for only two classes now. How will I get into college if I don't graduate from high school?"

"Alexandria," Raquel said. "I promise you'll graduate. You still have two years to get in all the classes you need, and I promise we'll do better after this semester."

"I gotta get to class." Alexandria hurried down the hall. Sure, Raquel was confident everything would work out, but she wasn't the one who would be short credits.

And that didn't touch the problem of *paying* for college, now that they didn't have Dad's military income. Her grades weren't *bad*, but they weren't that good, either, and need-based grants were unlikely to cover all her expenses.

Fortunately, she had heard about a nice judo scholarship. Unfortunately, she needed to earn it. And though she was good enough to get her brown belt already, she couldn't prove her skills until the slash wound on her back finished healing. The mere thought of practicing throws made her cringe, and if the crazy guy who knifed her wasn't already dead, she'd be tempted to find him and kick him around the block. At least she had two years to try for her black belt, but at the rate the school was sucking up her time, she would need every spare minute she could get.

If she could dump the school on everyone else, her life would be so much easier. But how could she do that when she had promised Gil and Miknon that they were part of her family? She couldn't disappoint them. And with Nikos spending most of his time in classes or at work, she couldn't abandon Ian and Mom to do all the work. As for the other adults, Alexandria *liked* them, but she didn't trust the government or the military to always make the right choices.

As she passed the open doors to the other offices, she waved at all the leaders present. Ms. Stafford was packing her briefcase, probably to head to the building slowly filling with adult fae. She split her time between the school and the adults, since both age groups needed her expertise as a refugee specialist. Mr. Farrell was gone, as usual; the Office of International Affairs was much more interested in the adult population.

Mr. Riggs waved back at Alexandria. Poor Mr. Riggs, stuck with a nasty boss in the State Department *and* trying to make the last-minute school work *and* find housing for ten thousand fae by the time they all landed. Though Raquel got the day-to-day problems, Riggs suffered through all the red tape and the ire of his fae-hating boss. Alexandria was still steamed about Mr. Compton suggesting they send a nuclear bomb against the fae ship on the moon. Not on her watch, buster! Which wouldn't have worked, anyway, because the fae had magic shields. One more proof it was a good idea to keep this school secret for now. She shrugged her shoulder, feeling the half-healed scar stretch. They definitely didn't need more crazies ruining their chance at peace.

In the fae office, Chantelle was too busy talking to Abe to notice Alexandria run past. Alexandria didn't envy her trying to translate all the fae customs into something that would work on Earth. She was deeply impressed, though, at how many details Chantelle had stored in her brain without the help of a written record.

The bell rang, and Alexandria slid inside the classroom just in time. Mrs. Hahn smiled and waved her forward. The teacher's blonde hair was elegant in a French twist, but she wore practical running shoes and a simple peasant blouse.

The fae students looked wide-eyed from Alexandria to Mrs. Hahn. Though none of the humans students were troublemakers so far, the fae were strikingly more obedient. They followed the bell schedule without a fuss, and they never misbehaved in class. Alexandria wasn't sure if the ship discipline would eventually wear off, but in the meantime, it made it possible to have a large student-teacher ratio so everyone got a chance to learn. It also meant they were appalled if she was two seconds late.

Somehow, Miknon had beaten Alexandria to class, probably thanks to her wings and her penchant for finding shortcuts too small for humans. Now she tapped her foot impatiently on the teacher's desk, where she stood to be high enough to be seen from the back of the room. Beyond her, the windows showed clouds gathering in the sky. Considering the cool of the day, Alexandria would be surprised if it didn't rain that afternoon.

"Sorry," she said. "I was talking to Ms. Maxwell."

That got her more worried looks from the students. To them, "War Lady" was definitely to be respected, possibly to be feared. Alexandria smiled and shrugged, trying to demonstrate an unconcern she didn't feel. Her personal problems needed to stay away from the fae.

"Anything I can do to help?" Mrs. Hahn asked. The science teacher had arrived on Friday, late like many of the teachers due to the sudden creation of the school, but she was already taking an interest in her students and teacher's aides.

Alexandria shook her head. "Nope. I'm ready to go."

She pulled her microphone from her pocket, plugged it into her phone, and turned on her recorder. This was the fun part. Any new Fae words that emerged in the class would be captured for Ian's dictionary, while fae science tidbits would go to Therese Ortiz at the Minor Planet Center. Friday had been occupied with introductions for teacher and students, and orientation for Mrs. Hahn.

"Okay, class," Mrs. Hahn said. "We're going to talk about—" She stopped and put a hand on the desk. Her pretty face turned white, then greenish, and she pressed one hand to her stomach.

"Are you okay?" Alexandria asked.

"Oh, dear," Mrs. Hahn said. "I think the time has arrived to tell Ms. Maxwell about my good news. I'll be back." She put a hand to her mouth and stumbled from the room.

"Congratulations," Alexandria called after her.

Once the teacher was out of earshot, Alexandria chuckled. Poor Mrs. Hahn. Lucky Mrs. Hahn, too.

"What wrong?" Miknon asked.

"Mrs. Hahn is feeling sick because she's going to have a baby," Alexandria explained. "Um, Miknon, what's the word for an infant?"

Miknon shrugged, so Alexandria tried alternate explanations until they found the right Fae word.

In the front row, a fae raised his hand. "She doesn't want the baby?"

"I'm sure she does," Alexandria said. "But pregnancy can be hard on a human woman."

Miknon didn't know the word for pregnancy, either, and Alexandria's explanations got nowhere.

The door opened, and a human boy entered. After examining the room, he stood awkwardly by the door, a frown deepening on his face. Well, if he wanted to wait for the official teacher, that was fine. Alexandria was busy, anyway.

Finally, she gave up trying to discover the Fae word for pregnancy and put her hand on her stomach. "The baby is inside Mrs. Hahn," she said.

The fae gasped. "She ate a baby?"

"No!" Alexandria took a deep breath. "This should be a health lesson, not a science one," she muttered.

But the fae weren't taking health classes, so where else were they supposed to learn anything? If only Mrs. Hahn would come back!

"Excuse me," the boy at the door finally said. "Is Mrs. Hahn here? I have a message for her."

All the fae stopped talking and waited for Alexandria to deal with the visitor. Compared to a regular high school class, it was practically unnatural. Even Miknon froze, looking like a doll on top of the desk.

"She stepped out for a minute," Alexandria said. "Can I give it to her?"

"No." The boy scowled. "Why do all these students get to wear costumes to class, but I can't wear my hobbit feet?"

Alexandria blinked. Seriously? Had he slept during orientation last week? And he was speaking English perfectly fluently, without an accent, so language wasn't to blame. Anyway, it was a requirement for all the human students to speak English adequately. Even if he hadn't paid attention in orientation, had he ignored his roommates so much he missed their differences? Even the most human-looking of the fae weren't identical to humans.

"This is a fae class," she said. "Like you were told about in orientation."

"I tried to sign up for a fae class," he said, "and they told me I wasn't eligible. I don't see why I can't be in one."

"Because you aren't fae?" Alexandria waved her hand at the students, who were still watching silently. "Now, if you don't mind, we were in the middle of a discussion. You can leave the message with me or wait quietly for Mrs. Hahn." She raised her eyebrows at the boy, who sniffed and flopped into a chair.

"Okay," Alexandria said to the fae. "You were all born little, right?" She demonstrated size with her hands, then bit her lip. "Were you born?"

Maybe they didn't have pregnancies. Maybe they were spawned or hatched or something. Since no fae had been born during their interstellar travel, maybe the kids didn't know how babies were created. A frantic glance at Miknon didn't help, though the fairy was obviously thinking hard.

"Of course they were born," the messenger boy blurted. "Everyone is born except robots! This is the stupidest class I've ever seen. And it's still not fair they get to wear their costumes."

"They aren't costumes," Alexandria repeated. "These are fae. What you see is what they actually are."

"They are not," the boy shouted. He pointed at the far end of the room. "He's got horns." At the back. "She's got green skin." He marched to the teacher's desk and poked Miknon. "And dolls in high school are stupid."

Miknon swatted his hand away, and the boy flinched.

"What the—" He grabbed Miknon and held her in front of his nose, squinting.

"Hey, hey." Alexandria moved toward the desk, hands out. "Put her down, please. You need to leave now."

"Animatronics?" The boy grabbed one of Miknon's wings and tugged.

Miknon screamed. Alexandria lunged closer, but she didn't dare tackle him while he was holding Miknon.

"Put her down," she bellowed, slapping the security button on the wall.

Once Miknon was free, she could tackle the stupid kid, though the fall would hurt her back again. At least this opponent wasn't armed.

The fae students shouted, and someone threw a book at the boy's legs. He staggered, and a cloud of books flew through the air. The boy fell to his knees under the barrage, and Miknon kicked him in the nose. His grip loosened, and Miknon struggled free. As soon as the fairy was out of the way, Alexandria threw herself on the boy.

"Hold still," she shouted.

But he wiggled and fought, and Alexandria scrambled for a better hold on him as they rolled on the floor.

The classroom door slammed open, and security officers — undercover military — streamed in, guns at the ready.

"Everybody down," Alexandria shouted in Fae, still fighting to make the boy hold still.

On the desk, Miknon flattened herself, and the rest of the fae doubled over in their wheelchairs or threw themselves into the bottom of their wagons or baskets. Some slid from their chairs and cowered behind them. Smart.

The boy under Alexandria punched her. Not smart. She leaned harder on him, but he wedged a leg against the desk and got enough leverage to roll her over. Her shoulder slammed into the floor, shooting pain through her wounded shoulder. She howled and used her judo skills to throw him off.

As she scrambled for him again, a gun appeared right by Alexandria's cheek, pointed at the head of the boy. He froze, eyes wide.

"Okay, Alex," the soldier said. "You can get up, because this punk won't move a muscle, isn't that right?"

The boy blinked. His lip quivered, but he said nothing.

With a groan, Alexandria rolled off the boy and struggled to her feet. The slash on her back ached again. Yeah, throws in judo class were still a bad idea. She rolled her shoulder, wincing, as the security officers dragged the boy to his feet and marched him out the door.

On the way, they lectured him about the NDA he signed to attend the school, threatening him with prison if he talked about anything after his sorry self was kicked off-campus permanently. And if he wasn't okay with expulsion, they could skip straight to prison, where he could get the psychological help he obviously needed. Alexandria suspected they'd also take him for a chat with a fae mind-magician, to make sure he didn't reveal the secrets.

Alexandria sank into the teacher's chair and rubbed her face. "Miknon, are you okay?"

The fairy flexed her wings and winced, then nodded. "Okay."

The door closed, and Alexandria dragged herself to her feet. "Is everybody okay? You can get up now."

One by one, the fae sat up. The door opened again, and everyone jerked to face it, cringing. Oh, great, now the fae were scared out of their wits. Great job convincing them that Earth is peaceful.

Mrs. Hahn paused with her hand on the doorknob. "Oh, what happened?"

"I'll tell you later," Alexandria said. "Miknon and I need to see the nurse, so I guess class is done for the day. Um, just sit here and be soothing. Answer questions if you can, or practice counting in English." She rolled her shoulder again. "Sorry. Do whatever you want, but Miknon and I really must go to the nurse."

Mrs. Hahn took a deep breath. "Counting, right. We can do that. You will talk to me later?"

"Yep." Unwilling to raise her burning muscles to shoulder height, Alexandria cradled Miknon like a baby. "Everybody, you'll be fine now."

Despite skeptical looks from several of the fae, she faked a smile and left. After the nurse checked her shoulder and Miknon's wing, they needed to have a chat with Raquel about screening the human students better. If that boy wasn't the only one who still didn't believe the fae existed, they'd better find the others fast and get them out of the way.

CHAPTER 3

IN WHICH MORE FAE LAND ON EARTH

SEPTEMBER 10, 2022

"YOU SHOULD COME," Gil said.

He spoke in Fae for privacy, since Sharrukin's human roommates still spoke only a few words of their language. Ashur was tending his garden, as usual, so nobody would overhear their conversation.

The prince didn't open his eyes. He lay on his bed, arms behind his head. His previously waist-length hair had been cut like Ian's, long enough to cover his ears and swoop down over his eyes. He looked surprisingly human without his pointed ears showing, though his hair was too bright of a gold.

"You're doing fine without me," he said.

"They're your people," Gil said. "Imagine how happy they'll be to see you're still alive."

Shar slowly turned his head and opened his eyes. Gil fought to meet his piercing silver-blue glare, which was even more terrifying than Alexandria's. And unlike Alexandria, the prince did have magic.

"I've been strictly forbidden to reveal myself." Shar gestured to his wheeled chair by the bed. "Taras says if my enemies see me weak like this, they'll try assassinating me again. I'd like to see them try!"

"None of us want that," Gil said, "but Nik is sending your allies first." The king's secretary, who shared a use-name with the human Nikos, was canny enough to sort out the troublemakers and keep them on the ship until last. "And the humans will help protect you."

"I should be able to protect myself," Shar growled. "I hate being weak."

Sighing, Gil sank into the closest chair. Even though he could now walk, his legs still got tired faster than he liked.

"All of us are weak right now. You're no different. Come build alliances so when the lords return, your inheritance will be secure." He removed his necklace and dangled it in front of Shar, offering the king's signet ring that served as his badge of authority. He would happily return it to the prince, authority and all. "Or stay here but go make friends with the humans. You know we need Ki on our side, too."

Gil had human friends, yes, but the treaty with Earth was still temporary. If this school failed to connect the humans and fae and teach each side the other language, the peace would fall apart. And the humans had already said they wanted to negotiate with the fae leader, who was not Gil. Shar knew all that, and repeating it was useless.

"*You* are building alliances with Ki," Shar said.

"We need you, too."

Shar's glare intensified. "Until I am approved by the lords or become an adult and can take the throne myself, I cannot overrule my advisors, and on this subject, they will not yield."

He would not reach his two-hundredth conjunction for almost another thirty.

Gil held out the ring again. "You don't have to be king to lead. Earth wants our leader to sign the treaty."

"The treaty is not ready yet," Shar said. "I promised to keep my father's promises to our people. And I will fulfill his oaths as soon as I am not a child." He growled the last word and rolled to face the wall.

Gil sighed and replaced the necklace, gold ring clinking against his silver family emblem. Apparently, he would have to convince Taras and Shalla first. He rose and nodded at the humans studying at their desks.

"Can we help Shaun with something?" Touji whispered, nodding at Shar. The short, slim boy had black hair and narrow dark eyes.

Gil shrugged. "Not today. Keep try, okay?"

"Hai," Two said, returning to his studies.

Kirill nodded. "Tak, I will."

The taller boy had short brown hair and brown eyes and wore glasses. He cast another worried glance at Shar before turning a page in his book.

Gil made a mental note to ask Ian what the unfamiliar words had meant. English was so complicated.

The magic box in Gil's pocket rang, and he pulled it out and fumbled with the buttons of light as he exited the room. "Hello?"

"Hello," Ian's voice said, almost as clearly as if he was beside Gil. "It's almost dark. Are you ready to go?"

"Yes. Be I down soon." He hurried to the deck-transfer, letting Ian turn off the magic message.

When he exited onto the bottom deck, all the others were waiting by the front door. His foster family was dressed as usual, but Mak-swill wore her uniform again. War Lady motioned toward the door, and her helpers streamed out. By the time he reached the door, only his family and a few fae were left in the hall. To his surprise, Shalla, Miknon, and the healer Merodach were accompanied by Mother.

Gil bent to hug Mother in her chair, then transferred Miknon to his shoulder. "I didn't know you're coming with us."

Mother wrinkled her nose. "I want to help. I should be out of this chair in a conjunction or two, so I wish to see how the landings work."

As the humans each pushed a chair, Gil hurried to open the door.

"We can use all the help we can get," he said.

Once the fae were loaded into Mak-swill's barge, Gil joined Ian's family in Nikos's bright blue barge. Truck, it was called a truck. Which was also what the big flat barges were called. English made no sense. Which reminded him about the mystery words, but when he asked Ian, his friend laughed.

"Two is from Japan," Ian said, "and Kirill is from Ukraine. Two said 'yes,' and I'm pretty sure that's also what Kirill said."

"So many words." Gil made a face at Ian.

Ian laughed again. "No, you don't have to learn every language on Earth. Don't worry about it."

The trip to the landing site in a neighboring town went quickly, and as darkness fell, everyone was in position. From the trucks, they watched the flames descend, one, two, three falling stars. By now, the dragons knew the way without the guidance of their drivers, and they smoothly followed the lights along the river until they splashed down and waded to the shore.

Mak-swill's soldiers swung into action, removing more than two hundred sleep-spelled fae from the barges as soon as the doors opened. By the time most of the fae woke, they were already in the long buses waiting to take them to housing.

Gil hurried from bus to bus, giving his welcome speech and introducing the leaders who would be working with the fae. This time, there were no emergencies for the healer, so as soon as the dragons were hidden in the big box trucks — and Gil didn't have to urge them inside — the caravan departed.

Nikos drove after them to the building where the fae adults lived for now. He parked, and everyone got out again. After several landings, everyone knew their part in orientation by heart, and within an hour, all the latest batch of fae were settled in their rooms. In the morning, the humans and more experienced fae would start the newcomers on language and cultural lessons and teach them how to turn on lights and water and so forth.

Gil's foster family made it home for bed only a little later than most days, and he shifted to wolf, curled up on his bed, and fell asleep almost instantly.

IN THE MORNING, Nikos dropped the Fitches at "church," then took Gil and Miknon to the school. While the siblings visited and answered questions, Nikos sat at a dining table and studied for his classes unless he was needed to clarify something. With his friends around him, Gil lost track of time.

"Hey, Gil," Alexandria said behind him.

Gil jumped and squeaked. Apparently, Nikos had already retrieved his family.

"Sorry." The girl's mouth twitched. "I'm setting up my telescope in the courtyard so we can look at the moon, which is full for the next three days. I don't mind everyone using it, but it's important that people don't change the settings or knock it over or anything. Do you mind making sure all the fae understand?"

"Okay." Gil switched to Fae and raised his voice. "Alex is putting her magic spyglass outside. If you wait for her help, you can look at the worldlet where *New Kunisu* is sitting. If you touch it without her permission, remember that she has a stonegazer's eyes."

She didn't have a stonegazer's magic, but they probably wouldn't remember *that*. Her precious telescope would be safe. The fae murmured and pulled back a little. Alexandria squinted at him, lips compressed, as she obviously filtered through the words she had and had not understood.

Gil smiled back blandly. If she deciphered it, he hadn't *actually* threatened anyone.

Finally, she grunted and stalked off. Miknon pinched Gil's ear.

He shook his head to free himself. "She wants it safe, right?"

Waving his throwing circle, Ian gathered together a bunch of humans and took them outside for a game of toss-and-catch. If Gil borrowed an office or hygiene room, he could ditch his clothes and shift to wolf. Then he'd be fast enough to chase any throw.

But before he could leave, Mother rolled into the room and headed straight for Gil. In her new chair, she could push herself by turning the wheels by hand. Most of the shifters had gotten the new chairs as an intermediate step to walking, since switching forms tended to strengthen their bones considerably faster than the fae who were stuck in one shape. Gil and Miknon had bets placed as to which shifters would be on their feet first. Gil thought Ram's competitiveness would win.

"I need to talk to you," Mother said. "I've decided its time I moved out of the school."

"Great!" Gil beamed. "Helen will be thrilled to have you."

He had been begging Mother and Ram to move in with his foster family and build connections faster, but Ram didn't like humans and

Mother was uncomfortable. If they were past that now, it meant his hopes of alliance were that much closer.

Mother winced. "I mean I'm going to live with the adults. They need more help there than the school does."

"Oh." Gil's excitement crumbled like dry leaves. Instead of being closer to him, she would be farther.

"The mage and the pilot are going with me," Mother said, "but the Companion is staying here. The healer will split his time."

After so much time among the humans, the fae habit of using titles instead of names sounded odd to Gil, and he concentrated on that peculiarity to avoid the pang of separation he already felt. Until he came to Earth, he had never spent more than a few hours away from his family. The worst part of their original escape hadn't been the risky ride on a dragon or slashing his hand to fake their deaths. It hadn't even been the possibility of landing among enemies. No, missing his family had been worse, and their reunion had filled his heart again.

"That's a good idea." Miknon softly touched the back of his neck, comforting him as always. "I'm sure they'll appreciate your help, Mother, and we are old enough to manage without you. We will miss you, of course."

Gil swallowed hard. "Yes, we'll be fine. You won't be that far away, and we'll come see you every week."

"What about Ram?" Miknon asked.

Ears perking forward, Gil looked around for his brother. Though the human and fae students had combined in large and small groups throughout the dining hall, he couldn't see Ram.

Mother sighed and laced her fingers together. "Ram is staying here."

"He could move in with us," Gil suggested.

Mother shook her head slightly and wrinkled her nose.

"Okay," Gil said.

Sooner or later, Ram would have to overcome his prejudice against the humans, but that was one reason for the school in the first place.

"You could share a room with him here," Mother suggested.

Gil grimaced. "Ian and I learn more words when we share."

Mother looked at Miknon.

"According to human customs," Miknon said, "I can't share a room with Ram. I'll stay with Alex."

Gil exhaled in relief. At least he would still have her close by. "When are you leaving?"

"Today," Mother said softly. "I just told Chantelle and Mak-swill. They're working on moving Ram from the third deck to the fourth. If you want to suggest good roommates for him, I'm sure they would welcome your opinion."

Today. Another pang hit Gil's heart, and he stood to cover his flinch. "I'll go right now, then. Don't leave before I say farewell?"

"Of course not," Mother said. "I still need to pack my things and talk to some other people. I'll be here for a while. And I'll want to see Ram settled in his new room."

Gil nodded stiffly and headed for the offices. He found Mak-swill in Shalla's office, already discussing rearrangements. Some roommates weren't working out, and one student had been expelled, so it was a good time to consider changes.

The women nodded to Gil but kept talking. Mak-swill referred to the writing in her hand, but Shalla merely stared at the blank wall as she thought. Gil took a seat and listened until they got to Ram, or Rafe, as the humans knew him.

"What about Nate?" he asked, using the human use-name because of Mak-swill. He was sure she was trustworthy, but Nashuja wouldn't believe that yet, and Mak-swill still didn't understand how important it was to keep their names private.

"Which one is Nate?" Mak-swill flipped through her list.

"The hydra," Shalla said in Fae.

"The dragon with many heads," Gil interpreted.

"Oh, the little dragon." Mak-swill raised her eyebrows. "Are they friends?"

Gil shrugged. "Rafe is more interested in training than in friends. But Nate is *my* friend, and he's very nice."

Mak-swill stabbed her finger on her list. "Nate is currently with Okoro Dambe, Yuri Berezin, and Wes Smith. Will it create problems to move out Wes, or should we move Nate?"

Shalla rolled her eyes. "Not at all. Wes despises Nate. But he doesn't like any of the Browns, so..." She pursed her lips in thought. "Let's put him with Vince. That will keep Wes from pushing around someone smaller than himself."

Mak-swill merely nodded and made several notes, but Gil smothered a chuckle. Vince, as he was known here, was a troll. If Wes tried anything, Vince would flatten him.

The women kept talking, and Gil excused himself. Now that Ram had a new room assignment, Gil and Ian could help him move his things.

By the time he collected Ian and they arrived on the third-deck room Mother and Ram shared, Mother was already there with a packed box. Ram was not packed and obviously not happy.

"I don't see why—" He broke off his near-shout and glared at Ian. "What is that doing here?"

"*He* is here to help," Gil said mildly. "He brought a crate to transfer your clothes."

Mutely, Ian held out the soft box, supposedly made of the same stuff as their books. Despite their continued claims that Ki didn't have magic, Gil didn't understand how that could be so.

Ram spun his wheeled chair so his back was to Ian. Gil shrugged and moved to the drawers on another wall. The humans had supplied all the fae with clothes, as much to their tastes as possible, but most of the refugees only had a few outfits, so packing for Ram took no more than a minute.

Too late, Ram spun around again. "Don't touch my things!"

Gil snorted. "Really, brother?"

Ram's ears turned bright red. Unlike Mother and Gil, the pale skin he inherited from Father showed embarrassment well.

"I thought—" he spluttered, glancing from Gil to Ian and back.

"Oh, Rafe." Mother sighed. Even under stress, she remembered his new use-name, which Gil found difficult.

Gil dumped the box onto Ram's lap and grabbed the handles of the chair. "U.N., would you please open doors for us?"

With a quick nod, Ian darted for the deck-transfer. He kept that door open until everyone was loaded, then pushed the button for the fourth deck and dashed ahead to open the door to the room. Gil checked the room numbers as they turned the opposite direction of Shar's room. That was good; Ram would probably recognize the prince, so keeping them separated was a good idea.

By the time the others caught up, Ian had already explained the situation to the occupants. While the highborn Wes piled his belongings onto his lap with evident relief, his human roommates stripped a bottom bunk and remade it with fresh sheets. To leave space in the room, Mother and Ram watched from the doorway.

"Don't worry," one boy said. "I don't snore."

The other roommate snorted. "Much."

That started a brief wrestle, which ended almost as soon as it began, with no obvious winner but both boys laughing.

"They look like fun," Gil murmured to Ram.

Wes snorted. "They aren't." He didn't bother to lower his voice, though he did speak in Fae. "Push me out."

With an eye roll, Ian obliged, wheeling him down the hall and around the corner.

From the other lower bunk, Nate bobbed a head. "They fun." He spoke in Human, though the words were highly accented by the shape of his mouths.

The humans slapped hands with each other. "Yeah, man."

"I'm Yuri," one said. Other than his height, he was medium in every way.

"I'm Okoro." His hair was cut too short to be anything but a shadow, and his eyes were dark.

Both boys were tall and muscular, and they stared at Ram with obvious curiosity.

"So, what are you?" Yuri asked.

"Rafe," Ram said, as Ian reappeared in the doorway.

"Nice to meet you," Okoro said, "but like, *what* are you? An elf like Wes, or something else?"

Ian giggled, and Gil made a mental note to ask him what an elf was.

"Werewolf," Ian said, "but a nice one. He's Gil's brother."

In unison, the humans looked from Gil to Ram and back again several times, foreheads wrinkling.

"O-kay," Yuri finally said. "If you say so."

"I look like Mother," Gil explained, motioning to her. "Rafe looks like Father."

Not that he remembered Father, who had been murdered when the twins were only a day old, but that's what Mother said.

Ian shrugged. "We haven't figured out fae jen-ett-icks yet." Gil bumped his elbow, and Ian nodded. "I'll explain later. Anyway, have fun." He slipped into the hall and waited.

Mother leaned across the chair arms to hug Ram. "You will be fine," she promised.

"I don't want to be with stinking humans," Ram hissed.

Gil smiled at the humans, who fortunately didn't speak much Fae yet. "Give him some time to adjust."

They nodded, but Nate rolled his necks into a ball, burying his heads in the middle.

Mother waved Gil off, so he wandered into the hall to Ian. It was a good thing Nate was easy-going, because it seemed like Ram was determined to be difficult. Wes wasn't any happier, which was fairly common for the highborn, alas.

Wes and Ram didn't like the humans, and Shar wasn't allowed to help yet. Could Gil convince the fae to make friends and thus future allies, or would all his efforts fall apart in the end?

CHAPTER 4

ABERNATHY

As IAN EXITED seminary with Alexandria, he slid his sunglasses up his nose.

Alexandria glanced at the cloudy sky and raised her eyebrows. "What, again? That's the third time this month."

"Yeah." Ian closed his eyes halfway and followed his sister as much by feel and sound as by sight.

The English teacher for his fae classes still hadn't shown up, and the stress of teaching twice a day and interpreting for a third class was murder on his migraines. Not that the students were difficult, because the fae were motivated and disciplined, but he didn't know if he was teaching the right things in the right way, and he never seemed to know enough words.

Before he could ask, Alexandria added an electrolyte drink mix to his water bottle. Maybe it would help, and maybe it wouldn't, but they always tried. And Mom had his prescription meds at school. He downed the drink as quickly as possible, then let Alexandria guide him the rest of the way to school while he tried to keep his eyes closed and his stomach under control.

Ten minutes later, he was steered into the nurse's office. She was gone, and Mom was still at breakfast, so Ian lay on a cot and covered his eyes with the pillow.

"I'll find Mom." Alexandria turned off the light and quietly closed the door.

A few minutes later, the door opened. Ian waved without uncovering his eyes. "Migraine." Whether Mom or the nurse, she would know what to do.

"What does that mean?" a male voice asked in Fae.

Ian peeked from under the pillow. A slender man with a narrow face settled into the nearby chair and tapped his fingers on the arm. He was paler than any human, but dressed in ordinary jeans and buttoned shirt. With the ache pounding inside Ian's head, he couldn't identify the fae or remember why he was here instead of with the adult fae at the other building. His vision swam so badly that he could barely see the guy.

Ian switched to the Fae language, trying to remember the right words. "My head hurts. A lot. My eyes—" His vocabulary failed him, and he twiddled his fingers to indicate sparkles. "My stomach—" He resorted to gestures again, swirling his hand.

The man pursed his lips and tilted his head, examining Ian through narrowed eyes. "May I touch you?"

The question was odd, but if he planned to hurt Ian, would he have asked first? Unless he was one of the mind-readers Gil had warned about.

His brain hurt too much to sort possibilities. "I — guess?"

The man removed the pillow from Ian's face. "Close your eyes."

Slightly suspicious, Ian closed them only most of the way. The man touched him lightly on the stomach, then the eyes, then his head. His fingers were cool, but the touches were so fast that Ian felt guilty for suspecting him of mischief.

"Ah," the man said. "I see. Excuse me."

He pressed on Ian's forehead, and everything went black.

Ian woke to the sound of the door closing. Mom sat in the chair at his side, holding a glass of water and a pill bottle.

"Here you go," she said.

"Thanks," Ian mumbled, sitting up. "Where'd the guy go?"

"What guy?" Mom asked.

"The fae guy. He was here before... I fell asleep? How long have I been out?"

Mom wrinkled her forehead. "I don't know, honey. I came as soon as Alexandria found me." She checked her watch. "You usually get here about ten minutes ago."

"Ten minutes?" Ian reached for the pills and water, then froze. "My migraine is gone."

"That's wonderful, honey." Mom's voice was as confused as Ian felt.

His migraines almost never disappeared so quickly. She shrugged and dropped the pill bottle back into her sweater pocket.

Ian drank the water anyway, then stood. His head felt completely normal, his vision was fine, and his stomach was quiet. "That's so weird."

The door opened again, and the nurse came in. "Oh, good, you're up. Miles said you should be fine, but I wanted to check just in case." She made a face. "I mean, they're not even human."

"Who is Miles?" Ian asked.

Mom nodded. "The fae healer. I see. Well, I'll have to thank him the next time we talk."

"So what did he do?" the nurse asked. "I'd love to have a better remedy for you."

Ian blinked at her, reaching for his backpack. "I have no idea."

The bell rang, and he ran for the locker room so he wouldn't be late to swim class.

After lunch, he walked into the first of his English classes, mentally rehearsing the most recent vocabulary. The table at the front was still empty, so he dropped his backpack onto the chair and picked a whiteboard marker. He wrote his name on the board, then waited for the bell to ring.

At the last minute, he erased it and wrote his nickname, though "U.N." looked ridiculous. It *was* ridiculous. He didn't know all the United Nations official languages, and he wasn't fluent in everything he was learning. But the last time he used his real name in a fae class, Gil had lectured him afterward.

As usual, his class watched him with startling concentration. Even with fifty students at once, he never had the behavior problems common in the human classes.

"Good afternoon," he said.

"Good afternoon," they parroted back.

"Now that you know a little English," he said in Fae, "it's time to start learning to read and write."

Quiet gasps bounced around the room. Yeah, better head off the panic right now.

"In English," Ian said, "reading and writing *isn't magic*. And anyone can learn it."

His class looked very skeptical.

Ian pointed to his name on the board. "This is my nickname. I will teach each of you to write your own name." A hand went up. "Or the human name you are using," Ian said. The hand went down. "But first we need to learn the letters and the sounds they make."

He wrote the alphabet in big letters. "This is the letter A. It makes several sounds, but for right now, we'll only learn two. Say the sounds with me, and write the letter in your notebooks."

Reluctantly, the class repeated the short and long A sounds and copied the character.

"Good."

Ian rehearsed the whole alphabet, then taught them the alphabet song, which required yet another disclaimer of no magic. He made them sing it over and over, alternating the song with writing someone's name on the board.

Halfway through the class, the students were finally starting to relax. Ian called on an elf and asked him the name he was using. Before he got a chance to write it, the door flung open. A man paused in the doorway, examining the room. He looked to be in his fifties, with highly polished shoes and unremarkable light brown hair in a standard haircut. His fancy vest didn't quite cover his suspenders, his pocket protector, or his plump stomach. Behind his glasses, his gray eyes were like ice.

Without looking at the students, he stomped in and dropped a fancy leather briefcase on the table.

"I am here." He unlocked the briefcase and flung it open dramatically.

"Is there no proper desk? Shabby." Pulling picture frames from the case, he lined them across the front of the table. "My credentials, of course." He polished the glass of one, then relocked his briefcase.

Ian turned and motioned the elf back to his seat, using the opportunity to get his irritation under control. None of the fae could read, so what difference did the man's credential's make? And who was he, marching into Ian's classroom?

With a sour look, the man dropped Ian's backpack onto the floor and sank into the chair. "Students should be sitting."

"Excuse me," Ian said, "who are you?"

The man smoothed his vest. "I'm Abernathy, of course. Mr. Abernathy to you. I was selected by the United States government to learn a top-secret language and teach it to others. Not that *you* would know anything about that. I know ten languages, including ancient Babylonian, Akkadian, and Sumerian. If you've ever heard of any of those." His sneer relayed his skepticism.

"My contact is Ian Fitch, so, young man, sit down or go find me Mr. Fitch! Where's the substitute teacher for this class? What is the administration thinking, leaving you unattended? Never mind, I'm here now so we can finally start learning. Sit!"

"I'm Ian Fitch," Ian said.

Behind him, the class gasped at his use of his real name. But what choice did he have? The teacher obviously wouldn't accept his nickname, and Ian needed his expertise since Greek was the only ancient language he knew. Being fluent in three modern languages and working on four more didn't help him find connections to Fae. Ian desperately wanted help, but did Mr. Abernathy have to be so rude?

Mr. Abernathy sniffed. "Don't be ridiculous. Go find Mr. Fitch."

Ian dug into his pocket and handed over his ID badge.

Mr. Abernathy examined it, front and back, and held it up to the light. "What kind of practical joke is this? You don't look old enough to be a student."

Ian winced. Technically, he wasn't. He reached for his badge, and Mr. Abernathy slid it into his vest pocket.

"Excuse me," Ian said, "that's mine."

"I will show the principal what mischief you are up to," Mr. Abernathy said. "Now sit!"

"I'm not taking this class," Ian said. "I'm teaching it."

Examining him from head to toe, Mr. Abernathy grunted. "You couldn't possibly be teaching. How old are you? Ten?"

Ian pressed his lips together to keep back a retort. He was short for thirteen, but not *that* short. And he had earned his place here.

Mr. Abernathy didn't wait for a response. "When I came down the hall, I heard the alphabet song. Is that what you're teaching?" He sneered at the class.

Ian clenched the whiteboard marker hard enough to cramp his fingers. "Yes, we were learning the alphabet so they can learn how to read."

"How kindergarten!" Mr. Abernathy said. "Any stupid teacher could do that. I'm here to unravel a new language and make it available to the world."

"But they need to learn to read."

"I've had enough of you," Mr. Abernathy said. "March to the principal's office and tell him you need detention. Or expulsion for practical jokes."

In the front row, Zee raised her hand. "Is there a problem?" she asked in Fae.

"This is the new teacher," Ian explained. "He doesn't like my teaching ways."

"But you are good," Zee said. "We usually learn from magic songs without having to sing them, but the singing works."

"He doesn't care, but I'll go talk to Maxwell. You listen to the new teacher, okay?"

"Okay," Zee said. "War Lady will fix it."

The rest of the class nodded.

"Stop babbling nonsense and go to the principal's office," Mr. Abernathy barked.

Ian slapped the marker onto the ledge of the whiteboard. "Principal's office, yes sir."

He marched out, though he refrained from slamming the door. At the office, he blurted the whole story, then collapsed into a chair, panting for breath.

Ms. Maxwell checked her calendar. "He just got here? We knew he'd be late, but he was supposed to be here two weeks ago. Why didn't you tell me?"

Ian shrugged. "We were okay." In the loosest sense of the word.

"And he walked into your class without talking to me first?"

"Yep. I guess it doesn't matter, because he's an expert in ancient languages."

"Ridiculous!" Ms. Maxwell stood and fluffed her puffed sleeves. "He can only read them, not speak them."

She hurried to the classroom, heels clacking on the floor. Ian's shorter legs could barely keep up, though she waited for him outside the room before entering. The sound of shouting echoed through the door, and Ms. Maxwell frowned. She nodded at Ian and yanked open the door.

The students all turned their heads to look at them, sheer relief sweeping over their faces. Mr. Abernathy was red-faced, scowling at the class.

Together, Ms. Maxwell and Ian approached the table.

"Mr. Abernathy," Ms. Maxwell said, "so glad you could make it!" She paused. "Though it is well past September tenth when you said you would arrive."

Mr. Abernathy smoothed his vest. "I had to stay to accept the award for my latest paper."

"Oh, dear," Ms. Maxwell said, "I'm devastated to hear the U.S. Postal Service has stopped working." Mr. Abernathy sputtered, but Ms. Maxwell kept talking. "But that's not important. I hear you're confused, and I believe I heard you yelling at my students."

Drawing himself taller, Mr. Abernathy frowned. "They were ignoring me."

"I see." Ms. Maxwell nodded. "Why were you speaking to them in English when you don't know what words they understand yet?"

"Well—"

Ms. Maxwell waved at Ian. "Why don't you let him explain what they are learning?"

"He was teaching them the alphabet song!" Mr. Abernathy exclaimed.

She turned to Ian. "Oh, that's a good idea. How was it going?"

"Great," Ian said. "We memorized half of it already, and half the class can spell their names." He turned slightly, raised his voice, and switched to Fae. "Can those of you who know how to write your names please hold them up?"

Notebooks rose all over class.

"Good job, U.N.," Ms. Maxwell said.

Mr. Abernathy sniffed. "My apologies. Apparently I was told the wrong classroom. I'm not a special ed teacher. I'm here for my expertise in ancient languages."

He pulled his briefcase from under the table, unlocked it, and settled his "credentials" inside.

Ms. Maxwell crossed her arms. "You did get the contract, right? It listed the classes you're teaching. Did you listen to the sound clip we sent you?"

"Yes." Mr. Abernathy adjusted his glasses. "There was a resemblance to ancient languages, though they were mispronounced."

Ian nearly snorted. Mispronounced? First, nobody actually knew what the ancient languages sounded like, and second, how could the fae mispronounce their own language?

"Oh, I see." Ms. Maxwell nodded, but her fingers tightened on her biceps. "This class will teach you their language while you teach them English. We hoped your knowledge of ancient languages would increase the speed of learning in both directions, though it isn't exactly the same."

She smiled, lips stretched across her teeth in a near-grimace. "As it says in the contract, if you can become the best translator, we'll put you in charge of the training program. If you don't want to teach this class, we'll exercise the exit clause and let you return to your old job immediately."

Mr. Abernathy huffed. "Fine. I came all the way out here and already got an apartment, so I guess I'll stay and lend my expertise."

"We offered to house you with the students," Ms. Maxwell said.

"Too chaotic." Mr. Abernathy waved away the suggestion. "I need peace to study."

Ian rolled his eyes. Living with Gil was teaching him faster than anything. But the fae would probably be *overjoyed* not to have to live with this pompous jerk.

Mr. Abernathy polished his glasses on his sleeve. "And now that we've settled *my* conditions, this student claims to be Ian Fitch and was pretending to teach the class. He even had a fake badge!"

Ian fumed. Just because it was a stupid badge didn't mean it was fake.

"Oh, dear, may I see the badge?" Ms. Maxwell asked.

Mr. Abernathy sneered and handed over the badge. Without looking at it, the principal passed it to Ian.

"All of that is correct," she said.

"But he's a kid," Mr. Abernathy spluttered.

"And he's the best translator we have so far." She crossed her arms again. "You *will* work with him." Maxwell patted Ian's shoulder and walked out.

Mr. Abernathy scowled at Ian. "Mr. Fitch, you might have pulled the wool over everyone else's eyes, but you haven't fooled me. We will follow my lesson plans from now on."

"I was teaching the basics," Ian explained.

"That is completely inadequate." The bell rang, and Mr. Abernathy slammed his briefcase shut and locked it. "We need actual lesson plans. It's a good thing I'm here now." He marched from the room.

Ian's sigh was lost in the collective one that filled the classroom. As the fae rolled out, they nodded or waved at Ian.

He tried to smile back. This would be a long year. His head was already pounding again.

CHAPTER 5

IN WHICH ZAK ASKS QUESTIONS

OCTOBER 7, 2023

FROM HER SEAT in the front row, Zakiti studied the wall-sized slate, trying to match Alex's translation to her own knowledge of the area around Ki. Four worlds, then a band of stones, then four more worlds, all evenly spaced. Well, the seer's mural on the walls of the fae ship had also shown seven like that, though they had been unevenly located in reality.

That ring of stones was where Father was headed, to retrieve the rest of the fleet. He had never been farther from her than a few decks, and now she couldn't even talk to him. He wouldn't be back for many conjunctions. She didn't have his knowledge or his company, and every day she woke feeling more alone than ever. Worry gnawed at her every time she thought of him in a small barge with dangerous and hateful lords. Some of those lords had murdered her grandmother. But surely Father was safe, if only because they needed his navigation skills for a safe journey.

Would he stay safe?

Would any of them stay safe, if they couldn't make a treaty?

While she fretted, the highborn in the class asked questions. Missus-hun and Alex answered all of them, though sometimes the teacher promised a future lesson instead of a detailed answer now.

"Are there any other questions?" Missus-hun asked.

Gil raised his hand. The other commoners inhaled a smothered gasp for his impertinence.

"Worlds named why?" Gil said.

"Good question," Missus-hun said. "We named most of them after people in mythology. Um, old stories." She looked over the class and bit her lip.

Alex grinned through the translation, though she didn't explain why. "We'll talk about mythology later, okay?"

"Okay," Gil said.

He turned and raised his eyebrows at Zak, tipping his head toward the teacher. Oh, no, she couldn't ask questions! She was just a commoner. Gil jerked his head again. Zak widened her eyes and frowned at him. He sighed and raised his hand again.

"Yes, Gil?" Alex asked.

"Everyone ask questions, okay?"

"Yes, everyone can ask questions," Alex said.

Missus-hun nodded vigorously.

Gil raised his eyebrows at Zak again and elbowed Shar. The prince elbowed him back but nodded at Zak. To prove Gil was wrong, she raised her hand. The highborn fae in the class scowled at her, and she lowered her hand.

"Yes, Zee?" the teacher asked cheerfully.

"Why the little one?" Zak asked, managing the human words. "Is too small for world."

"That's Mercury," the teacher said. "It is very small, but we still count it as a planet. We used to count an even smaller one, but then we reclassified Pluto as a dwarf planet."

She had to wait for Alex to struggle through a translation. The fae merely shrugged. Neither Mercury nor Pluto had been in the seer's vision. Zak hadn't seen Pluto on the way in, and they hadn't gone as far as Mercury. It was just strange to see the different ways humans looked at things.

Zak raised her hand again, tentatively. The highborn in the class gasped, but she left her shaking hand up until Missus-hun called on her again.

"That picture isn't to scale," she said in Fae, not knowing the human word.

"What is scale?" Alex asked.

Zak brought up her hands to measure an invisible item. "Size, but compared?" She moved her hands in and out. "The worlds aren't that close together."

"Ah!" Alex translated for the teacher.

Zak hunched her shoulders and waited to see if she would get in trouble for correcting them.

Missus-hun nodded. "That's right. It wouldn't fit on the board if I drew it to scale, because the planets are so far apart."

Most of the fae looked confused. Their old worlds had been much closer together, close enough for the dragons to take them from one to the other. On the journey, they hadn't been informed of the technical details.

Gil and Shar nodded. As prince, Shar was updated on every step of their voyage, and Gil stuck his nose into everything.

Lacking a hand, Nate raised a head and waved it side to side. The highborn glared at him, and Nate spared another head to flick a tongue at them. Brave hydra, considering what they could do to him.

"Yes, Nate?" Missus-hun asked.

"Visit you the...plan-its?" he asked.

Missus-hun laughed. "Nobody has. They are too far away, and most of them are unlivable. We might eventually visit Mars in the future." She tapped the red world on the board.

"How know you—" Nate waved a head. "Stuff?"

"Magic," one of the highborn asserted confidently.

Alex shook her head. "No magic."

"That's a good question," Missus-hun said. "Let's talk about how we study the planets and stars."

The rest of the class was spent learning about "astronomy" and "telescopes" and "radio." The highborn kept saying "magic" until Missus-hun drew sparkles on the board and slashed a thick line through it.

Zak listened intently to the description of radio, because it sounded a lot like her grandmother's contrivance that had navigated them here. The tiny human device Miknon had left on *New Kunisu* was probably also a radio, and she yearned to know how they made it so small. But when she dared to ask Missus-hun a question about how it worked, the teacher laughed and shrugged.

"Sorry, I don't know much technical detail."

Technical. Who would know "technical?" Zak added that to her mental list of things to learn.

The bell rang, and Missus-hun turned off the recording magic.

"If you need the recording from today," she said, "let me or Alex know. Your assignment for Monday is to memorize the names and order of the planets. I'll be in my office if you need help. Class dismissed."

The human students soon arrived to push their roommates, and Zak spent the ride to lunch pondering how to get more information, faster. If she had to wait for her classmates, she would never learn everything the humans knew.

In the dining hall, she and Gaby got their food and sat with Nate and a bunch of other commoners and humans. Alex was the translator for their side, while Miknon and Helen helped the other side of the room.

Zak had barely finished her first dish when Jin dramatically flung herself into the seat across from her and dropped her tray onto the table. Since Jin was Freya's assigned buddy, Zak saw her less than Gaby, except in their shared room mornings and evenings. Still, she was hard to miss. Her naturally black hair was colored with bright stripes, and her clothing was even brighter. And she always carried a small case with her magic wand in it. Floot, she called it, and music poured from it at a mere touch of her mouth. It had taken weeks for Zak to stop flinching when Jin practiced, sure the human was working magic of some sort.

"What's wrong with Freya?" Jin asked.

Zak looked across the room to where Freya sat with the rest of the highborn, looking perfectly normal. "Okay?"

"No, I mean why is she such a hoity-toity stuck-up snob?" Jin stabbed her food and chomped it violently, eyebrows raised.

Zak waved her hand at Alex, who hurried over. Zak pointed to Jin. "Need words, please."

Jin swallowed her mouthful, then repeated her question.

Alex sighed and rubbed her face. "Um, Jin wants to know why the elves don't sit with the rest of you."

Zak shrugged. "Because highborn."

Jin rolled her eyes. "They're not better than you."

"Yes," Zak said.

All along the table, the common fae who had been following the conversation nodded their heads. Nate bobbed all nine of his.

Gaby blinked. "No they aren't. Ms. Ellison made them stop cutting in line."

Zak checked to make sure the highborn weren't paying attention. "Lords, and have magic," she whispered intently.

She still didn't entirely believe the humans didn't have magic, but she knew the highborn did. And if the humans weren't careful, they would discover that the hard way.

Swallowing again, Jin waved her hand. "Okay, okay, I can sort of see the rank thing, though it's hoity-toity nonsense. My parents say political rank is still sort of a thing in China, and I know some countries still have royalty. But we're in America here."

"The fae won't all be staying in the United States," Alex said. "Once the fleet lands, they'll spread out across the world, however the treaty assigns them. That *is* why we'll teach other languages next semester."

Jin sniffed. "I still don't think it's fair."

"It isn't," Alex said. "They're supposed to be sitting with everyone else for the cultural experience, which is the *other* reason everyone is here. I'll talk to Mom about it."

Gaby stacked Zak's empty tray on top of her own. "Life isn't always fair, Jin. My dad's family left Mexico because the drug cartels were running his town. And think of all the refugees who fled warlords and other conflicts. When the powerful and the powerless clash, the powerful win."

Alex translated the conversation for the fae, who all nodded.

"Yes," Zak said, "Power wins."

"And how did the Whites end up the ruling race on other planets, too?" Jin asked.

Nate rippled his necks, and Zak shrugged. The humans looked pink and brown and cream to her. In case the humans' color vision wasn't good, Zak pointed out many pale-skinned fae among the commoners.

Jin glared at the highborn. "But they're all white."

And so was Jin, as far as Zak could tell. What was the difference?

"Are gremlins all green," Zak said, "but differ some races. Are brothers Rafe and Gil but different colors."

Jin threw up her hands. "I surrender." She dropped her tray onto the pile. "Sounds like you've figured out everything but the power, then." Music case in hand, she paused. "Oh, yeah, that's right. You also think boys are better than girls. That's stupid, too. When will you dress like a girl, Zee?"

Zak flinched.

"Jeans and t-shirts are the same for everybody," Gaby said. "What difference does it make how she dresses?"

"Well, I think hiding is stupid." Jin sniffed. "Whenever you want to stand up for yourself, Zee, we'll help." She flipped her hair and stalked away.

"Don't mind her," Gaby said. "She doesn't understand. Are you ready to go?"

Zak nodded. "Will ring soon the bell."

Gaby pushed Zak's chair out of the dining hall and to her next class.

"Is bad, dressing boy?" Zak blurted, plucking at her clothes.

"No," Gaby said. "However you want to dress is fine." She turned the corner and dodged a pixie on a miniature wagon. "But what would your mother think?"

"Oh, not have I mother," Zak said.

"Not ever? Gremlins aren't born?"

"Yes, born." Zak frowned. "But know nothing. Say Father nothing."

"Huh," Gaby said. "That's weird."

It *was* weird. Why hadn't Father at least told Zak her mother's name? Who was she, and what had happened to her? But with Father retrieving the rest of the fleet, she couldn't ask if Mother hadn't been selected in the evacuation lottery or merely died in childbirth. And if he hadn't said anything before now, would he be willing to answer her questions when he returned?

And what would Mother have thought of her disguise?

Gaby spun the wheelchair and pushed her through the door. "Here you go. See you after class." She parked Zak's chair and darted back into the hall.

At the front of the room, Misterabernathy frowned at the students until the bell rang. Then he picked up a color stick and wrote on the wall slate, speaking rapid human.

Zak and the rest of the fae students groaned silently — they had learned not to make a sound — and looked at U.N. The young human grimaced and nodded, but he had to wait for Misterabernathy to stop talking before he could translate.

"He wants you to learn the English word order of sentences," U.N. said. "Subject, verb, object. Yes, I will explain."

He took another color stick and picked an unused corner of the slate. "If we have a person kicking a ball—" He drew a person with a circle head and lines for the body, kicking another circle. "You would say 'Kicks he the ball.'" U.N. drew a foot, the person, and the ball. "But English says 'He kicks the ball.'" He drew the same three figures, reversing the order of the first two.

Shar raised a hand. "Is that the same for all human languages?" he asked in Fae.

U.N. blushed. "No. But Mr. Abernathy is teaching you English, so please try to remember."

Misterabernathy grabbed the dark block and rubbed out U.N.'s pictures with an angry retort.

U.N. turned even redder. "He wants you to learn from his words, not my pictures."

But his pictures were so much better than words they couldn't understand.

Based on the way the boy cringed from the teacher, Zak was sure Misterabernathy had also said something mean. Shar narrowed his eyes, but what could they do? They didn't understand enough words to prove it.

Misterabernathy started talking again, and U.N. tried to keep up with the rapid translation. When he had to define words to ask the class for the correct vocabulary, the teacher scowled at the slower pace. Zak, like most of the students, appreciated the chance to slow down. Unlike the highborn, who were used to memorizing poetry and magic, the commoners only learned the tasks they were set. And the teacher kept writing on the slate, which helped none of the students. Even the highborn that could read Fae couldn't read more than a few words in human.

If they couldn't understand the teacher, how would the fae learn fast enough to make a good treaty, one that was fair for both sides?

The rest of the class lasted far too long. By the end, U.N. wasn't the only one rubbing his head. When the bell rang, U.N. read the assignment from the slate, hunching his shoulders under the teacher's glare. Yet again, the students were supposed to write sentences. Well, Gaby would help Zak, and hopefully everyone else's roommates were as nice.

And there was Gaby, ready to push her to swim class. Too bad Misterabernathy never came near the pool, because there were enough water-related fae to make sure he "accidentally" never surfaced again.

Zak reluctantly removed her outer clothing to expose her swimsuit. Though she had chosen a bottom half that at least covered her thighs, the shirt left her arms bare and clung to her figure. No matter what boy's hairstyle she wore, she looked like a girl in this class.

Assistants carried the fae from their chairs to the side of the pool or threw them directly into the water. The selkies used the closest hygiene room and arrived with just a towel wrapped around their nakedness, shifting directly to seal-shape as the attendant dumped them into the pool.

Alex, dressed in a single piece of clothing that left her legs and half her back exposed, including her new scar, waved for attention from the water. "Now that you all know how to swim, we'll swim laps today. That means from one end of the pool to the other, and back again, over and over. You can use any stroke you like. Okay, go!"

Grimacing at the stench in the air, Zak eased herself off the edge and into the water. Immersing herself in water felt so wasteful, but at least they were using obviously ruined water for the purpose. And she did want to walk again.

A selkie zoomed past her and splashed her with its flippers. Zak coughed and stopped paddling, kicking her legs to keep her afloat while she wiped the stinky water from her eyes and spat it from her tongue.

"No splashing other swimmers," Alex bellowed.

The selkies barked at her and rolled in the water, effortlessly passing everyone else. Zak stretched her arms into a swim stroke and returned to her slow progress. It wasn't speed that mattered, but effort and time. Unlike the shifters, it would probably take her a long time to recover her strength from the lesser weight on the ship, but she had a long time before Father returned.

By the end of class, she had swum forty "laps" and was absolutely exhausted. Gaby pushed her back to her room, and Zak took a nap for the hour before dinner.

Her hair was still wet when she woke, but rebraiding it hid the messiness. In the dining hall, they sat at the first empty table. The highborn in the room sat among the commoners and humans, though many of them looked pained. Freya and Jin took places at another table, though Jin waved at Gaby and Zak.

"Do you need help with homework after class?" Gaby asked.

The human girl smiled as if there was nothing wrong with Zak's incompetence. As if Zak mattered, now that she was nobody and knew nothing.

"English," Zak admitted reluctantly.

Why did Misterabernathy have to make it so hard? Couldn't they learn the words first and then how to write them? She wanted to learn it all, but it was so complicated.

"Anything else?" Gaby asked. "I only have creative writing left, so I have time."

Zak shook her head. She wanted more math and science. The class was still learning how to count, but Gaby had taught Zak how to add, subtract, multiply, and divide simple numbers, and she had found a practice book for bigger numbers. Zak had already memorized the planets for today's science assignment. No, she didn't need help with *that* class. If she only knew human words and reading better, she would ask Gaby for more books. That was allowed, wasn't it? She always saw the human students carrying stacks of books.

"Gaby," Zak said, then paused. What if humans didn't want to reveal the secrets in their books?

"Hmm?" Gaby drained her glass and pulled her "cake" in front of her. Like most of the fae, Zak found it sickeningly sweet and took fruit instead.

"Ask questions okay?" Zak blurted. "In class? Here?"

Mouth full, Gaby nodded.

Zak squeezed her hands together and gathered her courage. "Ask I questions not for class?"

Gaby nodded again.

"Ask tick?" Zak said.

Gaby raised her eyebrows. "Tick?"

"Redoe?" Zak tried to remember the words. "Earth magic? Alex see stars?"

"Astronomy? Oh, tech! Technology. Radio." Gaby giggled. "Yes, you can ask tech questions. In fact, I have an idea. Have you finished eating?"

Zak stuffed her last piece of bread into her mouth and nodded. Gaby zipped her down the hall to the deck-transfer and pushed the button for the lower level. A quick trip to the middle of the building ended at a class-room Zak had never entered.

Gaby greeted the teacher at his little table and babbled much too fast for Zak to follow anything she said, gesturing emphatically.

Finally, the teacher started nodding. "Okay, okay. She can watch my class. In fact, I have a book she can read."

"No read," Zak admitted, feeling her face heat.

"I know." The teacher spun his chair and pulled a book from the shelves behind him. "This one has pictures." He held it toward her, jiggling it until she finally took it.

The cover showed Earth contrivances. Inside, the contrivances were labeled and diagrammed. And page after page showed their insides and how they worked. Yes, Zak would still have to learn to read, but the pictures would help, and the words were in short sections.

Tears stung her eyes, and Zak ducked her head to hide them. "Okay."

"That means she likes it," Gaby whispered. "Thank you."

Zak closed the book and held it out to the teacher. "Okay." She would read it every day she came to the class.

"Keep it," the teacher enunciated. "For you."

"Me?" Zak asked. The book wavered as her hands trembled.

"Yes."

"Thank you," Zak mimicked Gaby, trying not to leak tears on the book.

Gaby spun Zak's chair and exited the room. Zak hugged her new book to her chest. With this, she could learn faster. But could she learn fast enough?

Another idea struck her. Miknon had used an Earth contrivance on *New Kunisu* to communicate with Gil on Earth. If Zak could learn how to make one like that, maybe she could talk to Father before he returned with the fleet. Even if she couldn't hear his voice, he would know she was waiting for him.

CHAPTER 6

FLUNKING

OCTOBER 18, 2022

ALEXANDRIA ACCEPTED her upside-down test from the calculus teacher. She'd run calculations multiple times and decided she could still graduate as long as she got good enough grades to offset the fewer credits. And if Raquel and Mr. Riggs kept their promise to give her more classes after this.

She sneaked a peek at the grade. C minus! Quickly, she slapped it on her desk, sucking in her breath. Nooo. She'd tried so hard and was sure she'd get at least a B. She'd understood everything on the test — she'd thought — so what had gone wrong?

Oh, who was she kidding? Her homework had been no better, though she really had thought she'd discovered where she went wrong. She simply wasn't good enough. Sure, C's get degrees, but they don't get scholarships. If she didn't raise her grades, she couldn't afford college. Even the judo scholarship she wanted still asked about GPA.

Without looking at it again, she slid her test into her folder. At least her lifeguard class had little homework, but with all the translating and cultural teaching she did, her free time was limited. She could study calculus *or* practice her judo, but she needed to improve in both. She definitely didn't have time for a job to pay for college. And her duties at the school were already taking all her time.

Now that the slash on her back had healed, she was finally getting back into shape. She'd gotten her brown belt, which she could have gotten months ago if Dad had cooperated. But to insure a scholarship, a black belt would be better. If she spent more time practicing, she'd have less time for homework. But if she spent more time on calculus, she'd have less time for judo. And next semester, she'd have more than two classes and thus more homework. Aaaah!

She took a deep breath. With two years to get her black belt, obviously her grades were more important. And surely she was competent enough to master calculus and still help the students socialize. She snorted. At most schools, socialization was a secondary consideration. Since she was good at making friends, this was right up her alley. She could do this.

The bell rang, and Alexandria hurried to the first math and science class for which she translated. Mrs. Hahn motioned her over, and waved her hands at several open boxes.

"The tablets arrived," Mrs. Hahn said. "I'm so excited. This will make homework so much easier for the fae. I want to save class time for the lesson, though, so can you arrange for their human roommates to teach them how to use the electronics?"

"Sure," Alexandria said, "but you'd better tell the fae these aren't magic, or you know how they'll react."

The pretty, blonde teacher sighed. "Oh, goodness. When will they stop believing in magic?"

Alexandria laughed. "Probably never, since they use it."

"I'm sure there must be some other explanation." But Mrs. Hahn's forehead wrinkled.

Absently, she patted her stomach, which was still flat. As of last week, she'd said her constant nausea had faded to only the occasional bout of queasiness, and she had stayed in every class instead of dashing for the closest restroom.

The fae rolled into the room and were attentively ready by the time the second bell rang. Alexandria clipped her microphone to her collar and turned on her recorder. The class had been discussing the solar system for a while, and Ian's vocabulary list and Therese's fae science facts had grown rapidly. It was fascinating, but the time it took to sort the recordings between language and science occupied Alexandria's time even more.

Many of the fae teens — or whatever the equivalent was — didn't remember their home world well, but there were a few adults in the class who were willing to give information. Last week, the snake-scaled man had said Earth's sun looked about four times bigger than their home star, as seen from the surface of each planet.

"But your star is so bright, we would burn to a cinder if we were properly close," he dryly finished, pushing his sunglasses higher up his nose.

The fae liked the moon better than the sun, apparently because their old planets had been so close together that from the surface of any of them, the others looked like moons.

With every detail that Alexandria passed to Therese, the astronomer tried to identify their old planetary system. Not even Zee, one of the navigators, could tell them where it was. Unlike humans, who developed science and navigation before they went into space, and thus had vocabulary for it, the fae had used magic for transportation and only line-of-sight for navigation. At least, until their sudden exodus.

That meant many of Alexandria's questions were met with a shrug. She was tired of hearing "magic" as the only explanation, but it was all the fae could give.

Mrs. Hahn pointed to the mural on the whiteboard and continued the comparisons of the planets. Since they had talked about size on Friday, she tried explaining gravity today.

"And how much gravity did your worlds have?" she finally asked, looking at the adults in the class.

The snake-man shrugged. "About same as Ki. Hard to remember after so long on ship."

Alexandria waved her hand. "Yeah, about that. Gil says he was born just before your journey, but how long was that, exactly?"

If she could get a more exact time, Therese might be able to fine-tune her calculations.

Zee raised her hand. "One hundred fifty-seven conjunctions."

Mrs. Hahn gently cleared her throat. "A conjunction isn't a time period; it's when the planets line up."

"For them it is," Alexandria whispered. "Apparently the event is pretty frequent."

"Okay," Mrs. Hahn said. "Obviously, we need to discuss time. Let's start with days."

The class nodded.

"Days are when the sun rises and sets."

The class shook their heads again.

"Sun never move," Zee said.

Alexandria whispered, "We think their planets are tidally locked. No rotation, so no sunrise."

"Okay." Mrs. Hahn rubbed her forehead.

"Harmakis marks each day," the snake-man volunteered.

Mrs. Hahn sighed and looked at Alexandria for an explanation.

Alexandria cleared her throat. "They measure days by planet-rise." She turned to the class for the next question, though she knew what Gil had explained before. "How many hours in a day?"

"Forty-eight," the class chorused.

Most of them even said it in English, and Alexandria beamed at them.

"But how long is an hour?" Mrs. Hahn almost moaned.

Zee raised her hand again. "Says Chantelle, Ki hours about same as Kunisu."

Alexandria nodded. "Then your day is about as long as two of ours."

The snake-man pursed his lips. "Okay. Sleep I that way, yes."

"If we know hours and days," Mrs. Hahn said, "let's move on." She drew a monthly calendar on the board and dragged her finger from side to side. "We have seven days in one week. You?"

"Nine," Zee said.

"And months? Several weeks together?" Mrs. Hahn motioned down the calendar.

"Two weeks is conjunction," Shaun said. "When planets all line up."

Alexandria did the math. "That's actually pretty close to a month. Nine days of twice our length is eighteen Earth days, times two weeks is thirty-six. A bit long, but not bad for an estimate."

"What about years?" Mrs. Hahn asked. "A year is how long it takes to go around the sun." She drew an orbit on the whiteboard mural.

"How know how long?" Zee asked.

"Well, if you aren't being too technical," Mrs. Hahn said, "you can tell by the seasons."

"What are seasons?" the snake-man asked.

"When the weather changes," Mrs. Hahn said. "The temperature gets colder or hotter, and the hours of daylight increase or decrease." She motioned toward the window, which framed trees with reddening leaves.

The entire class shook their heads.

"Always same temperature," the snake-man said. "Always same light."

"Tidally locked," Alexandria repeated.

Mrs. Hahn groaned. "Right. No seasons. Then how do they tell years?"

"Why care years?" Zee asked.

"Well, it's easier to talk about longer times," Mrs. Hahn said.

"Tens of conjunctions," Zee countered. "Hundreds of conjunctions."

Mrs. Hahn threw her hands into the air. "What about birthdays?"

"Born only once," Zee said.

Mrs. Hahn dropped into her chair and laughed so hard she turned red. The fae looked so confused that Alexandria had to bite her lip to hide her own giggle.

Obviously, there were still lessons to cover. But when she got a chance, she wanted to talk to Gil's mother and discover exactly when Gil and Miknon had been born. Her new siblings deserved a birthday celebration, right? And even if she had to count the days, she could figure it out. There was probably an online calculator for that sort of thing, and the other fae might find it amusing. If nothing else, it would let them fill out annoying human paperwork in the future.

Mrs. Hahn took a deep breath and held it until she stopped laughing. "You know, I'm tired of the standard curriculum when we clearly need something more basic. Tomorrow, let's talk about seasons on Earth and what to expect. Alexandria, please help me pass out these tablets, and we'll teach as much as we can about them before the bell rings."

Alexandria beamed at her. Practical lessons would help the fae accli-mate much faster than the usual lessons, which assumed the people taking them already knew how the world worked. Mrs. Hahn was an excellent teacher.

By the end of class, Alexandria and Mrs. Hahn managed to teach the class how to turn the tablets on and off, charge them, and open a few programs.

"Please ask your buddies for more help," Alexandria said when the bell stopped echoing. "We'll practice more tomorrow."

She hurried to lunch, where she ate between questions and translations. Though each meal was divided into two periods, four hundred students plus teachers and staff meant every meal had almost three hundred people in it. And she was responsible to translate for half the room. No matter how much she liked socializing, it was exhausting. At least this school was smaller than her last one, which had eight hundred students. It was more home-like, too, with regular tables and chairs instead of cafeteria picnic-style tables and benches, though that was mostly to allow for half the students being in wheelchairs. Even the shapeshifters who *could* walk frequently rolled to save their strength.

After two more math/science classes, which went more smoothly now that Mrs. Hahn knew what to expect, Alexandria hurried to the pool for her lifeguard class. Here, too, she spent much of her time translating, though the swim teacher had carefully memorized a few important phrases in Fae. Alexandria didn't have even a minute to look at her calculus, though it was constantly on her mind.

By dinner, she was exhausted and frustrated, and when Zee asked her a question about the science class, she snapped, "Look it up."

Zee stared at the ceiling in confusion.

Gaby leaned forward. "Look it up means research, read, find the answer. I'll help you search the lesson on your tablet, okay?" She frowned slightly at Alexandria, then turned to help Zee, shoulders rigid.

Alexandria savagely bit into her hamburger. Oh, great, now she was a jerk.

The other fae watched her warily, and even the human students didn't ask for more translations. And not only was she shirking her primary job this semester, she was scaring everyone else away from learning. Way to go.

She finished her food, dumped her trash and compost, and returned to the table.

"I'm sorry, Zee. I shouldn't have yelled at you." She raised her voice so several tables could hear. "If you want to see some of the planets tonight, we can use my telescope. Wear a coat, because it will be cold after dark."

The remnants of Hurricane Ian had made everything damp, too. The only good part of the hurricane was watching her brother turn red when she teased him that the name wasn't a coincidence.

She glanced at the fae feet in her line of sight. "And shoes, or at least socks."

Gil wore sandals now that he was walking, as did a few of the elves, but most of the fae went barefoot. She should talk to Chantelle and Ms. Stafford about making sure they all had proper footwear before winter descended. Great, one more thing to do.

Gaby caught her eye. "Thanks," she mouthed.

With a shrug, Alexandria grabbed her backpack. "Time to hit the books." She tried to smile but was pretty sure she failed.

"Why hit?" Zee asked. "Angry at books?"

Right. Alexandria sighed. "It doesn't really mean hit." She pounded her fists together. "It's a way to say I need to study."

"The stars?" Zee asked.

"I wish. Nope, I have to do math."

"Math fun," Zee offered.

Alexandria's mouth twisted despite her attempt to stay calm. "I'm afraid it's less fun for me. If I don't figure this out before midterms, I'll be — in the compost heap."

Leaning back in her wheelchair, Zee studied her for a minute. "Can help Gaby you. Taught she me."

Gaby blushed and muttered something unintelligible.

"That's sweet," Alexandria said, "but Gaby is only a freshman, and I'm doing calculus. It won't make any sense to someone in algebra."

"Trig," Gaby murmured.

"Really?" That was even earlier than Alexandria had taken it. She looked at the younger girl with more respect. "That's great, but I'm still in calculus."

Gaby turned even redder. "I've been studying calculus on my own. I can take a look if you want." She waved her hands in negation. "But whatever. You can ask the teacher. I don't mind."

Zee kicked Alexandria gently with her bare foot. "Try Gaby."

Fine, she could demonstrate why this wouldn't work before she tracked down her teacher. Alexandria pulled her calculus book from her backpack, then topped it with her test. The C- glared at her like a tongue-sticking-out emoji. *Nyah, nyah, Alexandria is stupid.*

Gaby didn't even look at the grade, just at the equations. "Oh, I see what you did wrong. You've got a couple of issues, but the biggest one is that you forgot to use parentheses."

"Does it matter when I'm just subtracting f from g?" Alexandria asked.

"Well..." Gaby's pencil flew across the paper. "It changes the sign right here, so your sum is wrong."

Alexandria smacked her forehead. "Oh, dumb!"

"No worries," Gaby said. "It's a common mistake and easy to fix. Which leads me to your next problem. You can't distribute everything."

Sinking onto the chair next to Gaby, Alexandria leaned closer. "I'm not seeing where I was wrong."

On a clean notebook page, Gaby rewrote the equation and worked through it, explaining as she went. After three problems, it finally clicked.

The dining hall emptied, and Mom, Ian, and Gil arrived with the second shift.

"We can go to my room," Gaby said.

Alexandria gathered her books and slipped Mom a hug. "I'm studying upstairs, and I promised the fae a peek at the planets tonight. Is that okay?"

Mom nodded and squeezed her back. "I'll get some extra paperwork done while we wait."

The girls moved upstairs. Their other two roommates were absent, though the sound of a flute drifted through the hallway. Borrowing Gaby's desk while Zee read on her bed, Alexandria fixed most of the remaining problems by herself, then Gaby helped her with the last two.

With Gaby's continued help, the next day's assignment was finished as quickly. In less time than she would have believed, Alexandria's homework was done. Even more amazingly, she was pretty sure she understood it.

"Thanks, Gaby. You da best." Alexandria slid her homework into her backpack with relief bubbling in her veins.

Gaby ducked her head. "Glad I could help."

Without looking up from her book, Zee grinned. "Gaby is good, yes?"

"Gaby is very good," Alexandria agreed. "I wish I always had her help."

"I'm available after dinner every night," Gaby said. "My homework doesn't take long."

Alexandria gaped at her. Was the answer that easy? Well, not easy, since she still had to do the work, but that simple?

"I have judo on Tuesday and Thursday," Alexandria said. And Saturday, but that wasn't a school day. "Are you sure you don't mind?"

Gaby shrugged. "Monday, Wednesday, and Friday, then? Same time, same desk?"

"You're on." Alexandria almost skipped to the door. "I'll see you on Wednesday."

"Sooner than that," Gaby said. "Telescope, right?" She glanced out the window, where the autumn darkness was already deepening.

"Right, right, of course." Alexandria slapped her forehead. "You can be first in line."

"I've got to find socks for Zee first," Gaby said.

Zee grimaced and lowered the book to her nose.

Alexandria hid a chuckle. "In a few minutes, then."

She hurried downstairs, grabbed her coat, and headed for her precious telescope. If she could master calculus with Gaby's help, then she could still get into college and be an astronomer.

If they ever discovered how to use the fae knowledge of the universe, or could duplicate the speed of their spaceship, then the stars themselves might be within her reach. Yes, Earth should definitely make that a request in the treaty.

CHAPTER 7

IN WHICH THEY GO OUT

OCTOBER 29-31, 2022

GIL TURNED the page and snickered. The grandmother was surprised at the wolf's big teeth. As if a wolf would have small teeth! He turned another page. Almost finished, and he hadn't had to ask for help once.

"Hey, Gil," Ian said. "Want to play frisbee?"

He spun the flat ring around his wrist and bounced on his toes. Gil had asked when they would teach him the writing on the frisbee, but Ian only laughed.

"It says *one ring to rule them all*, but it's not a language we actually use." Then he laughed harder.

Maybe one day Gil would understand the joke. In the meantime, he loved playing with Ian.

"I have few pages left," he said.

"Sure, I'll wait. Let me see if anyone else wants to play." Ian wandered out, calling, "Nikos, Alexandria!"

By the time Gil finished the story, his three human siblings were ready. Miknon stayed inside with Mama Helen to avoid being flattened by the frisbee or spotted by an unfamiliar human.

The apartment grass was just big enough for the four of them to spread out for a proper game of fetch. Nikos had the strongest arm, and Alexandria's long legs were the fastest, but Gil was the best at catching. Ian missed half his catches and threw wildly, but he laughed the hardest at his own mistakes.

They kept up the game until Gil's stomach declared it was lunchtime. When they piled into the house, a heap of sandwiches already filled a large plate.

"Good timing, Mama," Nikos said.

Helen laughed. "I knew you'd be in soon. Hungry teens never miss a meal." She dropped a kiss on Ian's head, hugged Alexandria, and patted Nikos and Gil on the way to her chair.

After the traditional words over the food, Gil ate as quickly as manners allowed. His siblings chewed nearly as hungrily while Helen and Miknon updated them on administrative concerns for the school. Another student had been expelled, but everyone else seemed to be settling in.

"Oh," Helen said, "I almost forgot to tell you. I talked to their mother and did some math, and I have one of the dates you wanted, Alexandria."

Alexandria clapped her hands together. "Perfect! Do we have enough time?"

"Plenty," Helen said. "Gil's sixteenth birthday is December 23rd. Miknon is six to twelve months older, though Meg doesn't know her exact birthday."

Gil exchanged confused glances with Miknon. Sixteenth what? When?

"She can celebrate with me or Ian," Nikos offered. "March and April are about in the middle of that range. Or she can pick a different day, if she wants her own."

"What's a birthday?" Miknon asked.

"A celebration of the anniversary of the day you were born," Ian explained. "Every year on the same day, our family has a special dinner with cake and ice cream and presents."

"Why?" Gil asked.

"It's fun," Alexandria said. "It's a way to say we love you and appreciate having you in our lives."

Gil reached across the table and patted her hand. "We love you, too."

Alexandria giggled. "Well, my birthday is in a few weeks, so we'll have a party then. You can see what it's like so you can make choices for your birthday."

"Now that we've settled that," Helen said, "anyone have any ideas for field trips? I'd like to start showing the real world to the fae we can disguise as human. I wish we could take everyone, but some of them really won't pass no matter what we do. We'll have to take video for the rest of them, I guess."

"What about Halloween?" Alexandria asked.

"What about it?" Helen said.

"We could take almost everyone out on Halloween because the fae will look like they're wearing costumes," Alexandria explained.

"Coolest costumes ever!" Ian slapped hands with her. "Halloween with real monsters!"

"We aren't monsters," Gil protested.

"No, of course not," Nikos said. "But some of you are very different, and we don't want to scare the humans."

"I don't know," Helen said. "It sounds pretty complicated, and Halloween is only two days away."

"What's so complicated about it?" Alexandria asked. "They don't need costumes."

"Where will we find enough pushers for every wheelchair?" Helen asked. "What about the fae that can't pass even on Halloween? Do we take the adults from the other building? Where do we go? How do we get there? What about meeting the landing?"

"Military for pushing and security," Nikos said.

"Leave behind the trolls and hydra and make the huldrekin wear shirts," Ian said. "Add a little makeup or costuming if it will make the fae more human."

"Take the adults that have been here long enough to understand a little English," Gil said.

"Just walk into town a little to see the displays," Alexandria said.

"Only a few of us need to meet the landings," Miknon said.

Helen sighed. "Okay, I guess I can talk to Ms. Maxwell and Chantelle and make a plan."

"Great!" Gil said. "What's Halloween?"

By the time they washed the dishes and left to go to the school to finalize plans, Gil still didn't understand the "holiday," but he was excited at the chance to show the human world to his people. If Alexandria and her family thought the fae would be safe, that was good enough for him.

Not everyone was so easy to convince. Shalla nearly had hysterics, and Taras refused to risk Shar. Merodach asked about plagues, though he'd been successful so far at ridding the fae of everything they caught from the humans. If Mother hadn't been tentatively on Gil's side, the whole plan would have died right there.

Gil left the adults to argue and went upstairs to talk to Shar. If he could get the prince to agree, persuading the others would be easier. As usual, Shar was in his room alone, though this time he was exercising in a chair.

"They thought of a way to take us out in public and still maintain secrecy," Gil said without preamble.

Shar lowered the hand weight. "Good day to you, too."

Gil bowed elaborately. "Good day, Sire." He threw himself onto the other lower bunk and rolled to hang his head over the edge. Looking at Shar upside down, he repeated his message. "We're going to take almost everyone into the city to see one of Earth's celebrations. You should come. Not only is it a chance to learn more about the humans, but you can spend time with your own people."

After switching the weight to the other hand, Shar said, "Taras already put guards in all my classes, though of course he doesn't say why they're there. I'm followed every time I leave my room. Do you really think I can sneak away from them?"

Gil beamed. "That's the best part. This celebration encourages people to wear disguises. Nobody will recognize you. Though I think it's time to stop hiding your identity, remember?"

Shar dropped the weight with a sigh. "I'm tired of hearing your thoughts."

Gil rolled off the bed, landing on his feet. He bowed deeply, then headed for the door. "As you wish, Sire."

He closed the door softly and walked downstairs instead of taking the elevator. With every step, he fought for calm. Putting him in charge of the treaty had made perfect sense when he and Miknon were the only fae on Earth. Leaving him in charge *now* was a dereliction of duties. If Shar didn't take responsibility before the fleet arrived, how would he save his throne from the usurping lords? And the lords would rather conquer Earth than make the treaty. Learning the human languages and culture wouldn't help the fae be ambassadors if they didn't have a leader who would reinforce the quest for peace.

Everything Gil had fought for was at stake.

In the school offices, the meeting was drawing to a close. All the adults and the young Fitches looked satisfied, so Gil didn't bother asking for details.

"Do you want to stay here longer?" Nikos asked Gil.

Forcing a smile, Gil said, "I'm ready to go home."

He rode silently in the truck, ignoring the conversation around him. In response to Miknon's worried pat, he merely touched her hair and returned to pondering.

Two days later, the buses rolled in after school, full of the adult fae who would join the youngsters on the "field trip." Even though they weren't going to any field. Only those who had been on Earth long enough to speak at least a little English had been approved.

The students lined up at the doors for an inspection. The humans were dressed in a wide variety of outfits, some normal as far as Gil could tell, and some very odd. Some of them had painted their faces or added fake body parts, including a fair number of pointed ears.

The fae wore their own clothing, washed and mended, over warmer human garb, and most of them had combed their hair back to expose features they normally hid. As they passed War Lady and Mama Helen, some were sent aside for a bit of paint on their faces or an adjustment to their clothing. A huldrekin was sent back to his room to get a shirt to cover the large cavity in his back, though his long tail was approved with a chuckle. Anyone too big or too different to pass as human-in-disguise would be left behind. Nash claimed he didn't mind, but several of his heads hung low.

As people passed inspection, the fae were matched with a human partner. Usually it was one of their roommates, if possible, but War Lady provided adults to escort the adult fae and push their chairs. Every pair was assigned to a group that had a human in charge.

Gil joined Mama Helen's group, which included his siblings — fae and human — and Mother. Might as well be with the whole family except Miknon, who had gone to the latest landing. Even though Mother and Ram had the new chairs, Helen pushed Mother's chair while Nikos took Ram's. Zak, Gaby, all three of Shar's roommates, and a few adult fae with their partners rounded out the group.

Finally, everyone was ready.

"Let's go." War Lady motioned toward the door.

Gil turned to follow Ian, but a movement at the back of the hall caught his eye. War Lady headed for the latecomer and bent to talk to him. Or her, since the shadows hid the face. With a nod, War Lady straightened. She moved behind the wheelchair and pushed it forward.

"Helen," she called. "One more for you."

As they moved forward, the light revealed Shar. Though he wore a fae tunic, it lacked the princely trim he deserved. His hair still fell loose, hiding his ears and half his face.

"May I come?" Shar asked in Human.

"Great," Ian chirped.

He took over from War Lady, and the group headed for the door in last place. Silently, Gil squeezed Shar's shoulder. His prince responded with half a smile. Without comment, Taras peeled away from his assigned group and wheeled himself behind Shar. As another shifter, he also had advanced to a new chair.

As they exited the building in orderly lines, darkness had already fallen. Each group headed a slightly different direction into the city.

Gil shivered in the cold. The ship was always the same warmth, and even with the lessons about seasons, this felt unnatural. His experience with cold was limited to the times the ice mages would cool food or a sick fae.

"I don't see why I can't walk," Ram complained in Fae. "I walk around the school now."

"Give yourself time to build stamina," Mother said. "You don't want to break something by rushing too hard."

"I can vouch for that," Gil said.

Even though his leg had healed, it still ached sometimes. If he'd had access to a proper healer and had shifted less often while it was damaged, it might have been better, but the human healer had done the best he could, and the frequent shifts had been necessary. If that was the worst cost of peace, he wouldn't complain.

"Once I return to full strength," Ram said, "I won't have to put up with this anymore."

"With the chair?" Mother asked.

"I don't like humans breathing down my neck," Ram said.

"Sorry," Nikos said, also in Fae. "I'll let you push yourself." He let go of the chair handles and moved to the other side of Mother.

Ram sucked in a breath and stopped speaking. Gil turned his head to hide a grin. The purpose of the school was to share languages, so how could Ram not remember some of the humans could understand him? True, only the Fitches had any great competency so far, but that would change.

Shar frowned at Ram but said nothing. He scanned the rest of the group, and Gil hoped he was noting the way most of the humans and fae were cooperating.

"So," Gil said, "will you try to explain this Halloween again?"

Alexandria, who was dressed in a white shirt and pants with a blue circle on her chest that said "NASA," shifted her round glass bowl from one arm to the other. "It was a religious holiday a long time ago, to scare away the evil spirits, but now it's just for fun."

"What means religious?" Zak asked. "And holiday, and spirits?"

"Oh, boy." Alexandria puffed out her cheeks.

While she worked on defining the words, Gil examined the city. Windows held skeletons, people in pointed hats, and half-putrified corpses. Again and again, the humans had to reassure the fae that everything was pretend. Nobody was dead, nobody was injured, and nobody was in danger.

The crowd walking past them in both directions was just as odd, though not all were as distressing. The children carried bags or artificial pumpkins with faces, and shoved their parcels at adults in doorways.

"What are they getting?" Zak asked.

"Candy." Ian bounced on his toes. "Um, sweets, like honey?"

"Why aren't you getting any?" Ash asked.

Ian sniffed. "Thirteen is considered a little old. Too bad."

He wore black from head to foot, with a black hood and an obviously fake pair of swords strapped to his waist. Every time Alexandria looked at him, she rolled her eyes.

"Are we older than thirteen?" Ash craned his neck to look at the candy in the closest child's hands.

"Yes," Zak said.

Two highborn passed them, walking, and Gil almost grabbed their arms to pull them back into the group before he realized they were only humans in disguise. Which explained the walking. Ah, so this was how the fae could come out tonight. Anybody could look like anything, and nobody cared.

A huge fairy wandered through the crowd, sucking on her thumb. Stopping in the middle of the path, she began to cry.

Gil crouched in front of the distressed fae. "Are you lost?" Why hadn't she stayed behind like Miknon?

"Waah," the fairy cried.

"Are you hurt?"

The fairy stuck her thumb back in her mouth and hiccupped. Her stunted wings were gauzy instead of feathered like Miknon's, and someone had glued jewels to them. No wonder she couldn't fly, besides her extreme size.

Gil scooped her up and tried again. "Where's your buddy?" He didn't recognize her, so she must have come from the adult floor rather than among the students.

"Mama," the fairy said.

"Oh, there you are, Gil." Alexandria tugged on his arm.

He turned, and she squeaked. "Oh, no, Gil! Where did you find her?"

"I guess she followed us instead of staying behind with the others."

Alexandria raised her eyebrows. "She's not fae. She's a human baby. See, her wings are fake."

She tugged on bands around the fairy's shoulders that he had assumed were decorations, and suddenly the truth was obvious. The fairy was huge for a fairy, but tiny for a human.

"Oh." Gil said. "Right. Um, do babies walk alone on Halloween?"

"No! Her parents must be frantic."

Gil held up the baby at arm's length. "I don't remember being this small."

Alexandria laughed. "I'd normally assure you that everyone starts that small, but I think you should ask your mom."

"Lucy," someone cried. The two "highborn" Gil had seen earlier rushed up and grabbed the fairy from his arms. "Thank you for finding her," they said, and then all three disappeared into the crowd.

Alexandria dragged Gil back to their group, who had stopped to wait for them. Most of the humans were a little ahead, talking to other people on the street, but Ian waited with the fae.

The wind picked up, and the temperature dropped again. If the humans hadn't insisted on the fae wearing extra layers, Gil would anticipate several of them falling ill. Ian's hood blew off, and Shar's hair fluttered away from his face.

"That's Shar," Ram whispered. "That's Shar," he shouted, pointing. "He's alive!"

Alexandria stared at him in confusion, then at Shar. "What's wrong?"

"Who's Shar?" Ian asked.

"Hush," Gil said. "We know."

Ram glared at him, then examined the faces of every fae surrounding him. "You knew, Mother? You all knew? And you didn't tell me? But Lord Kishar rules now."

Not true yet, but that was what Gil feared would happen once the rest of the fleet landed. Particularly if Shar waited years to claim his throne.

"What's going on?" Alexandria asked.

Gil waved her off and crouched by his brother's knees. "Be quiet," he begged. "Don't tell anyone."

"Now is not the time," Taras said.

Ram clenched his jaw and narrowed his eyes. "Now is not the time," he ground out between his teeth. "But what about the humans?" He spat the last word like an insult.

Quickly, Shar grabbed Alexandria and Ian by the wrists. "Alex, Ian," he said, "forget." Power hummed in his quiet voice.

Ian blinked and pulled his hand free. "Are we ready to go yet?"

Alexandria scowled and wrinkled her forehead. Gil held one finger to his lips. She clamped her mouth shut, but her eyes turned green, a sure sign of trouble. As she turned away, shoulders stiff, Gil wondered how long the magic would hold her using only her short name. If Ian hadn't been so careless about using his real name, he might have had a similar resistance. But Gil hadn't expected Shar to be the one Ian needed to guard against.

"That wasn't necessary," he told Shar. "They are trustworthy."

More trustworthy than his own brother, but Ram had known who Shar was for his entire life. If Shar erased himself from Ram's mind, too much memory would disappear. Gil had to believe Ram was still honorable enough to keep his promise to wait.

"Keeping his secret is easier when fewer people know," Taras said. "Shar was right not to take the chance."

Gil scowled. When would the prince be allowed to take his rightful place? Would it cost them the treaty when the time came to sign?

CHAPTER 8

ANGER

TRAY IN HAND, Ian looked for a free seat in the cafeteria. Unfortunately, none of his family could sit with him. Gil had to translate for the other half of the students, Nikos was at his college classes, and the ladies all had first lunch. He missed spending all day with Mom in homeschool, but if he was attending a regular public school, he wouldn't have any of his family with him, either.

He waved at Gil on the other side of the room and found a place by Abe, Shaun, and their human roommates. At least the boys were friendly acquaintances instead of strangers, and by now, they could at least partly talk to one another, which meant Ian got a little more chance to eat before he was bombarded with questions.

Or he usually did. Today, Abe immediately started asking questions. Apparently Gil and Alexandria had discussed her birthday in biology class, and Abe wanted to know if humans really set food on fire or if Gil had been making up stories.

"We only burn the candles on the cake," Ian said, and then had to explain what candles were and why they put them on the cake.

Shaun grinned behind his long bangs. "Birthdays are as odd as years."

"How old is your sister?" Touji asked. Shaun's Japanese roommate had a suspiciously bland look.

"Seventeen today," Ian said.

Touji grinned and smoothed his hair. "Seventeen is a good age."

Lovely. Wait until he discovered Alexandria didn't have time to date anyone.

Kirill grunted. "In Ukraine, it is unlucky to celebrate your birthday early."

"Too bad," Ian said. "She has judo tonight."

And when they'd heard that Artemis had finally lifted off without being canceled again, they'd had two reasons to celebrate. Though the dragons had already brought almost four thousand fae, that still left more than six thousand on the moon in probable starving condition. Even the best telescopes could only see so much of the ship, and the rocket launch was the best bet to check on its status. Most of the fae coming down knew only their own jobs, not whether the ship was still sound. Granted, there was a limit to how much the astronauts on the shuttle would be able to see, but it was better than nothing.

"Next question," Shaun asked. "What are grades?"

"Ways to measure how well you are doing in a class," Ian explained.

"Missus-hun tells us we are doing well," Abe said. "Is that a grade?"

"Mrs. Hahn is a good teacher," Ian said. "She doesn't give you grades because you guys are still trying to learn English, so whatever else you learn is extra."

And grades made three reasons to celebrate last night, since Alexandria had waved a calculus paper with a B- on it. She was so excited that Ian hadn't brought out his A+ Spanish test to show Mom.

"Misterabernathy is teaching us English." A vine sprouted through Abe's hair and wrapped around his neck. "He says our grades are bad."

"That's not fair," Touji said. "He should grade you on basic competency. You talk to us well."

Ian rearranged the last of his vegetables on his plate, his appetite suddenly gone. Gil also translated for Mr. Abernathy but hadn't mentioned any problems with the teacher, so it must be Ian's fault. He didn't know Fae well enough yet, and kept having to teach the fae something more basic because he hadn't done a good enough job with their language lessons before Mr. Abernathy arrived. If he didn't cooperate with Mr. Abernathy, the entire project might fail.

Ian sighed. "Sorry. I'll talk to him." But he only had a few minutes to practice what to say.

The warning bell rang, and everyone collected their trays and garbage. Heart racing, Ian checked that his vocabulary notebooks were in his backpack, then dragged himself to English class.

As usual, the fae all came on time. As usual, Mr. Abernathy showed up right as the bell rang and swept in like a king, paying as much attention to his students as to the frost melting on the windows. Somehow, he still hadn't noticed the fae who looked inhuman. He jumped immediately into the lecture without a greeting or introduction, and Ian scrambled to catch up. He'd have to talk to Mr. Abernathy about grades after class.

Ian stopped translating as soon as he realized the speech about proper grammar and tenses had turned into a rant about using subjunctive mood correctly.

"This is something you don't need to know yet," he told the fae.

Pretending to translate, he rehearsed the difference between present and past tense in regular form. Hoping Mr. Abernathy wouldn't notice the English, he then listed irregular verbs as he thought of them.

Mr. Abernathy, despite being hired to learn Fae, didn't notice what Ian was actually saying in either language and kept talking with a great many emphatic scribblings on the white board. Finally, he slashed through the writing and turned to face the class, panting hard.

He caught Ian in the middle of tenses for "do."

"What are you saying?" Mr. Abernathy accused. "That sounds like English, but not any kind of sentence. Are you translating correctly?"

Ian hunched his shoulders. "They aren't ready for subjunctive mood. Can't we review present and past tense?"

"It's not my fault they aren't ready," Mr. Abernathy snarled. "If you had translated my lessons correctly, they would be up to speed."

Ian scraped up his courage. "No they wouldn't. They can only learn so fast. Your lessons are too advanced. And seriously, subjunctive mood isn't required in high school at all."

Mr. Abernathy slammed his fist on the table. "What do you know?

You're a kid. I'm the expert here. If you listened to me like you're supposed to, the entire class wouldn't be *failing*. Every one of them flunked midterms, and it's your fault!"

His face turned as red as Dad's used to, and Ian cringed farther away.

"They aren't supposed to be graded," Ian protested. "They don't need the high school credit, just the language knowledge." He inhaled for courage. "I need to talk to you about that, actually."

"Don't contradict me," Mr. Abernathy roared, throwing the whiteboard marker at Ian.

Ian ducked, and the class inhaled audibly.

"I ought to walk out now and make you responsible for these failures," Mr. Abernathy shouted. "Then everyone will see how useless you are. I'm the expert here. I'm writing the paper. You are nothing but a worthless aide who can't even translate properly!"

Mr. Abernathy had learned the little Fae he knew from reading Ian's vocabulary lists and notes on grammar. But arguing with Dad in one of his moods had never done any good, so Ian kept his head bowed and edged farther away.

Zee raised her hand, though it shook visibly and she hunched so badly that her head almost disappeared between her shoulders. "Stop yell U.N." Her voice shook as much as her hand.

"Talk proper English," Mr. Abernathy shot back. "And be quiet in my class if you don't want to be suspended."

Zee and most of the students cowered under his anger. Even the troll, Vince, who traveled on a flatbed wagon and still sat as tall as the others in their chairs, lifted his book in front of his face.

With no way to win the argument, Ian waved the class down. "You're the teacher, sir."

If he was any kind of good teacher, his students would learn more and be less frightened. But Dad had never cared, and Mr. Abernathy obviously didn't, either.

Mr. Abernathy nodded sharply. "That's right. I'm the teacher." The bell rang, but nobody moved. "What are you waiting for? Get out of my classroom."

Ian grabbed the closest wheelchair and pushed it into the hall. He got half a dozen out before everyone's roommates arrived to help. Once the prior students were gone and the next class was seated quietly, he took his place at the front of the room to translate again. For subjunctive mood, as if that would do the fae any good when they still confused past and present tense and forgot the subject usually came first in the sentence.

"I don't need you," Mr. Abernathy said. "Go away."

"Excuse me?"

"Go. Away," Mr. Abernathy enunciated, pointing to the door.

And leave the class at his mercy? Ian shuddered. They really wouldn't learn anything then, since Mr. Abernathy expected them to understand his English. But what choice did Ian have? Silently, he trudged out.

As he headed to the principal's office, he racked his brain for anything he could have done better. Mr. Abernathy would have been happier if Ian had obediently translated, but the lecture would have been wasted. Should the fae have been ready for subjunctive mood? How could they be already?

Ms. Maxwell was busy, so Ian waited with the secretaries until she became available.

When he entered her office, she passed him a bowl of candy. "Aren't you supposed to be in class? What's up?"

"Mr. Abernathy is upset about midterm grades," Ian said.

Ms. Maxwell chuckled. "I bet his students are more upset."

Ian wrinkled his nose. "Pretty sure there isn't *more* upset."

Leaning back, Ms. Maxwell grabbed a candy for herself. "He comes from academia, Ian. He's used to everything being graded and weighed, and his success hinges in part on their progress."

"They are making progress," Ian said.

"But they aren't meeting high school standards, let alone college, and he's having trouble adjusting. Try not to let him bother you."

Ian stuffed a mini chocolate into his mouth. Mr. Abernathy was just like Dad, angry and blaming everyone else for the problems. Ian had tried hard to please Dad, but it never worked. The only escape had been leaving Dad behind after the divorce. But Ian couldn't leave the school. He wouldn't abandon Gil.

Feebly, he tried again. "Mr. Abernathy doesn't like my help."

Ms. Maxwell sighed. "He never will, Ian."

Ian would never get it right, and everyone knew it. "But—"

The door opened, and a secretary stuck in her head. "Sorry, Raquel, but we need you to deal with someone."

Ms. Maxwell hopped to her feet. "Do the best you can, Ian. Nobody expects you to be perfect." She walked out, closing the door behind her.

"But he kicked me out of class," Ian said to the empty room.

He slumped in the chair and ate another chocolate. Even Ms. Maxwell thought he didn't know enough. He was failing Gil and the rest of the fae, and he'd never learn fast enough, teach fast enough. Tears pricked behind his eyelids, and the sweet chocolate turned bitter on his tongue.

Ian stayed in the principal's office until he stopped crying, then hunted down his algebra homework. By the end of the period, his own assignments were finished and he'd helped several fae with their homework. In one case, all he did was turn the electronic pages on the tablet, since every time Freya touched the screen, the tablet shorted out. He'd mention it to Alexandria and Mrs. Hahn so they could find an alternative. In the meantime, he soothed her complaints about useless magic, good for nothing except war and scrambling both magic and human contrivances.

The kitchen staff arrived to set up for dinner, and Gil bounced in shortly after, hair still wet from swim class. He waved from across the cafeteria and took his place to translate for one side of the room. Ian grabbed his food and found a seat in the other half.

Ian listened to the fae and human students chattering at each other, mostly in English but a little in Fae, and wondered what he could have done better. He'd written every word Gil had explained to him, and he'd almost memorized the whole list. Granted, his grammar was probably bad, but the fae understood him, which was the important thing.

But that wasn't the language that had the biggest problem. How could he help the fae learn English faster? He ate absently, not paying attention to what he put into his mouth, and for once, his translating skills were in small demand.

He was so lost in thought that he jumped when Gil said his name.

"Hi, Gil. Is dinner over already?"

"No." Gil frowned at him. "Zee tell me Misterabernathy yell at you. Again? He yell much?"

Ian shrugged. "He's not happy with the progress of his classes."

Folding his arms, Gil glared. "Misterabernathy is teacher, yes?"

"Yes," Ian agreed.

"Why your fault teaching is slow? Why not fault of teacher? Or students?"

"I—" Ian hung his head. "I guess I didn't teach enough English before he got here, and I'm not translating well enough now."

Gil stuck out his tongue and blew a raspberry.

Despite his distress, Ian giggled. "Who taught you that?"

"Not matter," Gil said. "Why not tell War Lady?"

"I did. She said to try harder."

Gil squinted at him. "Hmm. Why not tell Misterabernathy be better teacher?"

"No way," Ian said. "He'd blow up." And then he had to explain both the literal and metaphorical meanings of the phrase.

"We should 'blow up' him," Gil said.

"No," Ian said. "But you can tell me what you're doing so he doesn't yell at you."

After all, Gil translated for Mr. Abernathy exactly the way Ian did. The teacher couldn't possibly ignore Gil as much as he ignored the other students.

Gil shrugged. "He does not talk to me. He does not look at me. Highborn often ignore commoners."

"He isn't highborn," Ian said.

"Thinks he is?" Gil suggested.

Ian raised his hands in a helpless gesture. "Maybe." He raised his eyebrows as a thought hit him. "Or maybe he's a garden-variety bigot. Um, that means he might hate your skin color."

Maybe Abernathy thought he'd get in more trouble for yelling at a black kid than a white one and settled for ignoring him despite the translating.

Gil examined his ink-black arm. "Is wrong color for his garden?"

Ian snorted. "Sorry, garden-variety means 'ordinary.' It's the bigot part that's the problem."

"I don't understand."

Ram's Nigerian roommate, Okoro, leaned toward them from his seat farther down the table. "Sorry for interrupting. And eavesdropping. Listen, Gil, there's no understanding bigotry. Some people are reared to hate other people because of the color of their skin or the shape of their eyes. They believe stupid lies, and you can't change their minds. Try to stay out of their way."

Gil looked at Ian, who nodded sadly.

"It's like the way some of the elves feel about commoners," Ian said. "I'm sorry Mr. Abernathy is one of those people."

"You are his color," Gil said. "Why does he yell at you?"

"Some people are lousy excuses for human beings," Okoro said. At Gil's confused look, he rephrased. "Some people are just bad people."

"Mmm." Gil nodded. "I know some. But Ian, you are reason this school work. Don't let him treat you like that." He stood with a grin. "I will talk to him. He will stop if wolf tells him to stop."

"No," Ian begged, grabbing Gil's arm and holding tight. "Absolutely do not threaten him. That would endanger the school and the treaty. I'll be fine."

Gil growled and pulled his arm free. "I don't like bad people, but I will wait, for treaty's sake." He stomped off.

Ian pushed aside his tray and dropped his head onto the table. Great. If he didn't find a way to please Mr. Abernathy, Gil would bite the teacher's head off — maybe literally — and then they'd have bigger problems.

CHAPTER 9

IN WHICH THEY SEE MAGIC

DECEMBER 2-4, 2022

ZAK GLANCED at the part in her hand, then back at her book. Yes, it looked like a "battery," though she had no idea how it gave power. Now, how could she hook it to the navigation contrivance she was assembling in the back of the tech classroom?

"Need help?" someone asked.

Squelching a yelp, Zak jerked around.

A tall boy with brown hair and round windows over his eyes held up his hands in a cautious gesture. "Sorry, didn't mean to startle you. I just thought you might like a hand."

"I have two hands," Zak said.

The boy chuckled. "It's a way of offering help. You know, like an extra hand to hold something in place?"

"Oh." She narrowed her eyes at him. "I can do it."

He nodded. "Okay. I'm Shaun's roommate, and he told me you were a navigator on the spaceship. May I ask you questions about space? I want to work in the space program — if the Russians ever start behaving again.

Not as an astronaut, but as an engineer. Or an astronaut engineer, maybe."

Zak held up a hand to stop the flow of words. "What is spaceship? What is space if it is not—" She held her hands apart to indicate distance. "What is astronaut and engineer? And Russian?"

"Oh." The boy blew a puff of air. "Right. Space is the place between the stars and planets. A spaceship travels in space. So does an astronaut, but that's a person, not a ship."

Zak nodded. "Okay." All the surviving fae were astronauts, so she was nothing special.

"An engineer makes or works on machines," the boy continued.

"What are machines?"

The boy pointed toward Zak's contrivance. "Cars are machines, microwaves are machines, the tablet you use for homework is a machine."

"Contrivances," Zak said in Fae. "I am a contriver, what you call an engineer."

The boy repeated both Fae words. "Yes, that's why I wanted to talk to you."

"Wait," Zak said, "what about Russian?"

"Good memory." The boy raised his eyebrows. "A Russian is someone from Russia, a country on the other side of Earth. Right now, Russia is fighting my country." He sighed. "My family had to evacuate. That means leave, escape."

Zak turned over the battery in her hand. "We evacuated, too."

But only a tenth of the fae had fit on the ships, and most of the survivors were still in "space," waiting for Father to guide them to Earth, hoping to get a home of their own. If Zak and the other fae students could learn enough to forge the treaty with Earth.

"I'm sorry. I hope you will be safe now." The boy pulled a chair closer and sat, elbows on his knees. "So, may I ask you questions about space?"

"Yes," Zak said. "But first, can you tell me how this battery works?"

"Sure. What are you making?"

Zak patted the top of her contrivance. "A copy of the navigation system on our ship."

"Nice," the boy said. "But why?"

"Earth has same — machines, but ours only get information, and yours send signals, also."

"Like a radio or television?" he asked.

"Raydeeo, yes. I want to send message to Father."

"But his machine can't reply?"

"No." Zak bit her lip. "But he will know I still wait for him."

"Oh. Here, let me see that battery."

The two of them worked on the radio until the bell rang and Gaby came to get Zak, even though she had advanced to a self-push chair.

"That is my roommate," Zak told the boy. "I have to go to language class."

The boy looked at Gaby and back at Zak. "Wait, you're a girl?"

Gaby sniffed. "Rude." She spun Zak's chair and walked off. Once in the hall, she said, "Don't mind him. Sometimes it's hard for us to tell. Most of you have long hair and are way too pretty, Gil and a lot of the boys wear a skirt — sorry, a kilt, and Nate is all snakes."

Zak shook her head. She'd rather be a boy, anyway.

In English class, Misterabernathy, looking at the giant slate instead of the fae, declared, "I will not accept my students failing. From now on, unless I am doing research, we will only speak English in this class so you will learn properly."

U.N. started to interpret, and Misterabernathy cut him off. "English only."

Zak bit her lip, and the other fae sagged. How were they supposed to understand without a translation?

U.N. sighed and sat in a chair in the corner. He doodled in his notebook while Misterabernathy lectured, but sometimes he wrote a Fae word in English letters and showed it to the class to help them understand.

Misterabernathy rarely allowed questions, and when he did, it was only from the fae who looked most human and most male. Yet another reason to dress like a boy, if Zak actually wanted to talk to the teacher.

At the end of class, Misterabernathy glared at the ceiling. "And starting next week, I want the cos-play to stop." The bell rang, and he marched out.

Zak raised her hand. "What is cos-play?"

U.N. scrunched up his face. "Remember Halloween? He thinks you are all wearing costumes."

"How stupid is he?" Wes asked. "And what are we supposed to do without your help?"

The highborn had all struggled during class. The commoners talked more to their roommates and thus knew more English.

"I'm sorry," U.N. said. "Do the best you can. Talk to your roommates about ways to look more human. Nate and Vince and everyone who can't disguise yourselves, sit in the back." He rubbed his forehead as everyone's roommates came to collect them.

Zak survived swim class and dinner, and in her room, found Freya trying on every outfit she had.

"I need a new dress." The highborn held a perfectly good one under her chin and frowned at the mirror.

"You have enough clothes," Zak said.

Jin stopped playing her magic. "Didn't Ms. Stafford tell you no more?"

Freya flapped her hand. "She doesn't understand. I'll take Zak's share, since Zak doesn't need them."

Jin blew a rude sound on her magic wand — flute. "Zak deserves her own pretty clothes, thanks." After a cheerful trill, she returned to her practice.

Zak groaned and pulled her pillow over her head as Jin's magic continued. No, music, which was as beautiful as it was still unsettling.

THE NEXT DAY had no classes, so Zak went to the empty contrivance room. To her surprise, the tall boy was examining her radio. If he messed it up, she would punch the stupid smile from his face.

"Oh, hi," he said. "I hoped you would come back today."

"Why?" she asked bluntly. "You have more questions about space?" She wheeled her chair between the boy and her precious contrivance.

"Yes," he admitted, "but I also want to apologize for thinking you were a boy."

Zak shrugged. "Not matter." She was more used to being a boy than a girl.

The boy snorted. "Of course it does. My name is Kirill Kovalenko, by the way." He held out his hand for an Earth greeting.

Reluctantly, Zak held out her own hand and followed U.N.'s lesson. "Zee Brown."

Kirill shook her hand gently. "So, can I help you with your project? I could explain words or hand you parts?"

"I still girl," Zak said.

Kirill wrinkled his forehead. "I don't see the problem."

Truthfully, having someone to explain unfamiliar words in her book would be useful. In fact...

"Could we explain so Father make same contrivance?"

If he could send her a message in reply, maybe she would stop worrying about him.

Kirill frowned. "Maybe, but will he have the parts he needs?"

Zak sighed. "If work with Earth parts, I look for Fae parts."

Kirill rubbed his hands together. "It sounds like a challenge."

They worked for hours on the contrivances, and by the time she rolled into bed, exhausted, the battery was working, and she had sent a two-word message.

"Greetings, Father."

THE DAY after that also had no classes. Between breakfast shifts, Alexandria waved her arms for attention. "I've been wanting to introduce you to movies for a while, as an introduction to Earth culture."

"Oh, fun," Gaby said. "I think you'll like this, Zee."

U.N. stood on a chair. "Despite what *some people* think, you all know enough English now to watch with the captions on. And I picked the first movie."

Alexandria continued. "A movie is like a story with actions, and captions are the spoken words written so you can read them. I've been thinking about this since Halloween, and it might help you understand some of the cultural legends of Earth. This is a pretend story, not real, and one of the languages is also pretend. Your roommates will help you with English words you don't know, and you don't have to worry about the pretend language. I talked to your healer, and Miles has cleared popcorn as a treat."

"This is a really long movie," U.N. said, "a set of three, actually, so we'll start right after the second breakfast shift and take breaks for meals." He giggled. "Second breakfast. Never mind. Okay, everybody, enjoy the movie in the basement, and we'll see you when we get back from church." He hopped off the chair, and his human family left.

"Come on, Zee," Gaby said. "We'd better clean our room and finish our chores quickly so we won't be late for the movie." She spun the wheeled chair and pushed it into the hallway. "I think I know what movie we're watching, but maybe I'm wrong. This will be exciting!"

She chattered all the way to their room, forgetting to use words that Zak knew, so the gremlin let her babble wash over her. They made it downstairs in plenty of time, though Zak didn't understand why the humans wanted a contrivance to shine a big rectangle of light on the far wall of the large room. She accepted a bowl of white blobs and reluctantly put one into her mouth. To her surprise, it was pleasantly chewy and fragrant.

As everyone took seats or wheeled their chairs into place, the light on the far wall dimmed. Someone turned off the room lights. Her roommates sat on one side of Zak, and Kirill and Ash took the other side. A few rows away, Gil sat by Shar and Nate and several human boys.

In the darkness, a woman's voice said, "The world has changed," and words shone on the wall to match. As the voice continued, pictures appeared, and the fae gasped in surprise. Though their "tablets" sometimes had moving pictures, this movie was so large and realistic it was hard to remember it wasn't real.

The woman continued speaking, and the pictures changed to match her words. When the woman said three rings were given to elves, wisest and fairest, the images were similar to the highborn. Around the room, the highborn cheered or slapped hands. Zak sniffed. It was a pretend story; U.N. said so. The highborn might be fairest, but they were no wiser than anyone else.

The movie continued with more magic rings bound with power. That was silly. The circlets that enhanced the fae magic didn't have any actual power in them, and losing them wouldn't destroy a fae's magic. And a master ring with its own will was definitely not a thing.

Somewhere in the room, Gil laughed loudly and said, "One ring to rule them all, U.N.!" He was shushed by several irritated voices.

As the movie continued, Gil wasn't the only one who blurted out comments. Most of the adult fae sighed when Sam mentioned he was the farthest away from home he'd ever been. Ash choked audibly at the destruction of the trees, and Taras complimented the scout's two-handed fighting technique and use of fire. Merodach snorted at the mention of elvish medicine, and Freya complained she didn't get dresses that pretty. But mostly the fae and humans watched quietly.

Assuming the others were doing the same, Zak made a mental list of questions to ask later, like why one-hundred and eleven years was unnaturally long — after she converted the years to conjunctions.

The hobbits looked a fair amount like pukels and a little like gremlins or koboloi. So why would they be excited to see the elves, who seemed to be the human idea of the highborn? The highborn were nothing wonderful, and the commoners would rather be ignored.

As for Zak, she would rather visit that library with all the scrolls and books and papers. Think of the knowledge! Even the mage in the story knew the secrets were in writing. That's why the highborn didn't teach their writing to commoners. And yet, the humans openly shared. Their generosity with knowledge was their greatest asset for a successful treaty, whether they knew it or not.

When the king's heir was introduced in the council, Zak shot a discreet look at Shar. Would either king step forward and take the throne? Gil wasn't looking at Shar, either, but his ears pointed toward the prince. Zak turned back to the movie to avoid drawing attention to Shar, but it stopped without resolving the problem of the heir.

Zak sighed in disappointment, and Gaby bumped her shoulder. "Wasn't it great?"

"Everyone run to the bathroom if you need to," War Lady said. "We'll start again in twenty minutes."

"Hurry!" Gaby wheeled Zak's chair, and Jin grabbed Freya.

But everyone else was also rushing, and the halls clogged with the evacuation.

As soon as possible, they returned and took their seats, and the lights went dark again. This time, there was even more music, and Zak found herself breathing faster. Not magic, Jin said it wasn't magic. And yet, there was definitely something magical about its effect on her. Around her, the other fae shuffled as if they also felt it.

She shivered again as the movie people struggled through snow. Now that she had experienced cold as more than the occasional ice magic, she pitied them.

The pictures on the wall flashed by, on and on, and yet, when they stopped, Zak still didn't know if the heir would take his place as king.

"Time for lunch," U.N. announced. "You can run to the bathroom while we set out the food."

"Is it finished?" Zak whispered to Gaby.

"This one is," Gaby said, "but there are two more. It's a *long* series, twelve hours."

They all hurried to their rooms, then to the dining hall to eat and discuss the movie. So everyone could eat at once, those who didn't fit around the tables balanced their trays on their laps. It was awkward, but nobody wanted to take the time for their usual meal shifts.

Taras and Ram and several other warriors dissected fighting techniques, including the merits of using any weapon at hand, even a frying pan, and how a smaller fighter could combat a larger one.

Several of the highborn argued with Merodach about magic and what was possible or wise and who would actually have those powers. Two of them debated the merits of a seeing stone versus a bowl of water and if either would allow a glimpse of the future.

Vince, Nate, some pixies, a kobolos or two, and a few gremlins clumped together and discussed the glaring inaccuracies and horrible attitudes toward certain races. Trolls turning to stone in sunlight? Ridiculous! Elves glowing like pixies? Laughable. Clearly, legend had become myth, because the humans got everything wrong. No wonder Alex hadn't been sure if the fae were born or spawned. And worse, all the non-human-looking creatures were monsters. Was that really what the humans believed? How could peace win if Earth considered them monsters?

Near Zak, Shar and Gil held a whispered conversation, too low for her to catch more than something about bloodline and making things right. The babble on either side of her drowned out the rest, but Alex watched them with a frown.

"Do you suppose Beren and Luthien were the Starry Lovers?" Freya asked. "Or Aragorn and Arwen?"

"Don't be ridiculous," Wes said. "Neither of them were a commoner. Humans aren't even fae."

"Fine," Freya said. "But the humans obviously believe in mixed-race relationships." She and Wes both grimaced.

"I think it's lovely," Shalla said. The sirin raised her chin and stared down Freya.

"Who are the Starry Lovers?" Gaby asked.

Freya and Shalla took turns summarizing the forbidden story of the highborn and commoner who fled the fae worlds to be together. Zak and the other navigators had followed their map to reach Earth.

"Why would the humans and elves and other races work together?" Wes asked.

"Isn't that what we're trying to do here?" Shalla replied.

"Of course we would," U.N. protested. "Why don't the highborn and commoners like each other?"

Zak buttered her roll all the way to the edge, hoping someone else would answer. Gil was still whispering to Shar, who was scowling. No help there.

Finally, she said, "Commoners have less magic and are worth less."

Alex scowled, and her eyes turned bright green. Most of the fae within line of sight ducked their heads to avoid meeting her gaze.

"That's ridiculous," Alex said. "Everyone has different talents. Magic doesn't matter."

The highborn raised their eyebrows, and the commoners hunched their shoulders.

Never trust an elf, Zak thought. And yet, if the commoners and lesser highborn didn't make allies, what would they do when the lords came to Earth, the elf-witches of terrible power? They must place their hope in men and hope they would defend the small folk in real life as much as in the movie.

"So, did the fae get lost in space," Alex asked, "or did something happen to them on Earth?"

With a sudden jerk, Shar slapped Gil's face. "Stop!"

The room fell silent as he wheeled his chair in a circle and rolled from the room. Everyone stared at Gil, who was rubbing his cheek.

Gil took a deep breath. "So, U.N., you say there's more to this movie?"

"Yeah," U.N. said, forehead wrinkled. "Are you o—"

"I'm fine." Gil waved his arms for attention. "As soon as you finish eating, head downstairs."

He led the way, and Zak followed, along with almost everyone else. In the basement, Alex set the movie box in Freya's lap so she could rearrange the table that held it.

U.N. walked in the door and groaned. "Oh, no." He grabbed the box and stared intently at the front. "Yep, it's dead."

"How can it be dead?" Alex asked. "It was working less than an hour ago."

"You let Freya touch it," U.N. said.

Freya pouted. "I didn't mean to break it."

"Yeah, I know." U.N. sighed. "I'll go see if we have another one."

Zak mouthed, "Sorry" at her roommate. Sometimes having a lot of magic was worse than having almost none.

In a few minutes, a new magic box was hooked up, and the next movie started. Not long after, Shar slipped into the room and parked his wheelchair against the far wall. Zak didn't point him out to Gil.

Like all the fae, Zak watched the battles in horrified silence. Even her amazement at the thought of someone running for three days straight and still having strength to fight died at the menu of the orcs. Around her, gasps and groans echoed.

The picture stopped moving, and Alex's voice spoke in the darkness. "Please remember this is a pretend story. None of it is real."

The movie resumed, but the silence continued. By the time they went upstairs for dinner, Zak felt numb, and the faces around her echoed her shock. The conversations were quieter this time, and the fae spoke of war and the end of alliances and all life. Ash said nothing, but tears ran down his cheeks, and vines from his hair had wrapped themselves around his shoulders like an embrace.

Only a few seemed happy. Freya had stopped paying much attention after the kissing scenes, and now sat with a dazed smile on her face. Even when the lovers said goodbye forever, she merely shrugged.

"Can humans really mount horses like the elf did?" Wes asked.

"No," his roommate Yuri said. "It's all pretend."

"Good," Ram grunted. "I'm tired of amazing human feats."

"They still have more stamina," Taras said. "You should take them seriously, even before their contrivances come into play. Though our land was best, Earth is our only option now, and we're running out of time to make new alliances."

"I don't care." Ram shrugged. "It's all pretend, anyway."

Alex stood abruptly. "This movie was a bad idea. We should stop now."

U.N. tugged on her sleeve. "We'd better finish the movie for the happy ending."

Alex surveyed the room and winced. "Yeah, but we need to have a long talk about appropriate movies, U.N."

Hunching his shoulders, U.N. set up the movie box again. "I'll skip the intro, okay?"

Alex growled. "Good idea."

As the movie progressed, the story still dwelled on war and the loss of home, though there were promises of hope. The elf and dwarf became friends, allies gathered to fight together, and the treacherous white mage fell.

As the music dragged Zak's emotions in circles, she squinted hard at Jin, sure magic must be involved somehow. She also noted the devastating effect of the war contrivances. The human "tech" would be just as destructive against the fae.

Most of all, she noted how only the men counted for anything. How like the fae! Then, to her surprise, a woman and a pukel defeated a witch-lord. Oh, because it was all pretend. And yet, she wished it could be true.

U.N. was right about the happy ending, and when the lights came on, Ash was no longer crying, and his vines had retreated out of sight.

"Bedtime," War Lady said. "You can talk about the movie tomorrow."

Gil stood on his chair. "Sorry, I have one thing to say." He continued in Fae. "Though this movie is pretend, it is much like our reality. There is no going back to our world. We could battle, but who would win? I plead for a better way. Many of you know our prince was my friend. For my part." He didn't look at Shar, still against the wall. "We spoke often of his hopes to fulfill his father's promises and make a home for us here. Now is our chance. I beg you to form alliances with the humans and learn their language. Let us have peace!"

He hopped down. Ram sneered at him and wheeled toward the hall, and Shar turned his face away as he passed. Everyone stirred and prepared to leave.

Shar wheeled himself to the doorway, then stopped. Without turning around, he raised his voice. "I'm for peace." And then he moved on, letting the crowd into the hall.

As Zak passed Gil, she touched his elbow softly.

He patted her shoulder. "We are not alone in this fight."

In her room, Zak fell asleep and dreamed of music and hope.

Chapter 10

Cousins

December 24, 2022

Alexandria bowed to her opponent and congratulated the victor. As soon as she turned away, Mom and Ian swarmed her. Mom wrapped her in a hug and passed over her water bottle.

"It's okay," Ian said. "You'll get him next time."

Next time. It had taken too long for the slice on her back to heal, and even longer to get back into shape. This competition was supposed to let her walk out with her black belt, but no, she still wasn't good enough. What did she expect only three months after earning brown belt? Sure, she *could* have earned brown last year, but she hadn't really been practicing regularly enough since then.

"Yeah," she grunted. "Next time."

If she couldn't make progress, then maybe she should quit for a while. Homework and her responsibilities at the school would keep her plenty busy anyway; she just hated to give up.

They all headed for the door, and Jin rose from her seat at the wall. A local student like her roommate Gaby, she was a senior and had her own car. Zee had talked her into helping, though apparently it hadn't taken much persuasion when presented with an opportunity to drive.

"All done?" Jin snapped her gum. "Nice job crushing them."

"Thanks." Alexandria shrugged into her coat. If only she had crushed the last bout.

Jin held open the door. "Am I taking you back to the school for the party?"

An arctic blast of air swirled in. Yesterday had been almost warm, but today had topped at fourteen degrees, and right now was cold enough to believe in ice monsters. After one step outside this morning, Gil had switched to warm pants instead of his usual skirt.

Alexandria hurried out first, pulling up her hood as a barrier against the cold. Gulping from her water bottle, she stretched her legs to reach the car quickly.

With only two classes this semester, her GPA was almost entirely dependent on calculus, in which she was still only getting a B despite Gaby's tutoring. Too many poor grades at the beginning of the semester. If she didn't ace her final, her grade would still sink. So how could she have fit in more classes, when she didn't have enough time to study for the ones she already had?

"Sadly, no," Mom said. "Nikos is picking up his family at the airport right now, and we need to keep them away from the school. We already had a birthday party for Gil last night. The students can celebrate Christmas, or school break, or whatever, without us. But thank you for the ride."

"No problem, Ms. Helen." Jin unlocked her cherry-red sedan and hopped in to rev the engine.

And Nikos's parents expected to meet all his foster siblings. No way could they see Gil and Miknon, but that meant Alexandria had to be at home instead of supervising the school party like she ought to. At least it gave her more time to study. Stupid calculus.

When the last seatbelt clicked, Jin peeled from the parking lot and zipped to their apartment at only one mile over the speed limit. Alexandria and her family climbed out, and the red car zoomed around the corner as Mom unlocked their door. Alexandria and Ian huddled together for warmth, then crowded through the door right behind Mom.

"Well," Mom said, "I'll start dinner. With the slow cooker and fresh rolls, I'll have time to visit with Nikos's family." She wrinkled her nose a little. "And check papers."

Like everyone else, she had made compromises to make the school work. In her case, history was at least her expertise, though teaching was a change of career and she still hadn't had time to return to her Ph.D. program. Right now, she only had a week to finish grading the long reports her students had written.

The corners of Ian's lips turned down, and he ducked his face behind his long bangs. "I have to study the lesson plans for English so I'll be on track."

He hung up his coat and slumped toward his bedroom, shoulders hunched. Yeah, so maybe Alexandria should suck up her own self pity. Mom and Ian were as busy with the school as she was, and had just as little free time, even during vacation. And while Nikos spent a lot less time at the high school, he was going to college full-time and still worked part-time to pay a third of the rent. A third, though he was one person out of six in the apartment and didn't even get his own room. Until Mom got hired as a teacher, he'd paid half. Alexandria sneaked a hug around Mom's shoulders, then hung up her coat.

"Calc test," Alexandria said.

She refilled her water bottle and grabbed her homework from the counter. To be comfortable, she removed her judo belt and dropped it over the edge of the thrift-store couch, then turned sideways and settled cushions behind her back. Propping her book against her raised knees, she turned to the chapter for the upcoming test.

She'd rather be at the party, hanging out with Gil and Miknon and the other students. Being "in charge" of social activities wasn't as fun as simply attending, but it could be worse. She could be stuck making a dictionary, like Ian! At least she liked helping the students make friends with each other.

And calculus was her enemy. Time to crush some equations so she could play with Nikos and Ian during Christmas break, then devote time to the students when school started again. At the very least, she needed to find where she still needed help so she could make the most use of her tutoring with Gaby. Thank goodness the younger girl was still willing to help her, or Alexandria would have already flunked. But obviously, tutoring would have to wait until after Christmas, so she was on her own today. And she'd better hurry, because after dark, she'd have to go meet another landing party of the fae while Nikos kept his family distracted.

In a way, she was lucky. She got to spend the holidays with her family, and thanks to the secrecy, none of the other human students could go home until summer. Only about half of the fae parents had landed yet, so their kids were also alone. Well, alone with four hundred other students at a holiday party. That didn't include her.

She lost herself in studying, emerging only when a rush of cold air heralded the door opening. A crowd of people pushed through, laughing and talking in Greek and shivering as they removed coats. Nikos waved at her, but Mom and Ian came in to greet everyone, so she was spared the trouble of unburying herself from her books.

Nikos looked very much like his parents, though his father had brown hair instead of black, and he obviously got his shorter height from his mom. All five of the strangers had the same straight noses, brown eyes, and thick eyebrows as Nikos, and all the men were as tall as Alexandria or taller.

Nikos made introductions for everyone. His parents, Marina and Damianos, kissed Mom and thanked her for taking care of their boy. The young men were Artur, Vasil, and Takis, brought to the U.S. for a cultural experience as well as visiting their cousin. If Alexandria had to guess, she'd put Artur's age a little higher than Ian's, with the other two closer to her and Nikos.

"It was no trouble," Mom assured Nikos's parents. "Your son is a delight."

"So, you have three children with our Nikos?" Marina asked, surveying the room. "I thought Nikos mentioned sharing a room with two boys?"

She frowned at Alexandria as if suspecting her of bunking with her precious son. As if. Even if Alexandria was interested in intimacy or a boyfriend, Nikos was her brother. Gross.

"I have five," Mom said. "My two foster children are at the school right now. One of them turned sixteen yesterday, so he's celebrating with his friends."

Not quite accurate, but close enough. It explained why a school party was more important than meeting their guests and avoided the truth of Gil and Miknon hiding out from strangers.

Alexandria turned the page of her calculus text. Apparently finished with English lesson plans, Ian settled into the chair next to her and opened a Spanish novel. No fair that his Spanish was now good enough for that, while she continued to stumble through the basics. And since she had to use Fae more frequently, her inadequate Spanish was suffering. She could probably still remember most of the tenses, maybe, but her vocabulary shrank every month. Unlike Ian, her brain had a limit to how much she could dump into it and expect it to make sense.

Marina and Damianos followed Mom into the kitchen and settled down to talk while she graded history papers. Nikos and his cousins sprawled on chairs and floor in the living room and chattered in a mix of Greek and English.

Alexandria nudged Ian's arm with her toe and twitched her head toward the other boys. "Talk," she mouthed.

After all, he could speak a little Greek. She rolled her eyes. Sometimes she thought he could speak a bit of everything, but his actual language count was somewhere around seven. Eight? Nine? Whatever. Greek was on the list, and this was a good chance to practice.

Ian shoved her foot off the arm of his chair and shook his head a little. He hunched his shoulders and raised the book in front of his face, though no page turned. Oh, well. Maybe he'd lose his shyness in a while. It's not like she was diving in, either. She made a note for her next tutoring session and focused on another problem.

"So, tell us about this school," Mariana encouraged Mom, her voice easily carrying through the small apartment.

"It's an international school with a lot of exchange students," Mom said carefully.

Alexandria hid a snort. Yeah, including ones from another planet. Imagine what Nik's parents would think if they knew that! No way Nikos could tell them, even if it wasn't a state secret. *Sure, Mom and Dad, I go to school with space elves! And a werewolf!* They'd yank him back to Greece so fast he'd leave skid marks on the tarmac.

"Anyone from Greece?" Damianos asked.

"Just Nikos," Mom said, "and he's not a student, though we do appreciate his help."

No kidding. At least with him there at breakfast, they could divide the translating duties a little more. And he shared the housework and carted them around in his blue truck.

"Oh, he's always been such a good boy," Mariana said, and then she launched into a stream of memories about her precious son.

Mom made listening noises to accompany the flip of pages and the scratch of her pen.

Alexandria turned her page to the next equation, though it was hard to concentrate with all the company around. Her room would be better, but even though the visitors weren't there for her, she enjoyed the sound and feel of people around her.

In the living room, the boys were talking about the school, too. Unlike the parents, who were distracted by talking about Nikos, the cousins were determined to know everything and grew more and more restless when Nikos refused to tell them anything specific.

"The school sounds so boring," Artur complained.

Alexandria shifted a little sideways to hide her grin. Imagine if they heard about yesterday. One of the naiads had visited the chemistry class to deliver a message. Seeing what looked like a half-full glass of water, he helpfully used his magic to fill it the rest of the way so the teacher wouldn't get dehydrated.

Unfortunately, the flask had contained sulfuric acid for a demonstration of killing gummy bears. The resulting explosion ended class early for every room in the hall. Nobody died or had serious wounds, but Miles and the school nurse were kept busy patching small injuries. And then Ms. Maxwell gave everyone a dinner lecture about not touching things without permission, no matter what they were. Humans and fae alike should make no assumptions about what was safe.

After giving up on getting other information, the cousins wanted to know about any cute girls.

Nikos raised his eyebrows. "Most of the students are still minors, and I'm a legal adult. I have no business noticing who's cute."

Vasil winked. "You can *look*."

Nikos thumped the back of his cousin's head. "No. Besides, I spend most of the day at work or school."

Glancing at Alexandria, Vasil said something in Greek. Nikos frowned and replied in a stern voice. The cousins laughed, and Takis spoke in a suggestive voice.

Ian slapped his book shut and moved to stand in front of the couch. "That's my sister you're talking about so rudely."

Peering over her calculus and past Ian's arm, Alexandria frowned at the boys. What had they said to make Ian so mad?

"What?" Takis said. "What makes you think we're talking about your sister?" He added something in Greek, and all three visitors laughed.

Nikos hopped to his feet and stood shoulder-to-shoulder with Ian, nearly blocking Alexandria's view. "*Our* sister."

Fists clenched, Ian snarled back in Greek.

"Ooh!" Artur blushed, perhaps at being caught in his rudeness.

Takis gaped, and Vasil slapped his knee and laughed.

Nikos sighed and rubbed his nose. "Ian, I didn't teach you those words."

"I don't care." Ian crossed his arms. "They deserved it."

Even though Ian had been defending her, Alexandria bumped him with her leg as a reminder to watch his language. He reached behind and pushed her away. Fine, he could suffer when Mom found out.

"Okay, okay," Vasil said. "With such valiant protectors, your sister is lucky."

And she was. She loved all her brothers very much. In fact, the visitors were lucky Gil wasn't here. He *probably* wouldn't bite them, but she couldn't guarantee it.

"Better hope I don't tell her what you said," Ian retorted. "If she hears, she might throw you across the room."

The cousins erupted in laughter.

Nikos patted him on the shoulder and sat back down. "She probably wouldn't, Ian."

"Well, she could!"

Alexandria nudged Ian again, and this time he relaxed and sat. He retrieved his book, but instead of opening it, he stuck out the tip of his tongue at Alexandria. She settled for raising one eyebrow.

The cousins were still laughing.

Nikos shoved Artur, the closest of his cousins. "I've seen her take down someone two times. One was a school bully who was twice her size and the football star of the county."

"Ooh, I'm scared," Artur whispered before chuckling.

"And once she defeated a crazy man with a knife," Nikos finished.

His cousins stared at him, then examined Alexandria from head to toe with obvious skepticism. Yeah, nobody ever expected a girl to tackle them. It served her well in judo. Usually. Not that she personally knew her last opponent today, but either he was very well trained or he had sisters, because he hadn't hesitated to fight her at full strength.

Enough. This wasn't helping her study. Alexandria closed her book gently and swung up to sit properly, feet on the floor. She stacked her notes on her book and shrugged, feeling her scar stretch across the back of her shoulder. Nikos was exaggerating her win over the crazy. She had only taken him down long enough for someone else to shoot him, and she would carry the scar for the rest of her life. It was worth it to still have Gil around, but not something she wanted to repeat.

"It's no fun when the other person is armed." She grabbed her water bottle, then reached over the end of the couch to grab her judo belt from the floor. Throwing it across her shoulder, she stood. "Tell you what; I'll go to my room so you can say whatever you want."

Wide-eyed, the cousins stared at her and the brown strip draped over her uniform.

"They'll behave now," Nikos growled. "Don't let them chase you off."

Alexandria sighed. "I really do need to concentrate on studying for a while. Call me for dinner, okay?" Without waiting for an answer, she collected her book and notes and stalked to her room. Between supper with the guests and the fae landing, she was almost out of time today, and she still hadn't conquered the chapter.

CHAPTER 11

In Which Ram is Poisoned

January 24, 2023

Gil closed Shar's bedroom door to avoid eavesdroppers and sat in the farthest chair, out of arm's reach in case Shar decided to strike him again.

"Are you coming to the party?" he asked. "Everyone's excited about the 'semester' being done."

The prince lifted the hand weight again. "No."

"You can go as an ordinary highborn, you know. Why won't you even spend time with your people to build friendships before the council arrives? Aren't you lonely?" Gil folded his arms. "There will be pretty girls there."

Shar paused in his exercise for a moment before shaking his head. "Irrelevant. I am tired of hiding and lying. Until I can be myself, I refuse to fool my people and my allies. Until then, I will work on growing stronger. It's good advice. When it is time, I will take back my rule."

It was terrible advice. Whose advice?

"The lords won't just give it to you," Gil said.

"They promised to obey their leader," Shar said. "That will be me."

Gil tried one more time. "Your strength will come from your friends and allies. Come make some."

"I will not base friendships, alliances, or courting on lies." Shar raised the weight again.

Gil sighed. "I wish you good fortune, Sire, with your lonely plans. Let me know if you want help." He walked out, shutting the door behind him.

In the basement, the noise of the celebration already echoed through the halls. Too bad Ian had been hit with another of his headaches, necessitating Mama Helen and Alexandria taking him to their healer. But as usual, Alexandria had planned everything in advance, so the party was sure to go well in her absence.

As soon as Gil walked in, Ash grabbed his arm and pulled him over to join several of their friends. To his surprise, Ram was with them.

"Shaun isn't coming," Gil said.

Ash sighed, along with his human roommates.

Ram smirked. "Glad to see he's being sensible."

"Did you say something to him?" Gil asked suspiciously. Was he the source of the "good advice?"

Shrugging, Ram said, "Maybe. He doesn't have any friends, anyway."

And if he never went around anyone, he'd never make any friends! Gil clenched his fists, but a party was not the time to express his opinions to his twin, especially the way he deserved.

Instead, he turned his back. "So, what are we doing now?"

Kirill, one of Shar's roommates, pointed around the room. "Food over there, games over there, dancing on that side, and we'll have a movie later. Don't worry; this one is a children's movie."

"What do you want to do first?" Ash bounced in his chair and nudged Nash, the hydra, who bopped him with three heads at once.

All around the room, fae and humans mingled. Some of the fae, the lightest or the strongest, were now walking gingerly instead of being stuck in chairs. The shifters walked easily, or ran. Most of the rest had advanced to the self-push chairs, which freed their old chairs for the new fae landing every week. Gil could spot the occasional pilot by the way their magic lifted them without visible support. A few adults, fae or human, were scattered among the students.

"Food," Gil said. "I'm starving."

Tables lined one entire long wall. As the boys walked along, planning their attack, Gil noted multiple kinds of fresh fruit. One table was full of pastries with a sign marking them as approved by Merodach, the fae healer who had landed in the first wave. Another table had baskets full of popcorn. Some tables held food not yet cleared for fae consumption. Plenty of the human students carried food he didn't see anywhere on the tables.

"What's all that?" he asked, pointing.

Yuri, one of Ram's roommates, laughed. "Parents send their children food for Christmas or to celebrate end of school. It's okay."

"It's all junk food," Two said. "Not nutritious but tasty."

Shar's other roommate wiggled his eyebrows and pulled his own contraband from a back pocket.

A girl put her shiny green drink on the floor nearby, and Gil squinted to read it. "Sprite?"

He pursed his lips. Where had he heard the word before? Not in the food list... Ah, in his mythology book! He stopped abruptly and stared in horror.

"Sprite?" he squeaked. "Like pixie? Is that pixie blood?"

Ash froze, eyes wide, and Nash's heads all swiveled toward the green drink.

Ram's roommate, Okoro, grabbed Gil's arm, while the other humans reached for Ash, Ram, and Nash.

"No!" Okoro said. "It's just sugar water with some lemon flavor."

"Why is it called sprite?" Gil demanded.

Kirill shrugged. "I don't know. Why are other sodas called Dr. Pepper or root beer or 7-Up? There is no pepper or roots or beer." He chuckled. "Seven-Up really means nothing. Wait, I will show you."

He let go of Nash and ran for the green can. After pouring a little of its contents into a cup, he returned to Gil. "Look, sugar water."

Suspiciously, Gil examined the drink. It was clear and bubbly and smelled only of nasty fruits. He sneezed to clear the bubbles from his nose, then handed the cup to Ash. "It is a stupid name."

Okoro let go of him. "It's a very stupid name. Ready to grab some snacks?"

"Yes!" Ram bolted for the table of pastries.

Yuri and Kirill laughed and raced after him. They elbowed each other in an attempt to be first and ended up tripping each other and sliding across the floor.

Ram whooped in triumph and grabbed three orange rolls and an apple strudel. "I'm the fastest!"

Ash in his chair and Two and Okoro on foot made their way more slowly, but by the time Yuri and Kirill got to their feet with more elbowing, they also had plates and were busily filling them.

Nash sighed. "Ram is always like that. It doesn't help that both our roommates are athletes." He pronounced the unfamiliar word carefully. No common fae had time to waste on games and the highborn were too lazy to exert themselves. "And maybe Kirill, too."

Gil nodded. "Ram always has been competitive and physically able. Has he gotten used to having humans as roommates?" He grabbed the hydra's wagon handle and pulled toward the food.

"He hasn't gotten used to me," Nash said. "He says I'm soft."

"You mean you're nice," Gil said. "That's why I put him with you."

The hydra flicked out several tongues. "If you say so."

"I was hoping you'd be a good influence on him."

All nine of Nash's heads swiveled to look at Gil skeptically.

"Okay," Gil said. "It was just a thought."

They reached the food tables, and he filled a plate for him and another for Nash, then pulled the hydra to the ring of chairs the others had claimed.

Yuri was glaring at Kirill. "It wasn't my idea! I don't like it any better than you do."

"But your country started the war," Kirill said.

"*I* didn't," Yuri repeated.

"I should punch you in the nose," Kirill said.

Yuri stood, tall and straight. "I won't let you. I didn't do anything."

Kirill rose, nearly as tall and considerably more angry.

"Come on," Okoro said. "Neither of you are at fault."

"Isn't there a better way to solve this?" Gil said. "Practice your diplomacy, yes?"

Two laughed. "Hot sauce contest?"

"What will that prove?" Okoro asked.

"That I am better than he is," Kirill said. "I accept."

"Ridiculous," Yuri said. "It will prove nothing. But I will beat him regardless."

Gil threw up his hands in surrender. If they weren't fighting, what did a little contest matter?

The two boys stood almost nose to nose while Two ran from the room. He returned a few minutes later, hands full of bottles. He lined them up on a small table, and Yuri and Kirill took seats across from each other. Okoro added a bowl of thin triangles between them.

"What is hot sauce?" Gil asked. "Will it burn them?"

"It's just spicy," Okoro said. "Sometimes very spicy. The chips will help a little."

Yuri tipped the first bottle over a triangle until a single drop fell out, then popped the whole thing into his mouth. Staring into Kirill's eyes, he chewed and swallowed without expression.

Just as solemnly, Kirill copied him.

"That doesn't look hard." Ram grabbed a chair and took the third side of the table. When he ate a sauced chip, his eyes grew wide.

"Um, Rafe," Gil said, "maybe that's not a good idea."

Ram coughed. "It's fine," he croaked.

Yuri selected another bottle and repeated the process. Kirill and Ram copied him. On the third round, everyone's eyes watered when they swallowed.

"Rafe," Gil started. His twin held up a hand to stop him. Gil shrugged but shut his mouth.

After two more rounds, all three had red faces.

"Are you sure this is safe?" Ash asked. A vine crawled from the dryad's hair to wrap around his shoulders.

"Oh, sure," Two said. "The amount of toxin is too small to be a problem."

"Toxin?" Gil asked. "What does that mean?"

"Poison," Two defined. "Capsaicin and the caffeine in the sodas are both ever so slightly poisonous, but you'd have to eat way too much of it to do any damage. Tiny bits like this are just fun. And you'd have to drink about thirty of the sodas to have a problem." He grinned. "I had to do a report on caffeine in school last year."

Gil shared a perplexed look with Ash. Humans ate poison on purpose? For fun? But other than their red faces and hoarse coughs, the three looked fine after their fourth round of tasting, and none of the other humans seemed alarmed.

"Relax," Two said. "The plants produce the toxins to keep away tiny insects, not us."

After their next taste, the two humans and Ram panted for breath while their eyes watered.

Ash muttered, "I'll get Miles," and spun his wheelchair toward the door.

Hands shaking, Ram reached for the next bottle. He dropped the liquid onto a chip and stared at it.

"Rafe," Gil tried again.

Ram glared so fiercely that Gil gave up. If he was determined to be stupid, then let him suffer.

Yuri and Kirill swallowed their dose with sweat and tears running down their cheeks. After a deep breath, Ram popped his chip into his mouth. Unable to sweat, he panted, showing a reddened tongue. He dashed away a single tear, then bared his teeth in a vicious grin.

As Yuri reached for the next bottle, Ram shuddered and fell off his chair, jerking and shaking.

Gil dropped to his knees and pulled his brother's shoulders onto his lap. The closest students gasped and turned to watch, and the pool of silence spread through the room as Ram continued to tremble. His eyes were closed, and he did not speak. Gil clutched him tighter, trying to still the tremors.

"Oh, no," Kirill said. "I'll go get the nurse. Or the healer."

He darted for the door, but Merodach was suddenly there, right ahead of Ash. The healer knelt by Ram and gripped his cheeks to hold him still. He pried an eyelid open to examine Ram's eye, then checked his heart rate in his wrist.

"Tell me what happened," he ordered.

"Nothing," Yuri wailed. "We were just eating snacks."

"What kind of snacks?" Merodach trapped Ram's thrashing arm and bit gently at one finger. He swallowed a drop of blood to analyze it, narrowing his eyes in thought.

"Ew," several students said, and the crowd drew back.

Okoro pointed to the table. "Tortilla chips and hot sauce."

"What is hot sauce?" Merodach asked, pressing one hand to Ram's chest.

Two tapped on his phone and turned it to show a picture. "Some peppers are spicy and can be made into a spicy sauce."

"He said they're toxic," Gil accused. "He poisoned Ram."

"Not on purpose," Kirill protested. "We ate as much as he did." He poured a drop onto another chip and popped it into his mouth to demonstrate.

"Give me one," Merodach said.

Quickly, Yuri anointed a chip for him. Merodach chewed thoughtfully, then wiped his mouth on his sleeve. He stood and scooped Ram into his arms.

"I can fix this." He raised his voice. "But the fae should not eat food that has not been approved." He stalked out with Ram.

Gil squeezed Ash's shoulder. "Thank you, Abe."

He hurried after Merodach. Whatever the healer had done to speed his own recovery from space travel had worked well, and Gil had to nearly run to catch up. He punched the elevator buttons for Merodach, then followed him to the healer's office and helped arrange pillows on the bed.

"I'll call Mother," he said.

"Don't bother," Merodach said. "He'll be fine in an hour, though it's good Ash came to get me when he did. What were you thinking to let him do this?"

"Let him?" Gil squawked.

"I apologize," Merodach said. "Now be quiet and let me work."

Someone knocked on the door, and the healer raised an eyebrow at Gil. Obediently, Gil stepped into the hall, closing the door behind him.

"Is he okay?" Yuri asked.

Kirill and the other boys hovered behind him, all looking anxious.

"He will be," Gil said, "but Miles needs quiet for the healing."

Okoro grabbed Two and Kirill and backed up. "We'll leave him to it, then. Come on, Yuri."

The boys crossed the hall to the stairwell. Last in line, Ash grimaced at Gil, who leaned against the wall and sank to the floor. He might as well guard the door to make sure Merodach got the peace he needed.

When would Ram learn that things were different on Earth? Stupid, stupid! Gil knocked his head on the wall, then buried his face in his hands. Despite his differences with Ram, he still loved his brother, and losing him would be worse than losing an arm. At least he didn't have to worry Mother right now, though she was sure to find out eventually.

In a while, Yuri peeked from the stairwell, saw Gil, and disappeared again. A while later, Kirill did the same. The next to check was Okoro. Not long after, the door next to Gil opened.

Merodach exited, touching Gil on the head. "He's well now. I've asked him to stay in bed for the rest of the evening." He sighed. "Really, I just want to keep him out of trouble for a few hours. I'll be next door if anyone needs me." He slipped into the counselor's room and closed the door.

Taking a deep breath, Gil entered the healer's room. Ram reclined in one of the beds, arms folded and a scowl on his face.

Gil sank into the chair against the wall. "What were you thinking?"

"I can do anything the measly weaklings can do," Ram said.

Gil raised his eyebrows. "Weaklings? You did pay attention in science class, didn't you? Or while swimming? Do you listen to their conversations? They have strength, stamina, flexibility, speed... The humans aren't weak, just different."

Ram sniffed and rolled to face the wall.

A knock sounded at the door, and Gil wearily rose to answer it. The boys were back, shuffling their feet and bowing their heads.

"We're really sorry," Two said.

"We brought gifts to apologize," Kirill said.

Wordlessly, Yuri held out a wrapped package, and Okoro dangled a bottle of juice.

Gil swung the door open wide and motioned inward. "It wasn't your fault."

The boys lined up by Ram's bed and apologized all over again. Ram didn't roll to face them, but he did turn his head slightly to listen.

"We brought you apple juice and chocolate," Okoro said.

"Shaun likes chocolate," Kirill said, "and the juice is on the cafeteria approved list."

"Really, we're sorry," Yuri said.

Two stared at the floor. "It's my fault."

"You didn't know," Gil said. From behind the humans, he raised his eyebrows at Ram and tipped his head as a hint.

"Thanks for the snacks." Ram rolled enough to take both of them, then turned back to the wall.

Biting his tongue, Gil escorted the humans to the door. "It's okay," he said. "It was an accident. Go back to the party."

"Come when you can," Kirill said. "We're starting the movie in a minute. We'll tell Miles, too."

Gil nodded and smiled. As soon as he shut the door, he whirled on his brother. "Why didn't you say they're forgiven?"

"Because they aren't." Ram peeled the wrappings from the chocolate and took a giant bite. "Mmm, this is good," he mumbled.

"It was an accident," Gil repeated.

Actually, it was entirely Ram's fault for joining the humans, but it would do no good to mention that.

"Don't care." Ram crammed the rest of the chocolate into his mouth and rolled back to the wall.

"Gah!" Gil threw his hands in the air. "I'll check on you later."

He stomped out and ran down the stairs to the basement. As promised, the movie was already going, and he took a seat beside Merodach, whose eyes were closed and fingers were tapping on his crossed arms. Instead of human actors, the screen was filled with drawings that magically moved. Without seeing the first part, Gil was a little confused, but he grabbed a bag of popcorn and absently watched while he mentally ranted at his twin. What an idiot, for so many things!

Eventually, Gil started paying enough attention to understand a little of the story. This seemed to be another example of distorted human legends, though it wasn't as scary as the first movie. The wolf shifter on the screen was absolutely ridiculous, and Gil snorted quietly in the darkness. Half of the other creatures made no sense at all. Why would someone sew together body parts or walk around in bandages? But it was amusing, and the humans were laughing and chatting.

Then the man in the cape got angry and threatened the redhead. "I will suck every ounce of blood from your body."

Several students turned around and looked at Merodach, and one or two flinched. Merodach looked from them to the picture on the wall and back again. Gil looked at the movie, then Merodach, trying to decide what the humans were thinking.

It was the teeth that finally gave him the clue.

"That's their idea of a bloodworker," he whispered to Merodach, choking on the cruel words.

The healers would never drink all of someone's blood, never kill anyone. They *tasted* blood to diagnose problems so they could keep all the fae well, curing them of most illnesses and injuries, though they had lost the king despite their best efforts.

Gil and Miknon had caught a disease from the humans because they had been without a healer. Now that the bloodworkers were on Earth, no disease had passed between humans and fae. With the healers to keep the fae healthy, their natural life span ran up to three thousand conjunctions. Gil did rapid mental math. Three hundred Earth years, much longer than the humans could expect, poor creatures. And yet, they thought the bloodworkers were monsters.

He reached for Merodach in comfort, but it was too late. The healer walked away rapidly, hand pressed to his heart though his face was unreadable. Before Gil could stop him, he was through the door and gone.

Gil jumped to his feet. "Turn off the movie. What were you thinking? We are not monsters!"

"It's just a kids' movie," someone muttered, but the light went on, and the movie flickered off.

Without waiting for an explanation, a defense, or an apology, Gil stormed after Merodach to tell him the humans would learn better. He inhaled deeply and followed the healer's scent up the stairs and across the hall to Ram's sickroom. But his intended speech was cut off when he walked in the door and discovered Ram in a pool of vomit and Merodach frantically working over him.

"He ate something else," the healer said. "What did he eat?"

Ram vomited again, clearly unable to answer for himself.

"The boys brought juice and candy as an apology," Gil said, "but both were safe."

"What kind?" Merodach barked, shoving a basin under Ram's nose.

"Apple and chocolate."

"Chocolate!" Merodach whirled to stare at Gil before turning back to Ram. "Wolves can't eat chocolate."

"They said Shar eats it," Gil said weakly.

"Shar is not a wolf! Grab a clean blanket from the cupboard." Merodach wiped the dirty blanket across Ram to remove some of the mess, then picked him up and dragged the blanket to the floor. As soon as Gil put down the clean blanket, Merodach settled Ram with the basin. "When will you stop eating random things?"

Ram's ferocious glare was ruined when he vomited again, this time into the basin. Merodach rattled off a list of herbs he needed, and Gil ran to the cupboards to collect everything.

How long had Ram been sick while Gil was watching a stupid movie? Would his brother die from his own stupidity?

CHAPTER 12

LANGUAGE LESSONS

FEBRUARY AND MARCH, 2023

HAIR STILL DAMP FROM SWIMMING, Ian hurried to dinner and filled his tray without looking at his selections. He waved at Gil across the room and took a seat with Mom.

"Good news," Mom whispered. "Rafe's pneumonia is gone now, and the updated food signs have all been installed."

Ian nodded. Honestly, he almost thought Gil's twin deserved to be sick from his shenanigans last week, but pneumonia from aspirating vomit was too disgusting to wish on anyone. Maybe Rafe would be more careful about what he ate in the future, though.

Ian took a bite of his — ugh, apparently he'd grabbed the fish sandwich instead of the chicken. He dropped it onto the plate and shoveled some salad into his mouth before drowning his fries in ketchup.

All along the table, the fae and humans were chattering in a mix of both languages. Occasionally, he or Mom translated, but mostly the students managed on their own. In fact, many of the fae were advanced enough to take history classes either completely in English or with Ian translating. Those that still needed extra English practice all fit into a couple of basic classes and one advanced one, all taught by Mr. Abernathy alone so that Ian and Alexandria could take the classes they needed for high school.

Since formal Fae classes had been added this semester, it was nice that living together had given the human students a head start on learning the language. The new classes were taught in one of the biggest rooms so all the humans could fit into three periods. Gil taught with Miknon, then Mom and Miknon together, then Ian and Mr. Abernathy after lunch.

Ian's stomach churned, and he subtly pushed away his plate. Mr. Abernathy was worse than the fish sandwich.

Ian nudged Mom's elbow. "Now that Mr. Abernathy doesn't need my help with the English classes," he muttered, "maybe we should give him a new assistant."

"Nonsense," Mom said. "You're the best! The two of you combined will make great progress. With your help, he'll finish the Fae/English dictionary in time to send it with the ambassadors."

"But—" Ian started.

Someone asked Mom a question, and she turned aside to answer.

"Yes," Chantelle said on the other side of Ian. The beautiful fae with the long hair and musical voice nodded vigorously. "You are best, better than Abernathy."

Ian sighed and gave up. He pushed his tray farther away and leaned on his elbows, chin in his hand. Mr. Abernathy thought he was a ten-year-old kid who knew nothing — not Fae, not English, not teaching. Every time Ian made a mistake, Mr. Abernathy jumped all over him.

It wasn't like Mr. Abernathy spoke Fae perfectly, either, though he spent all his extra time working on his stupid book in his locked classroom. Let him stay locked up. Nobody wanted him around, anyway. He didn't believe in the fae, and anytime he paid any attention to them, which was seldom, he renewed his demands for them to stop wearing costumes to his classes.

But when Ian tried to tell Mom and Ms. Maxwell, they said to keep going. If they thought he could do it, then clearly he just needed to discover what he was doing wrong and fix it. What *was* he doing wrong?

Someone touched Ian's elbow, and he jumped.

"Sorry," Chantelle said. "You are worried about language?"

"Yes," Ian said.

If he could speak Fae better, maybe Mr. Abernathy would stop yelling at him for being stupid.

"You want learn more faster?" Chantelle asked.

"I'm trying!"

Chantelle patted his arm. "Yes, yes. I can sing language into your mind. You want, yes?"

"Like the alphabet song?" Ian asked.

"No, like magic." She wiggled her eyebrows and grinned.

"If you can teach languages by magic," Ian argued, "why didn't you do that at the start? Why don't you do it for everyone now?"

Chantelle wrinkled her nose and held up one finger. "To teach fae, I must know human language." A second finger. "To teach anyone takes much time." A third finger. "If your mind does not have space for it, the magic will *make* space. This is bad."

Make space, like overwrite other information? Ian gulped. Bad was an understatement.

"Are you sure this is safe?" he asked.

"Oh, yes," Chantelle said, "but will ask Miles. You know much now. Magic will only speed memory. Whatever I sing to you once, you will remember."

Ian's memory for languages was good, but not that good. Imagine remembering every word or grammar rule after only one lesson! At that rate, he could quickly learn enough to satisfy Mr. Abernathy.

"Yes, please," Ian said. "When can we start?"

"After meal each night?" Chantelle asked. "Zee or Gil can chaperone."

After quickly calculating his homework, Ian nodded. He always finished German and Web Design assignments in class, and Fae was just translating. That only left World History and Biology, because he didn't have time to do homework while he was translating, but neither of them were hard.

"Sure," he said. "We could meet in your office?"

Chantelle nodded and patted his arm again. "I see you there soon." She gathered her tray and pushed her wheelchair toward the door.

Ian waited for a break in the conversation, then tapped Mom's arm. "I'll study with Chantelle after dinner every night, okay?"

"Sure," Mom said. "I'll send Alexandria for you when Nikos arrives."

With a lighter heart, Ian cleared his tray, dumping the remnants of his meal into the compost bucket. With Chantelle's help, he'd be fluent in no time!

He hurried to the office and found Chantelle and Zee already there. He lay on the couch as directed, and Chantelle put her hands on his cheeks and stared into his eyes.

"Your name is U.N.?" she confirmed.

Nervously, he nodded.

"Ian," Zee corrected.

"Yeah, Ian." His heart sped as he remembered Gil's repeated warnings about sharing his real name.

"Ian," Chantelle repeated.

Ian closed his eyes and sucked in a breath.

"It won't hurt," Zee said quietly.

"Did you do this for navigation?" Ian asked.

"No," Zee said. "Navigation is too complicated. I had to learn it the hard way."

Chantelle shrugged. "If I not understand something, I cannot sing it. Are you ready?"

Again, Ian nodded. Chantelle took a deep breath and began to sing. As she recited a list of Fae words, Ian felt their meanings settle into his brain with a shock like static electricity. It didn't hurt, exactly, but it sure got his attention. Though she didn't give the English equivalents, his brain automatically supplied them based on the native meanings that rose to the surface. This list was of fae races, and he recognized Chantelle's among them. In English, she would be a siren, which was surprising because she had no mermaid tail but completely logical for her voice.

The song went on and on, and when Chantelle finally moved her hands, the clock on the wall said half an hour had passed. Ian's head ached, and the familiar sparkles of an impending migraine closed in around him.

"Ow." He pressed his hands over his eyes.

"Sorry," Chantelle said. "The magic is hard on some minds. We need not do again."

Ian reviewed the vocabulary list and found every word crystal clear in his brain.

"No, this is great." He kept his eyes covered to hide his wince. "Can you teach anyone else to do your magic?"

"Can a bird teach a human to find north without a compass?" Chantelle said.

"Are you okay?" Zee asked.

Ian nodded and immediately regretted it. "But please turn off the light as you go."

Someone patted his shoulder, and the door opened. The light went dark, and the door closed. Ian fell asleep with Fae words dancing like pink elephants through his brain.

When someone shook him gently, he startled awake in the still-dark room.

"Hey, Ian," Alexandria whispered. "Nikos is here. Are you ready to go?"

"Ugh, sure." Ian rolled to a sitting position and checked to make sure his head was still attached.

Surprisingly, his migraine had faded to half-strength already, and the beam of light shining through the cracked-open door hurt only a little.

"Here's your meds." Alexandria pressed a cup of water into one of his hands and a pill into the other.

Ian swallowed without protest.

"Zee told me what happened," his sister said. "Are you sure you want to do this?"

"Uh-huh," Ian muttered. "It'll be fine."

With a grunt, Alexandria hauled him to his feet and drew one of his arms over her shoulder. "Come on, brother mine. Let's go pour you into bed."

"Did you know Zee is a gremlin?" Ian said woozily. "And Chantelle is a siren, and Vince is a troll."

Alexandria dragged Ian down the hall. "I'm pretty sure everybody knows Vince is a troll."

At the front door, Mom shoved Ian's arms into his coat, and Nikos scooped him into his arms. Mom and Alexandria opened the school doors, then the truck, and Ian was asleep again before the engine started.

AFTER SOME EXPERIMENTATION the rest of that week, Ian and Chantelle settled on twenty-minute sessions every other day to reduce the risk of migraines. With Zee's help, they alternated vocabulary, grammar, and culture lessons, and Ian found his understanding of Fae expanding rapidly.

At the weekly fae landing on March 4th, Ian wrapped his arms around himself and pulled his hat lower over his ears. Though the daytime temperatures fortunately kept the river by the Bethlehem Sand Island from turning to ice, a snowstorm late in January had doubled the winter precipitation, and last night was nearly freezing. All during February landings when it was even colder, his breath had puffed out like an ice dragon's — except those weren't real, according to the knowledge Chantelle had been giving him. Even now, it was too cold and snowy for most of the fae to enjoy, so Miknon, Mom, and Gil's mother waited at the apartments to help once the fae arrived there.

With a splash, the first of the barges touched down. The dragon pulled the barge up the bank and waited, steaming, while practiced helpers unbuckled his harness. As soon as he headed for the semi that would carry him into town, the next dragon pulled her barge to shore. While she was unharnessed, soldiers were already knocking on the first barge to alert the travelers it was safe to open.

As usual, the door slid open and revealed rows of three-high bunks filled with mostly sleeping fae. Gil stepped forward, looking ridiculously cheerful and not nearly cold enough. He started his standard welcome speech as soldiers approached with blankets, but now the second barge opened, and it was Ian's turn.

"Welcome to Earth," Ian said in Fae. "You are among friends. Please allow these people to carry you to your next transportation."

The fae inside the barge squinted at him, and he knew when they recognized him as alien by the widening of their eyes. He continued explaining about the buses waiting to take them to their apartments, along with the physical therapy, language lessons, and cultural education they could expect.

At the end of his speech, he waited. From the way they shivered, it shouldn't take long. In fact, the usual dragon driver was already scooting off his bunk to exit.

"We are ready," a highborn said.

Ian found himself using the Fae word automatically, instead of the human term "elf." Since the man was awake and highborn but unfamiliar, he must be the mage that had kept the passengers asleep.

Ian nodded at the blanket-loaded military, and the soldiers swarmed the barge, wrapping the passengers warmly and carrying them to the closest bus.

Once both barges were unloaded and the passengers were waking on the buses, Ian, Gil, Alexandria, and Nikos each took a bus for another round of explanations. When Ian stopped for questions, the first one was how he spoke the language so well.

"The sirin helped me," he said.

With his new cultural lessons fresh in his mind, he was careful to use no name for her, even though everyone on the ship knew her. As the questions continued, he automatically identified each fae race, though they rarely looked exactly like the Earth legends. Most of them shivered violently, even wrapped in a blanket. One hairy fellow — a hinagon, Ian's mind supplied — wrapped his blanket around his neighbor and leaned back in his seat with a smile. Well, sure, this weather was easy for a yeti! Ian shoved his hands deeper into his pockets.

When nobody had more questions, he left the bus and joined his family in Nikos's blue truck.

"You were great," Gil said. "All of you were great, but Ian, they told me they thought you were native until they got a closer look."

"Thanks to Chantelle," Ian said.

"You were already great," Gil said.

Ian huddled into his coat, letting the collar ride up to hide his grin. Great, huh? Then it was time to demonstrate his new knowledge for Mr. Abernathy. On Monday. In the meantime...

"Hey, Nikos, you ready for your joint birthday party tomorrow?"

"Do I have to do anything for it?" Nikos asked.

"No," Ian said.

Nikos shrugged. "Then I'm ready."

"I'm making the cake in the morning," Alexandria said. "Mom already planned dinner based on your favorites and Miknon's."

Gil smirked. "I hid the presents."

"Only because you sniffed out every place *I* hid them," Ian complained.

Gil laughed.

"Nineteen years for you," Ian said to Nikos, "and seventeen for Miknon. I have to admit, it's weird thinking of someone smaller than me being older."

Alexandria reached her arm behind the seat and smacked Ian's knee.

"Ow," Ian said. "I know, I know. Besides, it's not *really* her birthday, since we don't know exactly how old she is. Or yours, since we need to celebrate on Sunday instead of Monday."

"I don't mind sharing," Nikos said. "My name day is more important in Greece, anyway."

"Miknon doesn't mind, either," Gil said. "I just have one question."

"What's that?" Alexandria said.

"You aren't making chocolate cake, are you?"

Laughter filled the truck all the way home.

AFTER LUNCH ON MONDAY, Ian headed for the Fae language class with a bounce in his step. If the fae thought his skills were native-level, then Mr. Abernathy would have nothing to complain about.

He took roll, a task Mr. Abernathy hated, then stepped back and waited for the teacher to start the lesson. The human students gripped their pencils hard and focused on Mr. Abernathy. Most of them wore frowns or scowls or wrinkled foreheads. Fortunately, the class was about to get less confusing.

Mr. Abernathy started lecturing, as usual. Ian watched the students, and when several looked perplexed, he stepped forward and explained the grammar rule in different words.

"Oh, got it," Gaby said.

She and the others made quick notes. Instead of thanking Ian, Mr.

Abernathy huffed and continued his lecture. A few minutes later, he gave the wrong translation for a word. Ian quietly corrected him.

Mr. Abernathy slammed his pen onto the table. "You're making that up," he said. "That's not what my notes say."

"I'm sorry, Mr. Abernathy, but that's what the fae told me."

And why wasn't the teacher happy to learn the correct word so his dictionary would be correct?

"You lying little twerp," Mr. Abernathy seethed. "I'm the expert here."

"Of course," Ian said. "Continue."

He stepped back against the wall and waited. Perhaps it would have been smarter to correct him after class, in private.

Face reddening, Mr. Abernathy returned to his lecture. The students watched him and Ian carefully while they scratched notes. It didn't take long before Mr. Abernathy made another mistake, and this time, it was something that would offend the fae.

Reluctantly, Ian cleared his throat and said the correct word.

"You are wrong," Mr. Abernathy growled.

"The fae said—"

Mr. Abernathy threw up his hands to cut him off. "And stop calling them the fae! It's ridiculous. People will think you mean the mythological fae."

"But I do," Ian said. "They are."

And thanks to Chantelle, he could name most of their races and match them to Earth legends. The other students rolled their eyes and ducked behind notebooks or hands. Only someone who was steadfastly not paying attention could have missed the completely non-human appearance of the pixies or troll or hydra. And even the human-like fae had telltale characteristics to betray them.

Mr. Abernathy's face turned purple. "To — to the principal's office, you hooligan!"

Resisting the urge to salute, Ian marched out the door. Not that Ms. Maxwell would punish him, but she wouldn't release him from this misery, either. He couldn't win. No matter how much Chantelle helped him learn, he'd never be good enough for Abernathy, like he had never been good enough for Dad.

CHAPTER 13

In Which Zak Gets Bad News

MAR 25-30, 2023

LATE IN MARCH, Gil appeared at Zak's dinner table, grinning as usual. "Do you want to join the greeters for the landing tonight?"

"Father won't be in the group," Zak said.

Until he arrived, she didn't really care who landed. For months, she had been sending messages into space for Father, but he had not replied. Of course he hadn't. But she still talked to him every day, reciting her English lessons or explaining Earth tech or talking about her fellow students. For hours, she chatted as she worked, hoping he might eventually hear anything she said.

"No, but as a navigator, you are one of the leaders," Gil said. "And I think it's important to show that the commoners continue to lead even off the ship."

"They won't believe you," Zak said.

"They will if you come with me and act like a leader."

"What about Shar?"

Gil sniffed. "He isn't a commoner. Come on, Zee, come with us."

"Okay, okay." She checked the time contrivances on the wall that took the place of the ship bells. "When do we leave?"

"You have enough time to get a coat," Gil said. "It's cold out there, and still raining a little."

And since he traveled into the school every day from outside, she took his advice. As she exited the school, a few raindrops drizzled down the back of her neck until she pulled up her hood. Though not as cold as earlier in the year, the air was chill enough to make her shiver.

Gil traveled with his foster family, and Zak and Freya rode in one of the big wagons with War Lady Mak-swill. Not that Freya was a leader either, but the highborn were apparently soothing to some of the newcomers, especially when they saw how many commoners were in charge.

Even seeing a highborn didn't soothe all potential rebellions. Gil and Mak-swill had to separate the less-cooperative fae at each landing, sending them to a different building where they could be kept out of trouble. Gil was overly optimistic; the highborn would never accept the commoners as equals.

The rain stopped as they waited for the dragon to land. Zak did her part despite her misgivings, welcoming the new fae and explaining what to expect when they reached their temporary housing. She rode with them to their new home, sitting among the commoners and answering their whispered questions.

Yes, they were treated equally by the humans. Yes, the children were all being educated together. No, the highborn were not in charge; the humans shared responsibility with a mixed council of highborn and commoners. Yes, there was plenty of food and water, though the fae did not yet own land. Yes, everyone would get some sort of wagon to move themselves around until their bones strengthened. Yes, they would be taught the language. All was well, all was well.

By the time she returned to the school with War Lady and the other students, she was exhausted, and she rolled into bed without talking to her roommates.

TWO DAYS LATER, Gil pulled all the fae from their classes for a special meeting. Reluctantly, Zak left behind the contrivance she was working on and followed him to the dining hall. Uncharacteristically grim, he shut the door and explained the humans had a new far-seeing device that they used to look at the stars and other planets.

"And recently, they found the fae worlds," Gil said. "At least, our best combined guess at our worlds." His lips tightened, and he blinked rapidly. "The James sees no atmosphere on Harmakis."

It took a moment for his meaning to sink in. No atmosphere meant no life. One of their worlds was dead.

Zak sucked in a stuttering breath, and all around her, the fae did the same. Heads bowed, everyone froze in stunned silence.

Gil cleared his throat twice. "Though they intend to keep studying the rest of the worlds..."

He trailed to a stop and rubbed his eyes. If Harmakis was dead, then either the rest were also, or they would be soon.

Somehow, knowing their worlds were dying was not quite the same as knowing they were already dead. Someone choked on a single sob, and that was the catalyst for them all to weep. Whether or not they made a sound, tears coursed down every cheek.

Zak's first memory had been of the ship, not their world, and yet Father had told her so many stories that she would have recognized it immediately. And now it was gone, all the air burned away by fiery streamers from their star. All the people — all the life — that hadn't fit on the ships had either been scorched to death or suffocated.

Including her mother, if she hadn't died earlier.

Zak's chest tightened until she could barely breathe, and sobs clogged her throat. She doubled over in her wheelchair and hid her face on her knees. Wrapping her arms around her legs, she wept silently for the mother she couldn't remember and the father she couldn't comfort. To let him concentrate on his job, she wouldn't tell him until he landed, and he would surely be among the last to arrive at their new home. Their only home now.

The harsh bell rang, but none of the fae left for their second class. Zak had physical therapy, and now that she was a competent swimmer and her bones were stronger, she was supposed to practice walking. But her knees felt too weak to even stand. All around her, the fae who could walk had collapsed to the floor, and the rest huddled in their chairs, shaking with bone-deep grief.

Not until the bell rang for lunch did they manage to collect themselves enough to let the humans in to eat. After wiping her cheeks with her sleeve and forcing down a few bites of food, Zak rolled her chair to her advanced English class.

The students silently took their places and wordlessly watched Misterabernathy. Nobody took notes, and nobody volunteered answers. Misterabernathy didn't seem to notice the class's unusual silence, and he continued lecturing without pausing for breath. His words swam over Zak like the incoming tide in Father's stories of the old world, just as overpowering and incomprehensible.

"Well?" Misterabernathy barked.

Zak blinked and looked up. The teacher was leaning over her, scowling so hard she wondered if his face could break.

"Sorry?" she said.

"What is your answer?"

"Li— listen I not." Was that the way she should say it? She bowed her head in embarrassment at her inattention and poor grammar.

"You—" He spluttered incoherently, then turned around and waved his arms at the rest of the class. "None of you are listening! Why are you in this class if you aren't listening?"

Ash sighed, and a vine drooped over his shoulder to the floor.

Misterabernathy turned purple. "I'm wasting my time with all of you! You are incompetent, pathetic losers! Not one of you can speak a proper sentence!"

Like her classmates, Zak stared at her desk and didn't try to respond. Misterabernathy's assignments were always difficult, much more difficult than any of their other classes or talking to their friends and roommates. What good did it do to struggle with them when they could never find the right answers?

If returning to their world was possible, Zak would have chosen that in a single breath. But that never was an option, and the final death of their world changed nothing but the ache in her heart. They had always been stuck on Earth, but most of its inhabitants seemed willing to try to understand them. Only Misterabernathy insisted they meet him on his impossibly high level.

Today, Zak didn't care.

The teacher continued to berate them until the bell clanged for the end of class. Silently, the fae students rolled, hopped, or walked out of the room. Zak's next class was world history, taught just to the fae, but Helen greeted them quietly and announced a day of mourning.

"I'll sit here and answer questions if you have any," she said. "Please don't wander the school, but otherwise, you may do as you wish. Stay and mourn together, or go to your rooms. Let me know if I can help in any way."

And for the entire class, she sat at the front, speaking only when someone approached her. For some, she answered questions. To others, she offered a comforting embrace or a distracting story from Earth history. The stories were always the best part of her class, especially when human history left the fae confused. Helen's tranquility and warmth soothed Zak, and when she left for her chore rotation, her grief had settled to a hard lump in her chest.

At bedtime, the lump dissolved into more tears.

FOR TWO DAYS, the entire school was solemn. Someone must have told the humans about Harmakis, because the other students offered quiet words of sympathy or silent pats.

On the third day, Zak rolled into her first class, still without her usual enthusiasm. Based on her off-hours work last semester, the tech teacher had requested her official enrollment in his class this semester. She was still working on her contrivance at the back of the classroom. At this point, her original contrivance had been blended with a modern radio to read the frequencies needed to navigate their spaceship. Ha, she had remembered the correct English words, too.

The ship's original contrivance filled a whole wall, but her adaptation was a fraction of the size. She had added parts to record the sounds she detected, then replay them for others to prove what she heard. Next time, the crew would believe her because she would have proof.

What next time? Once the rest of the fleet landed, the fae would be stuck on their new home. She would never fly another ship again.

Now she was trying to reproduce her new contrivance using only parts available to the fae. Every week, she sent another report to Father, explaining what she was doing. Of course, she had no way to know if he was receiving her broadcasts, much less understanding them, but she kept whispering her messages into space. If he *could* hear her, she couldn't afford to miss the chance to speak to him. And maybe, just maybe, he would understand and alter his contrivance to allow him to speak to her.

She tightened her grip on her pliers and took a slow breath to calm the flood of loneliness that swept through her. Patience. Sooner or later, Father would return to her.

The classroom door opened, and a young human whispered to the teacher.

"Zee," Misterbeltran said, "please go to the principal's office."

Misterabernathy burst through the doorway. "I don't need the principal to handle this! Zee Brown, you are expelled for cheating!"

Half the class gasped, and Kirill jumped to his feet.

Zak waved her human friend down. "What is expelled? What is cheating?"

"*Stay here* until I return." Kirill darted into the hall.

Misterabnernathy gloated. "Cheating is giving answers or turning in work that belongs to someone else. And expelled means you must leave this school!" He pointed triumphantly toward the door.

But Kirill said to stay. Zak reached behind her and set the brakes on her wheelchair. "I do my own work."

"Settle down, Mr. Abernathy," Misterbeltran said. "I've always found Zee to be honest. There must be a misunderstanding here. I'm sure we can get this worked out."

"Worked out? Worked out! She is expelled. What else is there to work out?" Misterabernathy threw his arms wide. "When I turned in the midterm grades this morning, I saw her grades for her other classes. She *might* — might — be getting a B in history, and any idiot can do well in PE, but there is no way that idiot is getting an A in your class! She must be cheating, and she will not be staying in this school!"

"Excuse me," War Lady Mak-swill said, appearing in the open doorway. "I believe that is for me to decide."

She marched in and stood between Misterbeltran and Misterabernathy. Kirill, panting hard, edged between the students and joined Zak by her contrivance. He put one hand on her shoulder and squeezed gently.

"You okay?" he whispered.

She nodded. "What is A for midterms?"

Misterbeltran raised one eyebrow. "It means you are doing very well in my class," he said. "You are highly proficient. That means you know what you are doing and do it well."

Zak nodded, still confused. Of course she did it well. She loved the Earth contrivances.

"Nonsense," Misterabernathy said. "She doesn't speak enough English to be proficient at anything."

Mak-swill frowned and folded her arms. "What does English have to do with machines?"

Misterabernathy turned purple. "I want her expelled! I want everyone flunking English to be expelled!"

Kirill's grasp on Zak's shoulder tightened, and she pressed his hand with hers.

War Lady's lips clamped together. "That is not how this works. We will not expel any of the Fae, no matter what grades they get. This school was created for them."

"That's not how schools work," Misterabernathy protested.

"But even if I were willing to expel anyone," War Lady continued, "we wouldn't expel them for flunking *one* class. Furthermore, Zee will stay because she deserves to stay."

Kirill's hand relaxed, though it stayed on Zak's shoulder. "Zee is one of the best students in this class," he said. "She can do more with less than anyone, and she's also teaching us about the fae machines."

"Yeah," another student said, and most of the class echoed her.

"I don't believe it," Misterabernathy said. "Prove it."

"She doesn't have to," Mak-swill said.

"Okay," Zak said. "I will."

"You will?" Misterabernathy asked.

"You will?" Kirill said.

Zak released her brakes and turned her chair. By now, she had struggled with the vocabulary enough to translate it into English, and she had rephrased her messages to Father so many times that she knew the explanations by heart. One at a time, she named the parts and what they did, in terms simple enough for anyone to understand the basics. She explained why she put them together the way she did, though Misterabernathy's eyes started to glaze.

Mak-swill took a seat and watched with Misterbeltran, but Kirill remained standing by Zak until she was finished.

"And now I make same machine with Fae parts," she said, "so Father can copy."

"Sounds to me like Zee knows what she's doing," Mak-swill drawled.

Zak nodded. She had been raised with contrivances. Once she learned about the Earth parts and how they worked, it was almost easy to integrate them into her work.

"But—" Misterabernathy started.

The bell clanged, and Mak-swill clapped her hands. "Class dismissed. That means you, too, Mr. Abernathy."

Nose held high, Misterabernathy left behind the other students. Mak-swill winked at Zak and followed him.

Kirill whooshed out a breath. "Good job."

"Of course," Zak said.

Kirill laughed. "Of course." He glanced around the empty classroom, then back at her. Running a hand through his hair, he sucked in a breath. "Is it okay if I ask how old you are?"

Zak put away her tools and calculated conjunctions into years. "Sixteen years. Seventeen in... June, I think you call it."

"Okay, okay." Kirill bit his lip. "Would you like to go on a date?"

"Like a month or a day?" Zak asked.

Kirill laughed. "No, an activity with me, um, like a girl and boy together?" He shuffled his feet and clasped his hands behind his back.

"Like courting?" Zak tried to clarify.

Red bloomed up his neck and across his cheeks. "Sort of, but not so serious. Is that allowed?"

After a minute, Zak realized her mouth was hanging open. "I have no interest in courting," she said. "Can we not be friends?"

"Tak," Kirill said. "Always friends." He cleared his throat. "But if you change your mind, let me know, okay?"

Zak spun her wheelchair. "Okay."

She never would. She still wasn't sure she wanted to be a girl. What would the lords do to her when they landed and discovered a girl had been navigating the whole fleet? Her grandmother had been killed for the same reason.

Besides, her machines took all her time. In order to learn enough to contribute to the treaty, she needed every minute to learn and work, not dally in courting.

CHAPTER 14

GOOD AND BAD NEWS

AFTER PLOPPING a generous serving of broccoli onto her plate and Ian's, Alexandria passed the bowl to Nikos. She didn't mind eating at school, but she preferred these quiet weekend meals with just the family.

"Yuck," Ian said.

"Eat it," Alexandria said. Her shrimp of a brother needed all the vitamins he could get.

Mom patted Ian's hand. "It's better than turnips. So, how was school this week?"

Every Sunday, they talked about successes and problems as a family. Most had to do with school, but together they handled whatever arose.

"Fine." Ian speared a broccoli stalk and glared at it, shoulders hunched.

Gil beamed. "I beat Ram in the PE race today."

Miknon shrugged. "I think I memorized all the history words for tomorrow."

"You're doing fine in class," Mom assured her.

"I'm getting A's or B's in every class," Alexandria said.

She loved physics and could see how computer science and 3D design would be useful for astronomy. English was okay, and comparing U.S. government to the fae customs was more interesting than she expected.

"That's wonderful," Mom said. "Do you think your GPA will improve enough for an academic scholarship?"

Alexandria grimaced. "Maybe, but judo is still my best bet. I just need to get my black belt in time."

Before school started, she had assumed that was merely a case of healing her back and then getting in some practice, but she continued to barely miss qualifying every time.

December hadn't been that big of deal, as much as it hurt, but with the end of school approaching faster every day and still no black belt, she sometimes woke from nightmares of flipping burgers or mopping floors. Technically, she had another year to qualify, but she hated leaving important things until the last minute. If only she hadn't thrown that bout last year when Dad didn't come to watch her. Drat Dad, anyway. She smothered the familiar pang of missing him.

"Oh, yeah," Nikos said. "I found another alternative."

To Dad? No, he was just in her head. "To a black belt?"

"To pay for college," Nikos clarified. "On Friday, I discovered one of my classmates is a high school student, so I asked him what he was doing in college."

Alexandria clenched her fork until her fingers ached. "And?"

"He's taking early enrollment classes." Nikos wiggled his eyebrows at her. "That's exactly what it sounds like, and apparently it's pretty common in this area. The best part is that because he's still getting credit for those classes in high school, the school is paying half the tuition. He said to ask your school counselor about the process."

"I never have time to leave campus to meet with him," Alexandria complained.

That was unfortunately true. Due to the needed secrecy, they had no counselor of their own, only one borrowed from another school. The military psychologist handled any humans that needed to talk to someone, and the fae took care of their own people. As for college applications, the fae didn't need that yet, and the exchange students handled them through their home schools. The few local students managed with the borrowed counselor.

Mom reached for her phone. "We will make time. Tomorrow right after school?" Her thumbs flew across the screen. "Great. Thank you, Nikos."

Mouth full, he grunted at her and elbowed Alexandria. She waited until the conversation switched topics, then snuck an arm around her favorite big brother for a quick hug. His idea to adopt them was the best idea ever. He winked at her and passed the potatoes across the table to Gil.

"WHAT DO YOU MEAN, you don't know if we have the program?" Alexandria stared at the counselor, heart sinking to her toes.

"The school has to apply by the deadline," the counselor said, "and with this being a new school, I don't know if it did that in September."

Alexandria whipped out her phone and sent a frantic text to Mr. Riggs. Fortunately, the lowly State Department secretary was much nicer than his cranky boss. She copied the text to Ms. Maxwell.

"While we wait for an answer," she said, "what do I need to do if we *are* eligible?"

The counselor slid her a list. "Decide which college to attend. Complete the application, send your transcript, and get a letter of recommendation. You only need a 3.0 GPA." He raised his eyebrows in a question.

Alexandria hid a wince. Drat calculus! Until the end of this semester, when she was sure she would have higher grades, she only had a 2.98 average. But that would be close enough, right? She could get several recommendations to compensate for it. Her sensei, Raquel as principal, Mr. Riggs from the State Department, Therese and her physics teacher for the science angle, maybe even Ms. Stafford the refugee specialist or Mr. Farrell from International Affairs. Quickly, she made a list in her notebook. If she asked everyone today, she could hopefully turn everything in by Friday.

Her phone beeped, and she opened her texts.

> We are eligible. I did all the red tape for
> everything I could possibly think of.

Mr. Rigg's accompanying emoji bared its teeth at her.

Smothering a chuckle, Alexandria showed the text to the counselor. Poor Mr. Riggs got stuck with all the boring paperwork, but when he was away from his terrible boss, he had a subtle sense of humor, and his efficiency shone like diamonds.

With relief, Alexandria pulled the list of colleges closer. The choices included Nikos's alma mater and the state college. She wouldn't mind going with Nikos, but the advantages to going to the state school were in-state tuition when she graduated, and not having to transfer for her astronomy major. She had enough saved from her summer job to pay the other half of tuition for a semester, and Mom could help with the one after that. By the time Alex ran out of money, she'd have earned more.

According to the info, the college would only let her take eight credits at a time, but there was a summer session of classes. If she started then, she could still get a full year of credits by the time she graduated high school. Then another year at the local campus before transferring to the main campus for her major classes, and she'd only be gone from home for a couple of years. Less, if she continued the summer classes.

She wouldn't need the judo scholarship for two years, so her failure to achieve her black belt wouldn't matter. It was a perfect plan.

"The deadline is June sixteenth." The counselor slid more paperwork across the table.

"No problem." Alexandria gathered up everything, set a return appointment for Friday, and nearly skipped from the building to the bus station.

FOR A DAY AND A HALF, Alexandria ran around talking to people about letters, arranging for her transcript to be officially sent, and completing paperwork. By Wednesday lunch, she was finally finished with her part, and she filled her tray and collapsed at the table in relief.

All around her, the fae slumped with frowns and wrinkled foreheads. They'd eventually rebounded from the bad news about their planet, and considering that most of them were now walking, even if unsteadily, the new gloom was surprising.

"Hey, what's wrong?" Alexandria asked.

Zee shrugged. "What do humans do with mean people?"

"Do with them?" Alexandria repeated in confusion.

"You don't have magic," Zee said, "same as commoners. I don't see you with weapons. How do you make them stop being mean? Or can they do whatever they want, like the highborn?" But she turned hopeful eyes on Alexandria.

"Wait a minute," Alexandria said. "Who's being mean to you? Have you told Ms. Maxwell or the teacher? Any adult?"

"Yes," Zee said. "They said to keep trying to get along."

"Well, that's sometimes good advice," Alexandria said, "but it depends. Has anyone been hurt?"

Zee pressed her lips together. "Only words."

"Words can hurt, too," Alexandria said.

All along the table, the fae stared at their plates and didn't respond.

"I think somebody had better tell me the whole story," Alexandria said.

Zee shook her head. "I should not have said anything. We don't want anyone to get in trouble, and we can't help without weapons or magic."

"I still think you should talk to Ms. Maxwell again," Alexandria said, "but let me tell you about Rosa Parks and Ghandi."

She spent the rest of lunch telling stories of civil disobedience to the wide-eyed fae.

THURSDAY AND FRIDAY PASSED QUIETLY, and the fae seemed a little happier at meals, so perhaps her advice had helped. By Saturday morning, Alexandria had everything submitted for early enrollment, including all the letters of recommendation she could convince people to write for her.

At breakfast, Ian drowned his pancakes in syrup, then just stared at them. Finally, he said, "Mom, is it okay if I grade English papers for the fae?"

Mom passed him a glass of milk. "I thought you didn't have any English classes this semester?"

"I don't. But the fae have started to give me their assignments anyway. Should I grade them or give them to Mr. Abernathy?"

"Why would they do that?" Mom asked.

Ian shrugged. "I don't think they like him. I hear rumors they've started playing little pranks on him with their magic, too."

"Oh, dear." Mom sighed. "I'll talk to Ms. Maxwell."

"They aren't hurting him," Ian protested. "They blow his hair in his face or move his notes or stuff like that. He hasn't even noticed it's them. He doesn't believe in magic, remember?"

Miknon squared her shoulders. "They're just standing up for themselves. Nobody likes Misterabernathy. Please, may Ian grade the homework?"

Alexandria squinted at her. Why didn't they like Mr. Abernathy?

"Ian, how's the Fae class going this semester," she asked suspiciously.

Ian's shoulders hunched. "Fine."

"Do you get along with Mr. Abernathy?" she pressed.

She already knew he wasn't a good teacher, no matter what Raquel said, but was he undermining their progress at befriending the fae?

Ian stabbed his pancakes and shoved a huge bite into his mouth. "Mmm mm mm-mmm," he mumbled.

Mom sighed. "Alexandria, leave your brother alone. I'm sure he would tell us if there was a problem. Ian, don't talk with your mouth full. I'm sorry, but Mr. Abernathy is in charge, and he needs to do the grading."

On the other side of the table, Miknon sighed and busied herself with her own food. Gil looked his usual cheerful self, so Alexandria concentrated on the fairy and her brother, but by the time everyone finished eating, they still hadn't said anything more about Abernathy. Fine then, she'd have to discover the truth by herself. Was he the mean person Zee had mentioned? Was he bothering only the fae or also her brother?

AFTER GLANCING AT THE CLOCK, Alexandria untied her judo belt and pulled on her jacket as she ran from the studio. Class had run a little late, and if she didn't hurry, they'd be tardy for today's dragon barge landing. They didn't even have time for her to change clothes like usual.

She ducked her head against the raindrops and tried to move a little faster without splashing the puddles. As soon as she slid into the truck, Nikos stepped on the gas. She hurried to buckle her seatbelt before Mom could remind her.

Gil waved his phone. "Can you drop me at the school on the way? Mak-swill needs my help convincing the highborn newcomers they don't get a separate apartment building or servants." He rolled his eyes. "They think they're being punished by living with commoners who aren't serving them, even though we explained everything when they landed. You can pick me up at the hotel after the buses arrive, okay?"

The school was on the way to the river, but the road to the newcomers' building was almost at right angles to their path. Gil's plan was practical, since he could afford to be late with Raquel, but they must meet the dragons on time.

As they traveled, Alexandria amused herself with mental math. With both dragons bringing passengers every Saturday, they'd increased the fae population on Earth by about two-hundred-fifty fae every week. That meant that they now had approximately nine thousand fae down and only one thousand still on the moon. Plus the animals Gil had tended.

Poor Mr. Riggs had to find a new building to house them every two or three months. The original hotel was used for the newest additions, with Gil's mother in charge of on-site arrangements. As the fae recovered and learned how to use Earth facilities, they were transferred to the latest building acquisition to continue physical therapy and language lessons.

They probably had another month of landings for those in the original spaceship, then sometime the rest of the fleet would arrive and they'd have almost three hundred thousand fae to bring to Earth. And before then, they needed to tell all the humans what to expect.

As far as she knew, Mr. Compton was already working with governments around the world, but the existence of the fae was still top secret to the general public. She wasn't sure if she was looking forward to when the secret broke or dreading it. For sure, it would be dramatic.

But for today, she knew the drill. Same old "Welcome to Earth" speech. Same old surprise from the fae that an alien spoke their language. Same old complaints about everything being different.

Nikos pulled into the school parking lot, and Gil and Alexandria both hopped out.

"Uh, Alexandria," Ian started.

"Look, I gotta use the bathroom, okay? I'll hurry."

She slammed the door in his face and ran inside. On her way back out, she almost collided with Gil's twin brother in the main doorway.

"Oof," she said. "Why are you lurking here?"

"I'm just looking," Rafe said. "You go to landing now?"

"Yup, and I'm late." She tried to move around him, but he matched her step.

"May I go?"

"Sure, I don't care. But hurry." She dodged him and rammed out the door without waiting.

He followed on her heels and hopped into the truck with barely a hesitation.

"Hi, Rafe." Mom raised her eyebrows.

Alexandria shrugged. "More help, right? Step on it, Nikos."

The truck pulled out at exactly the speed limit, and by the time they reached the river, the first dragon barge was already splashing down. Everyone hurried and took their places, huddling under umbrellas or daring the sprinkle. Ian made the standard speech, then everyone spread out to answer questions as they arose.

Halfway through Alexandria's Q&A, she glanced around to check on everyone and discovered Rafe whispering with a small group of elves on the bus. As soon as they noticed her gaze, they stopped talking, with guilty looks. What had they been saying?

Alexandria casually approached them. "Everything going well here? Can I answer anything from an Earth perspective?"

Most of the elves turned up their noses.

Rafe smirked at her. "I have it all under control. Go away, girlie."

Alexandria stuck her fists on her hips and took a deep breath to tell him what he could do with his control, but the bus driver leaned on the horn.

"All off if you're getting off," he called.

Rafe patted the nearest elf on the shoulder. "We'll talk later." He sneered at Alexandria. "Off, girlie."

The engine rumbled, and Alexandria settled for a ferocious glare at Rafe. She hurried back to the truck, followed by Gil's brother. All the way back to the school, she pondered the interaction but got nowhere deciphering his mysterious conversation.

They left Rafe at the school and picked up Gil from the apartments on the way home.

While Mom unlocked the door, Alexandria pulled Gil aside. "Hey, Gil, Rafe went with us tonight and was talking funny with some of the elves. Do you know what—"

Gil said a word Alexandria didn't recognize. "You let him go? Didn't you know he's on the side of conquering Earth? We kept him away from the newcomers on purpose. He must have evaded his watcher for the day."

"Oh. I didn't know." Alexandria felt like cursing herself, but Mom had turned to make sure they were following.

"Never mind." Gil sighed. "He would find a way sooner or later. I just hoped it would be later."

Alexandria followed him in and locked the door. Drat! But Rafe had seemed so normal. How was she supposed to know he was a secret rebel?

But he couldn't get into much trouble in just a few minutes, could he? What had he been saying?

CHAPTER 15

IN WHICH THEY CHOOSE AMBASSADORS

MAY 12, 2023

TWO WEEKS after Rafe snuck out to a landing, Gil walked into a school council of the human and fae leaders and took his place between Ian and Alexandria with Miknon perched on his shoulder. Other than the four foster siblings, the table was divided between humans on one side and fae on the other, though they faced each other with smiles.

Though sometimes exempt from meetings, Gil and his adopted siblings were present today to interpret if needed and give perspective from and about the students. According to Ian's frequent complaints, children were no more likely to be on a council among the humans than among the fae, but this was an unusual situation for everyone, and qualifications were more important than age.

Gil beamed happily at all of them. Most of the council meetings were boring, but today was an exciting day, one he had looked forward to for months. At last, the school was reaching its intended goal, and the students would harvest the rewards of their long effort. More importantly, the long-awaited treaty between Earth and the fae was almost within reach.

"Now that we're all here," Mak-swill said, "let's start with updates before we discuss today's goal. Ms. Stafford, how are the refugees doing?"

"Well enough." The small woman who took care of food, clothing, and supplies for the incoming fae flipped cheerfully through her notes. "We're about ready to need a new building, though. Are we expecting the same number today and next week as usual, do we know?"

"Just one today," Gil said.

Every week, he asked the newly landed fae for updates from the ship to supplement what Nik sent via the radio transmitter Miknon had left behind. The king's secretary worried about eavesdroppers, so he radioed only the bare minimum. Usually, the reports were fairly similar, but with most of the fae now on Earth, only a minimal crew was left to take care of the ship and zoo. Gil had been repeatedly assured that his old charges were being cared for properly, but before the last fae could leave, their workload had to be removed. Since the animals were the biggest chore left, it was time to bring them down.

"Just one barge with passengers?" Stafferd asked. "Are they bringing supplies in the other? I know the seeds still need to come."

"Just one person," Gil clarified. "The giant is coming down in one barge, and the other will carry fae animals."

The humans stared at him without moving.

"A... giant?" Alexandria finally asked. "How big is he? She?"

Gil gestured toward the ceiling. "He's about as tall as the school."

Tall enough to pick apples from the highest branches without straining, which his hundred hands accomplished as fast as people could carry the baskets. Wait until the humans saw how helpful he could be!

The smile fell from Stafferd's face. "Oh, dear. Four stories? Where will we put him? And do the animals look like Earth animals, or do we have to hide them, too?"

"I'd hide them." Gil winked at her. "Even the ones that sort of look like yours do not act the same. And you can put the giant in with them, as long as he has a clean corner to himself. The kelpies and a few other animals can be taken directly to the ocean and left to care for themselves. When the selkies and water fae are assigned territories, they'll track them down then."

More importantly, he didn't want humans annoying the kelpies and other dangerous animals before they knew how to be cautious. Drowned humans wouldn't improve the chances of a treaty. He'd spent almost a year persuading Earth that they could live peacefully with the fae, and he didn't want any accidents to ruin everything.

"Are there any more giants?" Mak-swill asked.

"Not on this ship," Gil assured her.

Rigz muttered and scribbled a note on his paper. He spoke for their current host country and had set up the school for Maxwell to run.

"I'll see what I can do about tall housing that won't be ruined by live-stock," he said. "At least it's warm enough that a barn might work. Maxwell, I recommend just the semi-trucks tonight."

Mak-swill sighed. "Yes, I don't think the buses will help much. Farrell, how's the international scene progressing?"

The rotund man didn't bother looking at his stack of papers. "Most countries have agreed to host fae refugees and ambassadors with the intent to discuss a treaty soon. None have promised a treaty, and nobody's happy about the refugees. I have the list of host countries here, whenever we need to discuss them specifically."

They debated a few more promising but inconclusive details about Earth politics, then ran through general school problems and health issues. Whenever Gil fidgeted too much, Miknon pinched his ear. Despite the importance of the meeting today, the ordinary troubles still had to be solved.

"And now to the main topic of the day," Mak-swill said.

Gil sat up straighter and folded his hands in his lap to keep them still.

"With less than a month until classes end," Mak-swill said, "it is time to choose ambassadors from among our students. Ian, do you have the language grades?"

"Right here." Ian patted a stack of paper, though he frowned as he did so.

Did he have another one of his headaches? Was he still worried he wasn't a good teacher? Or was Misterabernathy still being rude? Ian hadn't mentioned any problems recently, but his shoulders were perma-nently bowed. Gil mentally smacked himself. He should have checked on his brother earlier. And he could talk to Merodach about the headaches.

"And some kids learned other languages outside of class," Alexandria said. "We should take those into account."

"We'll do the best we can," Mama Helen said. She taught the fae in several classes and helped interpret, so she was useful in the meeting.

Mak-swill transferred her gaze to the adult fae. "And you are prepared to discuss your people?"

The four of them nodded and squared their shoulders. Shalla as king's housekeeper, Merodach as healer, Taras as chief guard, and Mother were the biggest leaders the fae had until the king's secretary or the lords landed, or until Shar revealed himself. Gil had never discovered why Mother was considered a leader even after Grandsire died. Though she was a perfectly wonderful, competent person, she was nobody important.

None of them had paper in front of them, because fae commoners rarely learned to read their own language, and none were good enough at writing English to make it worth the effort. They had learned spoken English, and their memories held all the information they needed. Gil would have congratulated them if he could decide how to not make it sound condescending.

"Okay," Mak-swill said. "As we proceed, please remember that we are looking for both language facility and a cooperative attitude. We are still seeking peace."

With a deep breath, Gil forced himself to not squirm. Even after months living together, not all the students could get along. Some of the fae preferred the plan to conquer Earth instead of negotiating for a small part of it. Some of the humans thought their tech was capable of blasting the fae to bits to "protect" their home instead of sharing. Gil didn't want to discover which side was stronger, because winning would come at too great a cost.

Couldn't everyone just be friends? Look how well he got along with Ian and Alexandria, who were now closer to him than his own brother.

What could he do with Ram, anyway? He despised the humans, based only on the fae lords' desires to conquer Earth, and wouldn't give the Earth students a chance to prove themselves. He had spent all year ignoring his roommates and being rude to his classmates.

Gil was tempted to thrash him, except it would set a poor example.

And Ram was trained as a warrior, while Gil was not, so who would actually get thrashed was uncertain.

"It would be nice to have three hundred interpreters," Mama Helen said. "I know, I know, they aren't all suitable. I just said it would be nice."

"That wouldn't be this year, anyway," Mak-swill said. "Only two-thirds of our students are graduating or returning home."

Gil was staying, as were Ram and Zak and all the youngest fae. According to Earth customs, children stayed in school until they were eighteen years old, or about one-hundred-eighty-three conjunctions. For the fae, that was still childhood, but while they attended an Earth school, they would follow Earth rules and be adults at eighteen.

"I consider that good news," Mama Helen said. "Over the next two years, we'll have a group of students who are even better, linguistically. And perhaps socially as well."

Now that the other fae spoke English well enough to need less translation help, Gil intended to use the next year to learn another language or two. Maybe three, since he was no longer in charge of the zoo, but it would depend what else the humans wanted him to learn.

"With so many fae leaving," Rigz said, "we're only keeping locals for the humans, to maintain the fae/human roommates. That's good in most ways, but it does mean we'll have fewer graduates next year."

"It will be fine," Mak-swill said. "But we really do need to discuss this year's graduates, if you please. I'd like to use the next few weeks to give our new ambassadors a little extra training."

One by one, they discussed two hundred students, both human and fae. Some were eliminated rapidly because their attitude toward the other race was unsuitable. Among the humans, the tendency appeared randomly, and they hadn't had to expel anyone since the first few weeks. Among the fae, the highborn like Wes were more likely to be antagonistic, while the commoners frequently had more human friends. Gil wasn't surprised, since most of the highborn were raised to feel entitled and biased.

"But we can't make a judgment call just by race," Taras cautioned.

The king's Companion looked more stern than usual. The strain of keeping Shar safe and secret had added to the problem of protecting the fae in general. At least one of the burdens would soon be lifted from him.

"Some of the highborn have adjusted to Earth better," he continued, "like Freya, while some commoners have not. We have already been sending the adult troublemakers to the farthest housing to keep their attitude from spreading. We must do the same with the students in a few weeks."

Gil sighed. His own brother was still in the problematic section. Fortunately, Ram wasn't graduating this year and wasn't eligible for an ambassadorial post, so Gil didn't have to admit he was a problem. But if Ram didn't change his attitude, he would be moved out right after graduation, and Gil wouldn't get to see him anymore. At least Nik, the king's secretary, had been wise enough to send down the more cooperative fae in the first loads, so by the time the more prejudiced arrived, they had little opportunity for mischief.

Feral shuffled a paper to the top. "We need the more popular languages of Earth most, of course, to fill the most positions in the countries that have agreed to host fae. That includes English, Mandarin, Arabic, Russian, Hindi, Portuguese, Spanish, French, German, and Japanese. What languages were your students able to learn this year?"

"What about African languages?" Mak-swill asked. "Are we excluding an entire continent?"

"English and French are pretty common as a second language in Africa," Feral said. "Beyond that, there are hundreds of African languages." He shrugged. "We'll have to make do with English and French."

"We have plenty of Spanish, French, German, and English," Mak-swill said.

"Jin speaks Mandarin semi-natively," Alexandria said. "Jinyuan, I mean."

"Freya speaks it with her," Miknon volunteered.

"How good is she?" Feral asked.

Miknon shrugged. "I don't understand either of them, but Jin doesn't cry."

Mak-swill coughed and held a hand in front of her face. Her eyes twinkled, but she said nothing. Gil winked at her, not bothering to hide his own smile.

"Freya is highborn," Shalla cautioned.

"Yes, but she has gotten used to us commoners," Miknon drawled. "A little, anyway. And she likes Jin's fashion sense."

"We don't have anybody perfect," Gil said. "Even if they annoy each other, they'll make it work. They didn't kill each other as roommates."

"How is Freya's English?" Feral asked.

Ian scanned his papers, then scowled and covered the page. "It's fine. I've talked to her myself. And Jin's Fae is good enough."

With Ian's arms across the page, Gil couldn't see what it actually said, but he agreed with Ian's assessment.

Feral made a note. "Okay, Freya and Jinyuan can go to China. Who's next?"

"Shaun learned Japanese from his roommate," Ms. Stafford said. "He's eighteen soon, isn't he?"

"Shaun is staying here," Taras said flatly. The humans waited a minute, but he didn't elaborate.

Gil shifted in his chair and bit his tongue. Shar's survival was still a secret, and until he decided to claim his throne, it would remain so. In the meantime, the fae who knew who he was would never consent to send him into the world, despite his age or him using his mind-touching to skim both Ukrainian and Japanese from his roommates. But he wasn't the only one rooming with Touji.

"Abe learned some Japanese. And Ukrainian." Gil rocked his hand back and forth to indicate Ash's moderate level of competency. Considering the dryad had learned three languages including English, without magic, Gil didn't care how poorly they were mastered. Besides, Ash would have Two to help him interpret. Together, they would be fine. "Where do you want him to go?"

"Japan," Rigz said. "I don't think we'll send any fae to Ukraine or Russia at this time. Sending the humans back will be enough for now. If the area calms down, we can send a team later."

"That leaves out Nate," Gil said. "He learned Russian."

"Uh," Alexandria choked. "I don't think we should send a dragon, anyway."

"Hydra," Ian corrected. "Dragons have wings."

"Whatever." Alexandria bumped shoulders with him.

Gil shrugged. A hydra seemed perfectly normal to him, and Nash was a lot nicer than dragons in the movies. And the highborn were less nice. The human legends got everything mixed up, but it wouldn't improve their chances of a treaty by scaring the humans.

"What about Portuguese?" Feral tapped his paper.

Everyone shrugged. Feral sighed. "Okay, let's see if any of the Spanish-speakers want to learn Portuguese. I think we'll have to do without Arabic or Hindi."

They continued discussing the students one by one, assigning human-fae pairs to as many countries from Feral's list as possible. Later, they would choose adult fae to accompany each of them, along with humans to assist and care for them. Nobody would consider letting the fae drive a car, for instance, and some of them couldn't use a microwave or phone without blowing it up.

The meeting continued for hours, long enough that they stopped to bring in food to eat while they talked. One by one, they matched fifty fae to human partners and assigned them as ambassadors to countries that were willing to discuss a treaty. Whenever the rest of the fleet reached Earth, the other ships would land in those same countries before dispersing to their final homes.

Assuming the treaty was signed.

But it would be. They were so close. All Gil's hard work was almost ready to harvest. With or without Shar's help, he would make a peace between Earth and the fae. His people would have a new home, and the commoners would be equal to the highborn.

Just a few more weeks, and then all would be well.

And he would have two more years to convince Ram that humans were worthy of peace and friendship.

CHAPTER 16

FINALS

MAY 26, 2023

IAN CRAMMED the last bite of lunch into his mouth and rose from the table. Everyone was talking fine today, so if he hurried, he could read another chapter of his book. He turned and discovered Zee right behind him. Perplexed, he stared at the gremlin, who didn't have lunch this period.

She held out a folded piece of paper. "Helen asks would you take this message to Misterabernathy, please? Before the bell rings. If he is not there, leave it on his desk."

Ian groaned and snatched the paper. "Fine." He stomped from the cafeteria, dropping his tray onto the stack as he passed it.

Zee followed him. "May I ask you questions now?"

"I don't care, but aren't you supposed to be in class with Mom?"

Zee shrugged. "Helen doesn't yell at people."

She quizzed him on English grammar as they walked through the hall. When they reached the classroom, the door was locked and nobody answered.

"Ha," Ian gloated. "I'll have to wait after all." He was in no hurry to talk to Mr. Abernathy.

Zee looked down the hall, then clasped her hands behind her back. "I will wait with you until we see Misterabernathy."

"Aw, nuts," Ian said. "I forgot they gave me a key at the beginning of the year."

The door was usually unlocked, except when Abernathy was hiding, and nobody wanted to interact with him more than necessary. With a sigh, Ian hurried back to his locker to retrieve the key.

The never-used key worked, and he let himself into the classroom. Abernathy's briefcase was open on the table he used for a desk, and the grade book sat in front of it. Ian dropped the note onto the book and turned to leave. He'd have to hurry to get his notebook before class started. Should have gotten it on the way.

Red ink caught his eye, and he turned back.

F.

F.

F. Every grade was failing, not just midterms.

Ian turned the record for a better look. The book was open to the English classes taken by the fae, and *every* grade was failing, even for the best English speakers. Better grades from before had been covered with red F's. Last semester's grades hadn't been great, but they hadn't been this bad.

"I don't understand." Ian pointed to the red letters, and Zee stepped closer to see. "Why is everyone flunking?"

"What are you doing here?" a voice barked from the doorway. "How did you get in?"

Ian and Zee jerked their heads up, staring in shock as Mr. Abernathy entered. As his gaze took in their stance at the grade book, the teacher's face turned red.

"Put that away!" He marched toward the table, fists clenched.

Ian slammed the book shut and clutched it to his chest. Zee side-stepped and looked anxiously toward the door, but her path was blocked by Mr. Abernathy.

"Why are you flunking everybody?" Ian asked. "You'll ruin their chances at being translators."

"Their grammar is terrible, and their accents are worse," Mr. Abernathy said. "And they don't listen to me anymore. They are terrible students."

"That's not fair!" Ian said. "They've been doing well. Their accents and grammar might not be perfect, but they're understandable if you listen. They've only been learning it for two semesters, so you can't expect perfection."

"Yes I can." Mr. Abernathy reached for the book, and Ian took another step backward. "After nearly a year, they should be almost fluent now. They would be if they would pay more attention in class." Unable to get the book, the teacher grabbed Ian's arm and squeezed. "Give me that book!"

Zee took a few steps toward the open door, then looked back at Ian. She wavered, shoulders hunched and one foot raised, biting her lip.

Ian held the grade book tighter. "I'm showing this to Maxwell. She won't let you get away with this."

"No you won't." Mr. Abernathy squeezed harder on Ian's arm. "It's mine. They brought me in to be in charge of this project, and you won't undercut me. The students won't talk to me, so obviously their English isn't good enough."

"Of course they don't talk to you." Ian tried to yank free without letting go of the book, but he couldn't get enough leverage. He winced at the pain but held on to the evidence. "You mock them. They talk to their roommates, they talk to me. I send you reports every month."

Mr. Abernathy sneered. "You are just a kid; what do you know?"

In a quavering voice Zee said, "Leave him alone."

"Get out of here!" Mr. Abernathy shouted.

Shrinking more, Zee ran for the door. In Fae, she said, "I'll get War Lady."

Ian glanced at Mr. Abernathy to see what he would do, but the teacher didn't even blink. Ha, some expert. He never did memorize the vocabulary once he recorded it for his dictionary, and he didn't pay any attention at all to the culture. Ian was willing to bet Abernathy had no idea who War Lady was.

Or, possibly, Mr. Abernathy hadn't heard Zee at all, since he was ranting so hard he was frothing at the mouth. He shook Ian, who stumbled backward, staying on his feet only because of Abernathy's grip on him. Insults poured out in a peculiar combination of Shakespeare and ancient Greek profanity.

Ian blinked back tears. This was like Dad all over again. He thought he had escaped when they left with Nikos, but bullies were the same everywhere.

Ian tried again to free himself, but Abernathy's hold was too tight. Anyway, running from Dad never helped. Alexandria won by standing up to him and then leaving.

Of course, Alexandria was older, bigger, and knew judo. Ian had none of those advantages, and Abernathy wasn't even listening to him anymore.

But he could hold on to the grade book. If he let go, there would be no proof of what Abernathy meant to do to his friends. He had to show Ms. Maxwell.

Tightening his grip until his arms ached from more than Abernathy's pinching fingers, Ian tried to close his ears. The teacher had expanded his insults to other ancient languages, which meant that at least Ian didn't understand all of them anymore. It didn't matter; the intent was clear. Abernathy despised Ian, just like Dad.

He didn't have the words or courage to talk back. He couldn't fight like Alexandria. But it didn't matter. If Alexandria could fight unarmed against a man with a knife, Ian could listen silently to a man with sharp words.

Just hold on.

Abernathy pressed him backward until Ian was against the wall. Every shake now rattled Ian's head, but he hung on to the book. *Don't listen, don't let go. Just hold on.*

You're useless, Dad said, his face imposed in front of Abernathy's. *You're weak. I can't believe you're my son.*

Tears streamed down Ian's face. He was nothing like Alexandria, but he had to be strong enough to save his friends. He couldn't let them flunk when they'd done so well, just because Abernathy didn't like them.

"WHAT are you doing?" The bellow echoed in the room.

Mr. Abernathy stopped shaking Ian and turned to face the doorway, but he didn't let go of Ian's arm.

Hands reaching for weapons she didn't wear at school, Ms. Maxwell stormed into the room, followed by Mom, Chantelle, and two of the school security guards. Marguerite was human military, and Lili was a tall fae with sunglasses and green braids tied up in a bun. Zee slid off the back of Marguerite but stayed behind the others. Mom clenched her fists and started forward, but the principal stopped her with an outstretched arm.

"I don't need you here for a minor disciplinary action of my teacher's aide," Mr. Abernathy said.

"He's not your aide, he's your co-teacher," Ms. Maxwell said, "and apparently you do need help. Ian, tell me what's going on."

She waved a finger, and Marguerite pulled her taser and swung out to flank Abernathy from one side while Lili approached from the other.

"*I'll* tell you." Mr. Abernathy let go of Ian and straightened his jacket, though he still stood close enough to trap Ian against the wall. "He's nothing but a kid, and he's not my co-teacher. I don't need to be lectured by a bunch of women and children about how to run my classes. I have four PhD's in ancient languages."

"He knows *this* language better than you," the principal said.

Mr. Abernathy turned purple. "He does not."

Ian stepped around Abernathy, dodging another grab for him. "You didn't stop Zee from going for Ms. Maxwell, so you must not have understood what she said."

When Marguerite blocked Abernathy, Ian hurried to Mom's side and held out the grade book to the principal. "I came in to deliver Mom's message and found his grade book open. He's flunking every one of the fae."

"Are you okay?" Ms. Maxwell whispered.

Ian nodded, scrubbing at the tears on his cheeks. What a baby. Dad never let him forget when he cried.

"It's none of your business," Abernathy blustered. "I'm not in the habit of listening to children."

"I know," Ian said. "All of your students are children, and they don't listen to you because you don't listen to them."

Abernathy straightened his tie. "I am in charge here."

Ms. Maxwell's eyebrows shot upward. "*I* am in charge."

Mr. Abernathy sneered. "As principal, you handle discipline — and ought to be concentrating on this juvenile delinquent — but I was brought in to handle the language because of my expertise."

"You were hired to help *Ian* with your expertise," Ms. Maxwell said, "which, in fact, you haven't been lending to this project."

Mom wrapped her arms around Ian and squeezed. He let go of the grade book with one arm and returned the hug.

Abernathy sputtered. "I've made a whole dictionary, and when I publish it, I will be famous."

Ms. Maxwell folded her arms. "You're not publishing it."

"Of course I am," Mr. Abernathy said.

"Nope." Ms. Maxwell looked at her watch. "As of right now, you are fired. If you don't leave quietly, security will escort you off campus."

With grins, Marguerite raised her taser and Lili touched her sunglasses. Ian found a similar grin stretching across his own face.

"Sunglasses are forbidden in school," Mr. Abernathy lectured the fae.

Ms. Maxwell laughed. "You really aren't catching on, are you? Let me put this in words of one syllable. You are fired. Go away. Nope, that was two syllables, too complicated." She rubbed her chin. "Be gone! Aha, that's better."

Ian snorted, not bothering to hide his amusement.

Mr. Abernathy shot him a look of utter scorn, then glared at Ms. Maxwell. "When I publish my dictionary, I will put in a foreword about how I accomplished it despite your obstacles. You will never work in the education system again. And if your people touch me, I'll see that the newspapers hear about your brutality." He brushed off his jacket and pulled himself to his full height.

Ms. Maxwell laughed harder. "I don't work in the education system. I'm an officer in the United States Air Force. And you should read your contract, because all the information from this project is top secret. All your papers belong to the U.S. government, so I will take all your drafts and notes, whether in hard copy or digital. You will publish nothing, and if you talk about anything to anyone, the NDA you signed will ensure you never see the light of day again."

Ian relaxed his grip on the book a little, but he stayed behind the principal. No, behind the USAF officer defending him. Even without a weapon, she was terrifying.

"You will be sorry," Mr. Abernathy hissed.

"Oh, I'm sorry I hired your sorry self," Ms. Maxwell said. "But you don't seem to understand. I'm doing you a *favor*. If I let the fae handle you, you will really never see the light of day again. See this young lady?" She pointed at Lili. "She's a gorgon."

"Don't be ridiculous," Mr. Abernathy said.

Lili reached up and untied her hair. As it uncoiled, the braids wiggled by themselves, hissing and coiling. Not braids — snakes.

Mr. Abernathy gasped and turned aside. The blood drained from his face, and he staggered back against the wall.

Ms. Maxwell's grin turned cruel. "She's perfectly willing to turn you into stone so my officers can carry you off campus without resistance." She quirked an eyebrow. "Since you're so kind to everybody..."

Chantelle nodded sharply. Lili touched her sunglasses again, sliding them slowly down her nose.

Shaking like an aspen leaf, Abernathy reached for his briefcase.

"I don't think you heard me," Ms. Maxwell said much too sweetly. "You aren't taking any of your papers. My security officers will search your car and your apartment. And remember, you can't talk about anything. Now go, and hope the fae don't decide to come after you when they discover how you treated their children."

Flanked by the two security guards, Mr. Abernathy marched out, sputtering more ancient language. Probably nothing nice, from the sound of it.

Once he was out of sight, Maxwell grinned. "That was great. Are you sure you're okay, Ian? Did he hurt you?"

Ian rubbed his head. "A little. He pinched my arms pretty hard, trying to get the book, and he shook me against the wall."

Mom brushed his hair aside and examined his head. Lips pinched, she shook her head at the principal.

"He was yelling like Dad," Ian murmured to Mom. "I wanted to run."

"I know," Mom whispered. "We heard him from the hall. I'm sorry."

"But if I ran," Ian said loud enough for everyone to hear, "I'd have to leave the book. I stayed to protect the book."

"You stayed to protect your friends," Mom said. "Well done, my brave boy. I'm so sorry you had to go through that."

Ms. Maxwell patted him on the shoulder. "Well done. I'm sorry I didn't understand the extent of the problem earlier."

Silently, he offered her the grade book.

She shook her head. "The class is yours now. I know you will do well."

Chantelle bowed slightly. "You are the reason this school is working. All of us know that."

Tears stung at the back of Ian's eyes, and he cleared his throat. Ms. Maxwell, Zee, and Chantelle left, shutting the door behind them. Mom wrapped both arms around him, and he buried his face in her collar and wept.

Dad was wrong. Ian wasn't useless. His talents were worthwhile in the right place.

Mom whispered soothing nothings until Ian stopped crying, then dropped a kiss on his forehead before letting go. "Are you ready for class?"

He glanced at the clock. "I still have a few minutes before lunch ends."

"Mm-hm."

He squared his shoulders. "If the class is mine, I have to fix Abernathy's grade book."

Mom rubbed his back. "Yes, but you can do it. You know all your students."

"I do." Ian smiled. "And I have all my notes. Thanks, Mom."

"Should I send Zee back in to help you?"

"Sure. Please get in my locker and send my notebooks with her." He recited his combination in case she had forgotten it.

She winked and left. Ian rifled through Abernathy's briefcase and found a red pen. By the time Zee returned, he was ready.

The gremlin handed him his notebooks. "I'm still not good with reading."

He handed her the pen. "No, but you're good with numbers. I'll do the reading, you do the writing."

Zee wrinkled her nose. "What if I mess it up?"

"Then we'll fix it." Without Abernathy in the way, they could handle it.

Zee nodded and pulled the cap off the pen.

Ian opened his first notebook. "Let's see. On the first assignment, Abe knew most of the vocabulary and all the grammar, but his pronunciation was terrible. Let's decide how to weight that..."

CHAPTER 17

IN WHICH FATHER CALLS

JUNE 2-3, 2023

A WEEK after Misterabernathy was removed, Zak was still thinking about the confrontation while she worked on her radio on the table. Other than U.N., who was the victim, everyone who had confronted the bully was female. Sure, War Lady had rank to protect her, and Lili had magic, but Helen and Chantelle had nothing. On Kunisu, Misterabernathy would have laughed in their faces. Even on the ship, where all workers were needed, the women had no say without the men. Gil's family had been bumped to the end of the food line when his grandfather died.

What was different about Earth? Why were girls respected here? And why wasn't she?

Kirill handed her the tool she needed before she could ask. Zak made an adjustment and tilted her head to listen. Yes, that sounded better. And yet, she still hadn't gotten a return message from Father.

"Maybe this will never work," she muttered. "Maybe I'll never be good enough."

Kirill handed her the next part. "Are you serious? You learned a whole new system of tech in less than a year, *and* a new language. You're the most competent person I know."

"But Father hasn't replied," Zak pointed out.

Father would have been able to make the machine work properly.

"He doesn't have the same parts," Kirill said. "Do you know for sure your substitutes will work?"

"No."

"Well, then." Kirill shrugged.

Maybe there weren't good substitute parts. Or maybe the lords wouldn't let him adapt the contrivance. Or...

"Maybe he sent a message when I wasn't here to hear it!" Zak bit her lip.

"Okay, no need to panic. We can add a recorder to this machine." Kirill ran to the shelves of parts and selected a handful.

"We can?"

"Tak, we can." He flashed her a grin. "We can do anything."

"Hand me those wires," she demanded. "Let's get it done."

Because she *was* good enough, and she would prove it. Even if Father never replied, she would have a whole new contrivance to show him when he arrived.

It took them an hour to assemble the recorder, and they were still integrating it into her machine when another thought occurred to her. If girls were as good as boys, then being a girl was fine, right? No one here cared. When the lords arrived, they would have to get used to Earth customs.

And if being a girl didn't matter, then she didn't have to hide it. Even the lady in the elf movie had revealed herself before she killed the monster.

"Kirill?" Leaning closer to the machine than really necessary, she peered inside.

A part appeared at the edge of her vision.

"Thanks, but..." She gulped. "Do you want to go to the dance tomorrow?"

"I'm going, yes. I like dancing."

Zak winced as she took the part. "I mean, do you want to go with me?"

He had once asked, and now she regretted telling him no. Especially since asking was harder than she had imagined.

"Sure, friends can go to the dance together."

Gathering her courage, Zak leaned back and looked him in the eye. "Yes, we are friends, but I mean as a date. Not a month, but—"

Kirill laughed. "Yes."

"Yes?"

"Tak, I would be happy to be your date. Not a month."

"Okay." She wiggled the part into place in her machine. "What should I wear?"

Eyes wide, Kirill shook his head. "I really think you should talk to your roommates about that."

"Okay. Pliers, please."

As they continued to work, a smile tugged at the corners of her mouth. By evening, her radio was connected to a recorder that would capture any messages Father sent when she was gone. Girls could do anything, and do it well.

"I LIKE THAT ONE." Freya pointed to the computer screen from across the room.

"I don't know." Zak wrinkled her nose. "It's very bright. Where's the rest of it?"

They'd been debating dresses all morning, and she was reconsidering the dance altogether.

"That's the whole dress," Gaby said.

Miknon chuckled. "There's enough fabric there to make a dress for *me*."

Jin coughed. "I don't think I recommend red satin with green skin."

Gaby sighed. "Maybe you should come help, then, Miss Smarty Pants."

Jin grabbed the laptop and clicked frantically for a few seconds. "This." She turned the screen to face them. The dress was a soft cream, with a flowing full skirt and a high bodice whose lace overlay turned into loose sleeves.

"The color is good," she said, "it comes in kids' sizes, and I think Zee would be more comfortable with more coverage like this."

"My arms and legs will show," Zak complained. "And the shape of everything else."

Her face grew hot. She would definitely look like a girl in that dress.

Miknon patted her shoulder. "That's normal. Not every girl wears their father's old clothes, you know."

"The sleeves come to the elbow," Jin said. "And the skirt comes halfway down the shins. It's a very modest dress."

Zak looked at her skeptically, and her roommate passed the computer to Gaby and hurried to her closet.

"Look," Jin said. "This is what Freya is wearing."

The narrow dress she pulled out was purple silk, very appropriate for a highborn, but the neckline dipped in both front and back, the hem ended at the knee, and there were no sleeves. On her bed, Freya lowered her magazine and wiggled her eyebrows at Zak.

Zak shut her mouth with a snap. "What are you all wearing?"

Gaby waved at her bed, which displayed a flared turquoise skirt and a puff-sleeved white blouse. "I'm not dating and not dressing up, thank you. I'm just going for the dancing."

"My flounced skirt and a sleeveless top," Miknon said. "Gil's wearing a copy of his old kilt. We thought we would show the humans a variety of traditional fae garb."

"Gil isn't going to Alex's judo competition?" Zak asked.

"I can't go." Miknon waved her hands at her tiny frame, obviously not human. "And Gil's been looking forward to the dance all month. Shaun decided to skip the dance, so he's going with Alex."

Jin put Freya's dress back into the closet and pulled out more silk, this time in an eye-blinding bright pink. "I'm going traditional, too."

She draped the ankle-length skirt over a chair and held the long embroidered jacket above it, overlapping the sides to demonstrate how it would look. The loose, flowing sleeves fell halfway down the skirt, and a matching sash was still on the hanger.

Gaby winced. "Is the color traditional?"

Patting the stripe of bright pink in her hair, Jin winked.

Zak waved her hands in surrender. "Okay, okay, I'll wear the dress. Um, how do we get it?"

"First, we need your size," Jin said.

She grabbed a long ribbon with lines and numbers and approached Zak with a mischievous grin. As she measured different parts of Zak's body, she recited numbers to Gaby, who compared them to a chart on the computer.

"Got it," Gaby said. "I charged it to Zee's school account, since she hasn't bought any new clothes yet. It will be ready for pickup in half an hour. Or should I have it delivered?"

"I can go get it," Jin offered, "if you two want to handle hair and makeup. I don't trust delivery to keep it out of the rain."

"I can help with braiding," Miknon said, "if you want a fae style."

Freya sat up and shut her magazine with a snap. "I can do makeup. All you need is a little lip gloss and eyeshadow."

"Sounds good." Jin grabbed her keys and purse and bounded for the door. "I'll be back soon."

"Hair first," Miknon ordered. "That way we won't ruin the makeup."

She pointed at Zak's hairbrush and raised her eyebrows. Silently, Zak pulled the elastic from her casual braid and loosened her hair.

FACE HOT, trying not to shrink into herself, Zak faced Kirill in the ground-floor hallway. The dress clung to her, except where it swirled around her arms and legs, and she had never felt so exposed. Behind her, the other girls blocked her from turning and running away.

Kirill held out flowers bound with elastic. "Don't worry," he whispered. "You look beautiful," he said louder.

He wore a crisp light blue shirt and black pants, and his hair was combed neatly instead of falling over his forehead like usual.

Gaby reached around Zak and took the flower. "This goes on your wrist, like this."

The creamy flower matched the dress perfectly. Either Kirill was very lucky, or someone had told him what color to get.

The other boys were dressed similarly, and the girls spread out to greet them. Miknon flew to Gil's shoulder, and Jin took Two's arm with the hand not holding her flute case. Wes didn't touch Freya, but he did give her a flower like Zak's, in a pale purple.

"Are we ready?" Jin asked, waving her flute case. Several of the students had volunteered to help with the music at the dance, including her.

Slowly, Kirill held his elbow toward Zak, who looked at Gaby in panic. Gaby widened her eyes and tilted her head toward Jin and Two.

Oh. Zak slipped one hand cautiously around Kirill's arm. He patted her fingers and led her toward the elevator after the others.

As they exited into the basement, Zak paused. Kirill raised his eyebrows in a question.

"Do you care—" Zak bit her lip, then let go before she ruined Freya's hard work. "Could we stop by the tech room, to check the recorder one more time? I know there's probably no message, but—"

Kirill patted her hand again. "It will only take a couple of minutes."

He turned right instead of left and led her to her radio at the back of the classroom. A light on the recorder blinked on and off. On and off.

"Did it break?" Zak asked.

"No," Kirill breathed. "You have a message!"

Clutching his arm tighter, Zak pushed the button to play the message.

"Greetings," Father's voice echoed oddly. "This is my second attempt at a message. I followed your instructions with a few adaptations. Hope it worked. The fleet will reach Ki in half a conjunction." He paused. "See you then."

The recorder went silent. In the quiet room, Zak's panting breath was clearly audible. Kirill turned to face her and gripped her other shoulder with his free hand, as if to hold her up. She inhaled, held her breath, and exhaled slowly.

"I'm okay." She blinked away the stinging behind her eyes. "Father is coming."

Tingling spread from her chest to her toes. Her stomach flipped upside down, and sparkles danced in her vision. Her body felt as light as it had on the ship, and she couldn't tell which way was up.

Kirill grabbed both shoulders and shook her slightly. "Zee?"

She took another breath and discovered she was trembling.

Grabbing Kirill's elbows, she smiled. "Father is coming!"

Her smile died. "The fleet — the lords will be here in half a conjunction! I have to tell the others." She pulled free and whirled for the door, then froze.

"I must tell Father I received his message." She threw herself at the radio and knelt in a puddle of skirts to press the necessary buttons. "Father, see you soon."

Barely avoiding her hem, she bounced to her feet and rushed away. Kirill stayed right beside her.

"The school offices are all closed for Saturday," he said as he flung the door open. "Most of the adults are either at home or dealing with the adult fae."

"Or with Helen and Alex. Oh! Or at the dance." Zak bolted around the corner toward the sound of music pounding nearby, grateful for the loose skirt that allowed her legs to move. "Some of them are chaperoning, and Gil is at the dance."

"Right. Let's split up to search faster." Kirill yanked the gym door open. "We'll meet back in the hallway."

Zak nodded and hurried inside. In the dim room, tiny lights glimmered on the ceiling and walls between paper streamers and colorful balloons. The crowd of humans and fae was split between those already dancing and those standing nervously along the walls.

"Have you seen Gil?" Zak asked the closest fae. "Or War Lady or Stafferd? Any of the leaders?"

Everyone shook their heads. She worked her way along the wall in one direction while Kirill went the other way, but nobody had seen any of the leaders, either fae or human. Those chaperoning were merely teachers. Eventually, Zak ran into Jin and Two and dragged them from their dancing to talk to her.

"Maxwell went to the newcomer building," Jin said in reply. "What's wrong? Where's your date?"

She frowned at the crowd, then smiled and waved. Kirill waved back and wound his way through the dancers.

"I guess Rafe is looking for Gil," he panted. "I gave him the message."

"You what?" Zak screeched. "Oh, no!"

Kirill shrugged. "They're brothers, right?"

"Wait, wait." Jin dragged Zak and Kirill farther from the music. "What is going on?"

Zak ignored her. "Kirill, tell me exactly what happened with Rafe."

"I saw Rafe," Kirill said, "so I asked him where Gil is, because you have a message for him. Rafe asked what message, so I told him. He said, 'Now is the time,' sneezed, and ran off. So he'll find Gil and give him the message, right?"

"Oh, no." Zak spun in a circle desperately looking for Gil, Miknon, or any of the fae leaders. Whatever Ram had planned, it was bound to be trouble.

"What message?" Jin groaned.

Two put a hand over her mouth.

"I don't understand what's wrong," Kirill said. "I'm sure Rafe can find Gil faster than we can. By the way, werewolves sneeze funny. *Kishar* instead of *achoo*."

"Kishar!" Zak pressed both hands over her mouth to keep from screaming.

Ram had run to warn the conquer-minded fae that Lord Kishar was almost here. If Ram wasn't stopped, they would start the war the school had been founded to prevent. Where was everyone when she needed them?

"Everyone, find Gil *right now*," she ordered.

Jin yanked away from Two, pointed her flute case like a weapon, and glared at Zak. "What. Is. Wrong?"

"Message from Father," Zak blurted. "Fleet almost here. Rafe is bad. Must stop him. Find Gil!"

"Wang ba dan," Jin swore. "Two, down the middle. I'll go right, Zee left. Kirill, you're the tallest; hop on a chair." She gathered up her skirt and ran.

"Sorry I goofed," Kirill said, grabbing a chair.

"You didn't know," Zak said.

Following Jin's instructions, they ran through the room, calling Gil's name. The dancers paused, and a ripple opened a space in the middle of the crowd. Sweating and grinning, Gil hurried to Zak, Miknon settling onto his shoulder. Though he wore a traditional fae kilt in crisp white, he had added a human t-shirt above it.

"Hey, Zee, glad you came." Gil brushed his hair back from his forehead and gulped air. "Did you want to dance?"

Zak waved at Two across the room, then dragged Gil into the hallway. "The fleet is almost here. Rafe heard my message from Father and ran off."

Gil's smile died. "He's gone to warn those on Kishar's side."

"That's what I fear." Zak clutched his arm. "Can you stop him?"

"Turn your back," Gil said.

Zak obeyed, and Miknon talked over the rustle of Gil's clothing. "Rafe is stronger, but Gil is fast. He might catch him."

Gil barked, and Zak turned around. The black wolf nodded once and bolted for the stairs. Jin and Two rushed into the hallway, trailed by Gaby and Kirill. They watched Gil scramble up the steps, then focused on Zak.

"What's the plan?" Jin asked.

"Gil will need help." Zak clutched her stomach, trying not vomit. They had to prevent war.

"No problem," Gaby said. "We can call the apartments and warn them not to let Rafe in. Miknon can help me translate."

"There's only one phone in those apartments," Miknon said, "to limit contact with the humans. And it only answers calls from approved leaders."

Which Zak and Gil were not, despite her status as navigator and his borrowed authority from the prince. No, only the adults counted, and they were all gone right now. Zak crumpled her skirt in clenched fists.

Gaby bit her lip. "Then we'll call the hotel and warn Maxwell and Meg." She held out an arm, and Miknon fluttered to her. "They can tell the guards to keep Rafe out."

"We can't count on that working," Zak said. "Some people are ready for a fight. All he has to do to alert them is shout through the windows. We need to bring him back, and Mak-swill is too far away. We need help faster."

"Go get Alex from the competition," Miknon said. "She's almost on the way. Run, Gaby."

Tucking Miknon close to her chest, Gaby ran for the stairs. The school was approximately halfway between the fae building for newcomers, where Mak-swill was now, and the one for troublemakers, where Ram was headed. The judo studio was a slight detour to the side. It was the best idea they had. Almost.

"I'll drive," Jin offered, digging in her skirt pockets for her keys. She tossed her flute case to Two, hiked her skirt to her knees, and ran after Gaby.

The boys followed at a breakneck pace, and Zak scooped up Gil's kilt and frantically chased after them.

CHAPTER 18

BOUTS

JUNE 3, 2023

STARING BLANKLY AHEAD, Alexandria fingered the envelope that had come in the mail just before they left. She'd brought the letter from the college with her. She hadn't been expecting an answer to her application so soon, and figured good news would energize her for her bouts.

"You're up next," Ian whispered.

Alexandria stuffed the envelope back in her bag and stretched her arms. She should have left the letter home. *Regret blah blah. GPA below our required standards.* So that was that. No early admission for her. No half-tuition scholarship. College would have to wait until she could pay for it herself.

With no time for a job, that meant she needed her black belt for a judo scholarship, and this was the last qualifying event of the year. If she didn't get enough points today, she'd have to wait months to try again. And win or lose, she must share the college's answer when they went home. Her family would know she wasn't good enough to be admitted.

"Kick some—" Ian clamped his mouth shut and looked sideways at Mom. "You can do it!"

Alexandria nodded and dropped into a stretch for her legs. Shaun raised both thumbs with a grin which might have been to encourage Alexandria or maybe just for remembering the human gesture. In jeans and a t-shirt, with his long bangs covering his pointed ears and half of his too-pretty face, he barely passed for human, but he stayed between Mom and one of the adult fae who had accompanied him and kept his mouth shut. He'd watched every bout with narrowed eyes and an intense expression, as if he was professionally evaluating the athletes. Maybe he was; what did Alexandria know about fae hobbies?

On the bright side, sticking around high school for another year would give her more time to get to know the fae better. And longer to raise her grades so she could at least get into college, even if she couldn't get an academic scholarship. If she had to go to school part-time while she worked, it was frustrating, but not the end of the world.

She twisted back and forth to loosen her back. That was another good point; her slashed shoulder was now completely healed, painless even during throws. She could fight as hard as ever without worrying that she would damage healing muscles. As she rotated, the door to the gym opened. Late observers, maybe. Parents who had to work or take care of other kids.

To her surprise, Jin and Touji rushed in, all dressed up for the school dance but with panicked expressions. Instead of taking one of the spectator seats, they headed straight toward her.

Jin grabbed her arm and tugged. "Gotta come with me," she whisper-screamed. "Now!"

"I'm in a competition," Alexandria whispered back.

"Rafe is trying to start a war," Touji summed up. "If you don't help stop him, Gil's on his own."

"Crap," Alexandria swore. What idiotic insanity had gotten into Rafe?

Mom's eyebrows shot up. Guess that wasn't a whisper. Mom turned farther and pursed her lips at the sight of Jin and Touji.

Alexandria shot a desperate glance at the competition floor. Her turn was in a few minutes, but she couldn't abandon Gil.

"Crap." She darted for the door, calling, "Trouble with Gil," in Fae over her shoulder.

The earlier rain had stopped, though puddles glistened in the sunlight.

Kirill was leaning against Jin's car, tapping his fingers impatiently. He yanked the door open and climbed inside as soon as he saw them coming. Jin and Touji jumped into the front seat, and Alexandria joined Kirill in the back. By the far door, Zee lifted her head from her knees just enough to grimace at Alexandria.

All the doors slammed, and Jin stepped on the gas. The bright red car shot from the parking space like a bullet. Behind them, Nikos, Mom, Ian, and Shaun ran from the gym and headed for the truck. Hallelujah, backup was on its way. Now all Alexandria had to do was stall Rafe for a few minutes.

"Okay, what's going on?" Alexandria asked, holding on to the door to keep from slamming into Kirill as Jin took the first turn at a speed that probably belonged on a race track. She scrabbled for the seatbelt, bracing herself with her legs until it clicked into place.

"Father called me on the radio," Zee said. "The fleet is almost here. Rafe found out, and he's gone to rouse the fae who support Lord Kishar. Gil is chasing him on foot."

Alexandria almost swore again. All this time currying peace with the fae, and now Gil's brother was trying to ruin it. If the fae attacked humans, no government would believe they meant to settle peacefully.

"Gaby and Miknon are calling Maxwell," Jin said, "but we have to delay Rafe long enough for the guards to lock down the fae."

"Wait a second," Alexandria said. "Why didn't NASA spot the fleet? We can see the ship on the moon."

"Magic," Zak said. "Now that they know you can see us, Kishar would have the mages shield the ships from your vision."

The car zoomed even faster. Behind them, the blue truck couldn't keep up; Nikos believed in obeying the speed limit. Zee whimpered, and the boys turned white. The fae apartments were only a few miles away, but at this rate, they'd reach them in only a few minutes. Or never.

"If you kill us," Alexandria gasped, "we can't stop Rafe."

"Funny," Jin said, gunning the car through a yellow light and screeching around a corner.

The light turned red. No way would Nikos run it, so their backup was now stuck. She and Gil were on their own. Alexandria cast a critical gaze at the other occupants of the car, dressed up for the dance and sweating bullets. Yep, no help there.

"There," Zee shouted, pointing out the window.

"He's on the right," Touji clarified, since the driver couldn't possibly take her eyes off the road at that speed.

Alexandria saw nothing for a minute, then a white wolf zipped between two parked cars, looking fortunately like a big Husky in the distance. At least the summer sun hadn't set yet. Chasing him in the dark would be a nightmare. Jin turned into a parking lot and cut through the block, still driving like a maniac.

"We'll lose the others," Alexandria fretted.

Without backup, how was she supposed to stop Rafe? Thank goodness, he seemed to be trying to stay out of sight. The last thing they needed was panicked calls to animal control. Maybe they'd be lucky, and people would think he was a big dog. A very big dog.

"Nikos?" Zee asked. "And who else?"

"U.N., Mom, and Shaun," Alexandria said.

"Shaun!" Zee bit her lip. "He shouldn't have come."

"Does anyone have a phone?" Alexandria asked. Hers was in her bag at the gym.

"Sorry," Kirill said, "I don't think any of us brought one to the dance."

"Nikos needs to drive faster," Jin said.

Alexandria bit her tongue to avoid a terrified retort. "Why didn't you take U.N. instead of me? He talks Fae better." She glanced at Zee and shrugged an apology for not counting her. "I guess talking isn't the plan?"

"Rafe won't listen," Zee said. "You'll have to fight him. He won't even listen to Shaun, or I would have brought him with us and left one of the boys behind."

"Thanks a lot," Touji said. Kirill merely nodded.

"Shaun?" Alexandria asked. "What does he have to do with anything?"

Zee looked out the window and didn't answer.

"There," Touji said. "I saw a flash of white."

Jin exited the parking lot, crossed the street, and careened into another parking lot behind the speeding white blur. Slamming on the gas, she pulled ahead, then curved into the wolf's path. Rafe backtracked to avoid crashing into the car, but then Gil was there, blocking his retreat. Rafe zigzagged, and Jin slammed to a stop right in his face. The white wolf reversed, but his black twin was on his tail. With buildings on either side, Rafe had nowhere to run.

Everyone piled out of the car and surrounded the two wolves. Rafe snarled at everyone, but whenever he lunged, Gil blocked him.

"Hey, Rafe, calm down," Alexandria said. "Nobody wants to hurt you. Just settle down and come back to the school, okay?"

Maybe he would be sensible and spare them all the trouble of taking him down. She'd spent all year trying to get the fae and humans to be friends, and no little punk would ruin all her work.

Rafe curled his lips back from his teeth. Guess that meant no.

Gil shifted back to two legs, and Alexandria immediately averted her eyes. This wasn't the first time she'd seen Gil naked, but she really wanted it to be the last. Jin untied her fancy sash and removed her embroidered jacket, revealing a silk tank top underneath. Grinning, she offered the jacket and sash to Gil.

"Everything will be fine," Gil said in Fae as he took the jacket. "The lords will see that peace is better. Don't ruin everything now."

Alexandria dared a glimpse. Fortunately for her peace of mind, the silk jacket reached to the middle of his thighs. And at least this time he could stand without breaking a leg.

Rafe growled and snapped at Gil. Alexandria revised her thought; at least Gil wouldn't break anything just standing. It remained to be seen if he would escape his brother without injury.

"Oh, that was rude," Gil said. "This isn't my fault."

Rafe growled again, and Gil tsked. "Such language."

"You can't win against all of us," Alexandria said, unsure if she was glad or sorry she couldn't understand the wolf dialect of Fae.

The white wolf bared his long teeth, and her healed shoulder ached with the memory of her last real fight, against a knife-wielding maniac. Maybe they could beat Rafe, and maybe they couldn't, but how much damage could the wolf do?

If only Nikos was here. He wasn't a trained fighter, but he was strong, and she could use all the help she could get. She glanced over her shoulder, but no blue truck was in view. Drat Jin's wild driving!

Zee sidled closer and stood on tiptoe to whisper in Alexandria's ear. "Stall him until Shaun arrives."

Shaun? Him again? Because he was an elf? Then why didn't Jin and Zee bring an elf from the dance to stop Rafe? Freya was probably at the dance, and if not, there were a lot of other elves hanging around the school. Or they could have brought Shaun from the competition.

Something stirred in her brain, and Alexandria struggled to identify the fleeting memory. What had she heard about Shaun?

Gil was still talking, still trying to persuade Rafe to give up his quest to rouse the fae.

"Who is Shaun?" Alexandria whispered to Zee. "I mean, why him?"

The gremlin's ears turned orange, and she looked away. She did know something! But what? Shaun was just another student who went to classes and shared a room like everyone else. He dressed normally, and nobody treated him differently.

Alexandria narrowed her eyes. No, that wasn't quite true. The fae had refused to send him as an ambassador, without saying why, even though he was old enough and had passed the requirements.

The lost memory fluttered at the edges of her mind again. It had been months ago. Someone had called Shaun something else and was upset about it, and then... And then Alexandria had just forgotten about it? What? Why couldn't she remember the details?

Rafe sidestepped, and Alexandria automatically moved to keep him from escaping.

"Come on, Rafe," Gil begged. "At least shift back and talk to me."

With a toss of his head and another growl, the wolf shifted. Zee looked away, and Alexandria firmly kept her gaze on Rafe's face as she removed her judogi jacket and shoved it at him. Thank goodness girls wore shirts underneath. He was as tall as she was, so maybe it wouldn't do any good, but standing there with nothing on was distracting.

"It reeks of human," he growled, though he slid it on anyway, wrinkling his nose.

Yep, he was too tall for it to meet the minimum demands of modesty. Alexandria kept her eyes up.

"I need popcorn," Jin murmured.

Alexandria opened her mouth to suggest he tie the gi around his waist, but Zee, closest to the car, opened the door and reached inside without taking her gaze off Rafe. She pulled out a bundle of fabric and tossed it to him. Unfolded, it was Gil's kilt, and Rafe redressed with obvious relief, dropping the jacket onto the ground.

Alexandria picked it up, keeping her protests silent. He was such a jerk.

"Okay," Gil said. "Can we leave now? If we hurry back to the school, you can apologize and make this all disappear. Come on, Rafe."

"My car isn't big enough for everyone," Jin said. "Are people going to sit on laps?" She raised an eyebrow at Rafe, and the corner of her mouth twitched.

"Gil and I can wait for Nikos," Alexandria said. "I'm sure he'll be here any minute, once he decides where Jin's crazy driving led us. Gil will have to ride in the back as a dog, but that's okay."

And the wait would give her time to question him about the oh-so-mysterious Shaun. Gil had never kept secrets from her — or so she thought — so the mystery was driving her crazy.

Zee gave her a highly skeptical look, but Jin and the boys nodded.

"Sure thing," Jin said. "We'll take Rafe right back to the school, and you can meet us there."

Gil slowly approached Rafe and put a hand on his shoulder. "Come home, brother."

Without replying, Rafe went to the car. He opened the door, staring inside with distaste, and everyone sighed in relief. He waved Zee into the car, and the circle broke up as the others headed for the other car doors. Thank goodness he'd decided to be sensible. Maybe all Alexandria's social efforts had made an impact.

"Well, I'm glad it's not cold," she said to Gil. "And that you have something to wear this time."

She smirked a little at the hot pink silk. True, fae fashions were different, and Gil seemed to love all colors, but to humans, he was a surprising sight.

"Sure—" he started.

Rafe slammed the door and whirled on his twin. Alexandria stepped between and parried his first blow. Without a pause, Rafe switched his attack to her, arms and legs flying almost faster than she could see.

Guess he didn't want to be friends after all.

She blocked him the best she could, but many of his blows landed hard. He had clearly trained to fight, and his style was unknown to her. Fighting a judoka was easier because she knew the moves, even if she didn't know what was coming next. Rafe was nearly unpredictable and so much faster that she had no time to try any counterattacks.

Dodging his next blow, she tried to grab him for a throw, but with no shirt to grab, he slid aside and spun a kick into her side. She grunted and backed up a step.

When she had signed up for judo, she intended to get some exercise, pacify her dad, and add a few self-defense skills. She hadn't expected to fight anyone besides other judoka or possibly an unskilled street tough who thought she was an easy target. Her current opponent outclassed her in every way. She had no hope of winning against him, but what choice did she have?

"Please stop," Gil pleaded, but Rafe didn't look his way.

Grimly, Rafe advanced, closing the distance between him and Alexandria. She glanced around for help, but found none. The humans present weren't fighters, and neither was Zee. She had never seen Gil fight, though he had once mentioned warrior training on the ship. Judging from his expression when he talked about it, it wasn't something he enjoyed.

"Stay out of the way," she commanded the others, who had piled back out of the car.

Not only could they get hurt, but they were as likely to hamper her ability to fight as to do any good against Rafe. No, Alexandria was on her own, and this was much more serious than a judo competition or a scholarship.

And then Rafe was within reach, and he yet again became a whirling tornado of blows and kicks.

Outclassed she might be, but she couldn't surrender. If she didn't stop Rafe before he roused the fae to war, Earth would pay the price for her failure.

CHAPTER 19

In Which There is No Way to Win

June 3, 2023

GIL COULDN'T LET Alexandria fight alone. Ram had always planned to emulate Grandsire, who had been the king's chief Companion before he died, the best of the elite. Even before the ship landed on the moon and everyone was forced into training, Ram had practiced often with the intent to join the Companions at adulthood. There was no way she could win against him, even though he had no weapons.

If he had a weapon, she wouldn't last a minute.

Gil dropped Jin's pretty pink jacket and shifted back to wolf. With buildings all around, he risked someone seeing him shift, but if he didn't stop Ram, the consequences would be worse.

"Everyone, think 'Shar,'" Zee instructed. "Keep thinking it. Or say it, if you like."

Shar was close enough to hear? That was good for them, but bad for Shar unless his guards were with him. At the least, Nikos would be driving his truck. Shar had enough mind-touching from his father to track his name to the source so Nikos could join the fight against Ram. As for the danger of revealing Shar's name, the humans would have no idea what the word meant, and if they figured it out, they had no magic to take advantage of it. And Ram already knew Shar's use-name.

Circling to the other side of Ram, Gil waited for an opening and lunged, snapping at his brother. His scant warrior training wasn't much help compared to Ram's expertise, but his teeth were just as sharp.

Mother would be appalled her sons were fighting each other, but what choice did he have? If the fae failed to find a safe home on Earth, they had nowhere else to go. Their old worlds were dying, or had already died, and neither the fae nor the humans knew of another habitable planet. They must stay here, and unlike Ram, Gil wasn't at all sure they could win a war against the humans. Even if it was a good idea, which it wasn't.

If only Ram would be sensible and stop fighting. It wasn't too late to get him out of this trouble, if he would only give up.

"What does Shar mean?" Kirill asked.

"Never mind what it means," Zee snapped, "just think the word as hard as you can."

"If you say so." Two narrowed his eyes and mouthed the word.

Ram kicked Gil in the side, sending him flying into a puddle. Gil staggered to his feet and shook his fur, then lunged again. He had risked his own life — and Miknon's, which was worse — to beat the lords to Earth and make a peace for all of them. They were so close, so very close. Their ambassadors would leave in less than a conjunction, and from there, it was just a matter of settling on terms both sides liked. Even the fae who wanted to conquer Earth would soon see that peace was more advantageous. Ram couldn't be allowed to ruin everything, even if Gil had to bite him back into sense.

"In the movies, the black wolf would be the bad guy," Jin said. "Shar, Shar, Shar. The two in white would be on the good side. I still need popcorn. Shar, Shar, Shar."

Zak wrinkled her forehead. "What does color have to do with the state of your heart?"

"Nothing," Kirill said, and Two shook his head.

"Shar, Shar, Shar," they all chanted quietly.

Alexandria shook her head as if to discard a distraction, and Gil snapped at Ram again to keep him farther from her. Unwilling to actually hurt Ram if he could avoid it, he bit nothing but air. His foster sister also blocked more than she hit back, though Gil was unsure if that was habit, defensive attitude, or inability to match Ram's blinding speed.

If Alexandria preferred defense, Ram wasn't handicapped by the same scruples. He launched himself at her as if she were his mortal enemy. As tall as she, but wider and heavier, he used every bit of his advantages as he fought her ruthlessly, aiming deadly blows at her head and torso.

Alexandria was also good, but her training was meant for formal competitions, not for lethal combat, and most of her life was spent in other pursuits. She dodged the worst of the blows or rolled with them to reduce the impact, but each one that landed left bruises, and many of them stole her breath for a moment.

Both she and Ram were hampered by their unfamiliarity with the other's style of moves, but Ram's extended training and willingness to hurt his opponents was obviously wearing her down. Ram was good, very good. Grandsire would be pleased with his skills, though not with his use of them.

For the first time ever, Gil regretted not practicing seriously with the warriors on the moon. He knew a little, but not enough to win, even with Alexandria's help. In fact, he wasn't sure if the two of them would survive this fight. And if they died, what would happen to Zak and the humans with her? Ram's derision toward humans meant he would have no problem killing them to continue his mission. He might regret Zak's death more, but he wouldn't spare her, either. What was the life of one commoner compared to the praise of Lord Kishar? Nothing, and less than nothing.

As Ram spun from Alexandria's grasp, he swooped up a rock from the ground. His next blow landed hard enough to make her cry out. Gil snapped at him again, aiming for an actual bite despite his regrets, but Ram dodged him. The wet road endangered footing, but Gil couldn't take the time to walk softly. At least Ram was in as much danger of slipping as any of them.

The others still surrounded the fight, bravely keeping Ram from escaping, even though they couldn't do anything else. Now Zak whispered frantically to Jin, who dove into the car and emerged with a black case. She pulled out shining metal and assembled her flute, then held it clenched in her fist.

What did Zak have in mind? If Gil shifted back, could he use the musical instrument as a weapon against Ram?

Maybe. And maybe Ram would take it and use it against him and Alexandria, and Gil didn't know how to fight with a flute, anyway. What was he supposed to do, poke Ram in the eye?

An engine roared, and a familiar blue truck zoomed into the parking lot, blocking Ram's easiest escape route. Now that the road was covered in both directions, Ram would have to dodge between cars and buildings to escape, and that would slow him. Ram seemed to realize the same thing, for he sped up his assault on Alexandria, still avoiding Gil's teeth without apparent effort.

Gil panted for breath. How could his twin possibly have enough strength and energy to fight both of them? At least Nikos was here now. Surely three of them could overwhelm Ram.

The truck doors opened, and several people jumped out. Nikos immediately ran to Alexandria's side. Ian and Mama Helen stayed by the truck with Shar. Mama had her phone pressed to her ear, listening intently. Ian clenched his fists but wisely stayed out of the fight. He couldn't help, and tripping over him would only mess up the fighters. Shar had trained a little with the warriors but was too valuable to risk in a real fight. He did have another advantage, if he chose to use it.

Yet again, Gil snapped at Ram, trying to distract him from Alexandria, who was staggering with exhaustion and pain. Nikos aimed a blow at Ram, too slow to connect. Even against three, Ram was holding his own and barely breathing hard.

They were going to lose. And then Ram would convince the fae to start a war with Earth.

Everyone would lose.

Shar shook back his hair and folded his arms, glaring at Ram. What was he waiting for?

Between one blow and the next, Ram looked sideways and spotted Shar. Instantly, he dodged his opponents and sprinted for Shar, shedding Gil's kilt as he ran.

In a moment, he had shifted, heading straight for the prince with bared fangs.

"No!" Gil darted after him.

If he killed the prince, Lord Kishar would bury Earth in war. Alexandria and Nikos whirled, but Ram was too fast. None of them could reach him in time. Why was Shar silent?

"Now," Zak shouted.

Jin raised the flute and blew two specific notes. Fifteen years of daily habit made Gil look which way his feet were pointed before the ship's gravity would come on. Shar did the same.

More importantly, the white wolf staggered as he checked the direction of the ground.

The humans, unconditioned to the notes, continued after Ram. Alexandria rolled and slammed into the white wolf, knocking him off his feet. Ram tumbled sideways, then regained his feet and headed for Shar again.

With a look of regret, Shar inhaled. "Naram, stop," he shouted in command voice.

Everyone trembled at the magic in his voice, and Ram collapsed. Nikos dropped on him, and without a moment of hesitation, the other students threw themselves on top.

Staggering with weariness and incipient bruises, Gil walked to the pile of bodies. Living bodies, at least. That was one good thing, though what he would do with his brother now, he didn't know.

Mama Helen hung up the phone and slid it into her pocket. In Fae, she said, "Maxwell got through. The apartments are all locked down. Nobody can get in. And the security guards have instructions to shoot any white wolf or dog that shows up." Her lip quivered.

Gil walked under her hand until she was touching his fur, leaning against her while he watched the heap of bodies. It wasn't her fault his brother was a rebel and a traitor. It wasn't his fault either, but his heart cracked in half. What would he tell Mother?

"Are you okay?" Mama Helen whispered.

Gil nodded. Though not as talented as his brother, he had at least managed to avoid Ram's teeth. Tomorrow the bruises would show, he was sure, but until then he could pretend he was fine.

"I'm sorry," Mama said.

Gil nodded again. Not as sorry as he was. There must have been something else he could have done to keep Ram out of trouble and convince him humans were worthy of friendship. But what? He had spent all year trying, and nothing he had said made a difference to his twin. When had they become so different? When had Ram stopped believing what Gil said?

"Gedovme," Nikos groaned. The only part of him that could be seen was a twitching foot.

"It's safe enough." Shar ignored the questioning looks and maintained his casual pose by the truck.

Only Gil knew him well enough to detect the distress in his eyes and the set of his mouth. Only he and Zak knew the prince could just as easily have commanded Ram to drop dead instead of stop. Punishment among the fae was swift and usually final. Shar's mercy left him with the huge problem of what to do with a traitor. Considering mercy also left Gil with a brother, he nodded his thanks. Shar lifted one corner of his mouth in a wry grimace.

"Right, sorry." Touji peeled himself from the pile and started helping the topmost people to stand.

Ian rolled off with the flexibility of youth and reached for Jin, who fussed over her dress a little and her flute a lot, blowing a tune to be sure nothing was damaged. Zak was next, bringing Gil's kilt to him. He hurried to shift and dress while Kirill rolled his shoulders and moved to one side of the heap. When Ian and Touji hauled Alexandria to her feet, she groaned and staggered.

Mama Helen moved to slide a shoulder under her daughter's arm. "Are you okay?"

While she checked Alexandria for serious injuries, Nikos lifted his head from Ram's furry shoulder and looked at Gil.

"Should I get up?" Nikos asked.

Deliberately not looking at Shar, Gil said, "Go ahead. It's safe."

Nikos narrowed his eyes at the prince, but he climbed to hands and knees, then after a pause in which Ram did not move, got to his feet.

Everyone stared at Ram, who lay on the black-pebbled road as if nailed there. Though he had originally stopped while standing, the weight of everyone on top of him had pressed him flat. Now, free of apparent restraint, he did not move a handspan, not even to arrange his limbs more comfortably.

Shar watched him, able to reinforce his command if necessary, but the only signs of life in Ram were the rise and fall of his ribs and an occasional blink.

"Huh," Ian said.

Alexandria stared at Shar, ignoring Mama's examination except for an occasional "ouch" at a sore spot. Like the other humans, she must surely wonder what magic Shar possessed that allowed such control over Ram. Unlike the others, she didn't seem — quite — surprised. Gil wondered how long the command to forget about Shar would hold without her full name to back his power. Not that he was worried; if she remembered, he would simply ask her to keep Shar's secret, even from the prince. She had always been trustworthy.

But that problem would have to wait until after they dealt with Ram. Gil sighed. Why did his brother have to be so stupid?

"Rafe," he begged, "will you please stop this mad campaign?"

Ram closed his eyes, the only sign of protest he could make.

"Rafe," Alexandria murmured. "That's not what... Shaun said." She narrowed her eyes at Gil, obviously second-guessing both names.

He raised his eyebrows at her in a silent plea to let it go.

She grimaced and sighed and touched a bruise on her face. "Are we finished here? Can we go find some ice?"

"Rafe?" Gil repeated. If nobody repeated his real name, the others might forget it, especially since events had been rather chaotic at the time. "Please come home."

With obvious effort, Ram jerked his chin in an awkward nod. Gil let his shoulders slump and looked at Shar. The prince stalked forward and leaned to whisper in Ram's furry ear. Though his voice was too quiet to overhear, everyone shivered when his power washed over their skin.

Ram pulled his feet under him and struggled upright. Most of the crowd flinched and prepared to fight again, but Ram stood silently, head bowed.

Gil put an arm around his twin's back and ran his fingers through the thick fur. "It's over, brother; come home."

It wasn't over, though, not really. First, he had to tell Mother, and he had no idea how to do that.

Then the prince still had to choose a real punishment, and none of the options were good. Gil could still lose his brother.

CHAPTER 20

BUSTED

JUNE 3, 2023

IAN BACKED up next to Shaun and leaned against the truck, since it looked like Rafe was finally under control. Poor Gil. He'd been so excited to have his brother on Earth, but his twin was such a punk. Rafe's roommates had tried to make friends with him. Ian had tried. In fact, he was pretty sure half the students had tried. Rafe just didn't like anybody.

But to betray Earth and the fae to the lords and fight his own brother? Gil and his mother had been working toward a treaty for almost a year now, and Rafe had almost ruined it in an hour. The news that the fleet was almost here was anticlimactic in comparison, since the arrival of the rest of the fae would only mean more of what they had already been doing.

"Come on, Rafe," Gil begged. "Shift back and get in the car."

The white wolf folded his ears down and turned his face away.

"Never mind," Nikos said. "He can ride in the back of the truck the way he is."

"I'll ride in the car," Shaun said. "If he can't see me, he might calm down more."

Ian scratched his head. What difference would that make? Rolling her shoulders, Alexandria glowered at the elf. That did it. She knew something, and Ian would pry it out of her. If she was trading places with Shaun, he'd have plenty of opportunity on the way back to the school.

While Nikos and Gil lifted the wolf into the truck bed, Ian scrambled into the middle of the back seat. With Gil on one side and Alexandria on the other, he could question both of them. Somebody would tell him what was going on, or he would scream!

It didn't take long for everyone else to pile into both vehicles, and Nikos pulled out in the lead without saying whether it was coincidence or to keep Jin from speeding again.

Seriously, how did that girl drive so fast without hitting everything on the road? On the way over, she'd lost them within minutes, and only Shaun's instructions on where to turn had reunited them.

And how had he known where to go? Alexandria was right — something was odd about Shaun.

"All right," Ian said. "Start talking. How did Shaun make Rafe stop fighting? Who is he? How did he know where you were? Why is Rafe crazy? What is going on?"

"Yeah, Gil." Alexandria folded her arms. "I want to know, too."

"I can't talk about it." Gil ran his fingers through his hair and grimaced.

"Bull—" Alexandria clamped her mouth shut and cast a guilty look at Mom in the front seat. "You have to tell us *something*."

Gil sighed and folded his arms. "Shaun followed us and stopped Rafe with magic. Rafe believes the lords are good rulers and their idea of conquering Earth is better than my idea of a treaty."

"Why do I think you aren't telling us the whole story?" Ian complained.

"I can't," Gil said. "I believe you would keep secrets, but they aren't my secrets. I can't betray the trust placed in me."

"Okay, kids," Mom said. "Leave him alone. You're not the ones he has to answer to. Gil, any idea what we should do with Rafe when we get back to the school?"

"The fae leaders will ultimately decide, but we might need to lock him up for a while. We can't put him with the rebels, and we can't let him roam loose. Do we have any empty bedrooms?"

"No," Mom said, "but we could lock him in the nurse's office for the night. That would be better, anyway, since all the bedrooms unlock from the inside without a key."

"Good enough." Gil sighed again. "What will I tell Mother?"

"That you stopped your brother from being stupid," Alexandria said.

Gil rolled his eyes and looked out the window. Ian leaned against his shoulder in subtle comfort.

Outside, the sun was sinking toward the horizon, though the sky was still bright. Behind them, Jin drove as sedately as a grandma, thank goodness. Rafe's white wolf head drooped over the edge of the truck bed.

What a mess. His sister was annoying, but at least she wasn't a traitor. If Alexandria were going to jail, Ian would be tempted to bake her a cake with a file in it. Not that it would actually work nowadays, but it would be pretty funny. And then he would find her a lawyer.

Poor Gil. Did the fae have lawyers? Would they do any good? Based on stories from the commoners, there didn't seem to be any way to fight the decisions of their leaders. Seriously, they needed a good slap of equality. When they sent off the ambassadors this month, that really needed to be at the top of the list.

Nikos glanced in the rearview mirror and turned on his blinker, pulling to the side of the road and parking.

"What are you doing?" Ian asked. "We need to get to the school."

Nikos jerked his head toward the window and unbuckled his seatbelt. By the time he climbed from the truck, an animal control van had parked in front of them.

"Oh, no," Ian groaned.

While Alexandria and Mom climbed out their side, Ian shoved Gil out his side. The dark-uniformed officer was met with a row of Fitches standing between him and the truck bed. On the sidewalk, passers-by stopped to gawk. A few whistled at Gil in his white kilt and bare chest, and little kids reached to pet the doggy. Fortunately, none of them came close.

Jin parked her car behind the truck, though she and her passengers sensibly stayed inside. Shaun ducked so only the top of his head showed, and Zee wasn't visible at all.

"What's the problem, officer?" Nikos asked.

"I don't see a collar on that dog." The officer frowned and stood on tiptoe for a closer look.

"Yeah, sorry." Nikos looked very ashamed of himself. "He escaped us. But we'll put his collar back on as soon as we get home."

"Hang on," the officer said. "Is he a wolf hybrid?"

A lot of phone cameras in the surrounding crowd were suddenly pointed at the back of the truck. Ian turned around and glared at them. They did not need people taking wolf pictures to show their friends.

"Sure," Mom said, "but when we got him in Kansas, a vet told us they were legal."

That had been Gil, actually, but she told the lie without blinking. Ian didn't know if he should be appalled or impressed.

The officer scoffed. "Maybe in Kansas, lady, but not here. I gotta take him in."

"Oh. Okay." Mom wrapped an arm around Gil. It looked comforting, but she was squeezing tightly. "When can we pick him up?"

"Pick him up?" The officer adjusted his belt. "Lady, you can't keep a wolf-dog. It's illegal, I said. Title 34 of the Game and Wildlife Code."

"Can't we at least keep him for the night?" Alexandria asked the officer. "Give the boys a chance to say goodbye." She reached around Ian and gripped the back of Gil's neck. "If not dog, can't take," she said in Fae.

Ian nodded vigorously. Once Rafe shifted back, nobody would know he was a wolf. And he wouldn't be wandering around free, anyway. All they had to do was get him back to the school.

"We'll keep him locked up," Nikos promised.

"Sorry, buddy," the officer said. "He's not legal. Now give me the dog, or I'll have to call backup and arrest you for having an illegal animal and obstructing an officer."

Ian let his lip quiver, lifting his chin so the officer had a good view of the tears he was dredging up.

"But he's my dog," he whimpered.

He reached toward Rafe to enhance the story. Rafe, who spoke English well enough to follow most of the conversation and had certainly heard Alexandria's plan, snapped at Ian's fingers. The crowd gasped, and more phones came up.

"Stop that," Gil said in Fae. "Be a nice dog, please."

Rafe growled and bared his teeth. Didn't he care that he was in danger? Ian was trying to save his life!

"Nice try, kid," the officer said. "He's clearly a dangerous animal. I've gotta take him for public safety, see? Can't let a dog attack people. We'll put him down painlessly, okay? Now step out of my way."

"Put him down where?" Gil asked. "We'll pick him up from there."

Ian tugged on his elbow until Gil bent low enough for a whisper in his ear. "Put down means kill."

"No!" Gil shouted.

He jerked forward, stopping only when Mom's grasp on his shoulders kept him from moving. From Jin's car, a loud gasp hinted at an equivalent explanation to Zee and Shaun.

"You can't do that," Alexandria blurted. "He's not a hybrid. He's a real wolf and protected as an endangered animal."

The officer groaned. "Okay, then we'll test his DNA. If he's a wolf, or has enough wolf genes, he'll go to the wolf sanctuary. He'll be much happier there, and he'll be alive. Are you satisfied? Now will you please step away from the animal?"

"He could escape from the sanctuary," Ian said in Fae. "It's made to keep in animals, not sentient beings with fingers. For that matter, I'm not sure the pound will hold him, either."

Gil sighed. "So he would run right back to the rebels."

"We can't let them test — him, either." Alexandria clearly didn't know how to translate DNA, but neither did Ian. "Once they know he's not really a wolf, they'll go back to plan Kill Him."

Ian turned and spoke rapidly in Fae to Rafe. "You have to shift back now."

"Are you crazy?" Alexandria hissed in the same language. "Not in public. We signed an NDA."

"He's got to shift," Ian said. "It's the only way to protect him. He doesn't deserve to die just for being fae."

Whether or not he deserved it for trying to kill Ian's sister was a different question, to be answered later.

"What are you saying?" the officer asked.

Nobody answered him.

"But then everyone will know about us," Gil said.

Ian shrugged. "Yeah, but they'll know soon, anyway. The fleet will land in a week or two."

"We have to consult with Maxwell and Chantelle and so forth," Mom hissed. "Not to mention the trouble we'd be in for revealing a State secret. Do you want to grow up in jail?"

Ian stuck out his tongue at her. No, he didn't even want to visit jail, thank you.

"Hey," the officer demanded, "what's going on?"

Nikos spoke in English. "How long do we have before you test his DNA?"

The officer shifted to his other foot. "As soon as I get back."

"Can we get permission that fast?" Mom said in Fae as she dialed her phone. "Can we follow you to Animal Control?" she asked the officer in English before he could demand a translation.

The officer rolled his eyes. "I don't understand the problem here. This is a wolf, not a stray kitty."

Mom listened to the phone and grimaced before hanging up. "Voicemail."

"He's not that dangerous," Ian lied. "He's just having a bad day." In Fae, he yet again said, "Shift."

"U.N.'s right," Gil said. "And the fae never signed an NDA. Please, Rafe, shift."

Rafe growled again and snapped the air beside his brother's face.

"Are we done here?" The officer glanced at the setting sun. "I'd like to get back before dark, if you don't mind."

Gil ducked past the officer and stuck his head in the back window of Jin's car. "Shaun, please tell him to shift."

He clutched the items on the chain that always hung around his neck, even as a wolf. It was unclear to Ian whether he was comforting himself with his silver family emblem or calling on the authority of the dead king with the gold ring. But surely that authority was only for specific things, not in general?

"Helen is right," Shaun said. "You should talk to the leaders."

"You know very well—" Gil clamped his mouth shut and banged his forehead on the car. "Please, Shaun. Don't let them take my brother. What's one week sooner? Please."

"If the humans take him," Shaun said almost too quietly for Ian to hear, "then we don't have to punish him."

Ouch. Ian turned to look at Rafe, whose ears twitched and then laid flat. Was that his reasoning? Take the problem away from his brother? Or was he just too stubborn to give in?

Face twisting in pain, Gil fell to his knees. "There are other options if he lives, but none if he dies. Plea—" The last word disappeared in a sob.

"Come on," the officer said. "Either you give me the wolf or I just take him and give you a ticket."

Shaun pressed his hands against his forehead as if he had a headache. Ian couldn't blame him. He wiggled around the officer and wrapped his arms around Gil.

"I'm sorry," he whispered. "I'm so sorry."

A sigh ruffled his hair. When he looked up, Shaun waved him away from the door. Ian dragged Gil with him, and the elf climbed out of the car.

Shaun nodded politely to the officer and approached the back of the truck. "Shift."

Had he been using telepathy with the leaders, then, to get permission?

Gil sagged against Ian, nearly falling onto the street. With an extra heave, Ian hauled him back to his feet. This would be a lot easier if everybody wasn't so much taller!

Ram flattened his ears and turned away.

Gil ran to the truck. "If you don't shift, they'll kill you. Please don't do this. You don't deserve death."

Ian grimaced. Only because they stopped him from betraying his entire people. And what if they hadn't caught him in time? He would feel the same if it was Alexandria in trouble, but she wouldn't be so stupid, either. Of course, the whole question of capital punishment was a different story, and Ian would rather not see anyone die. Not even Dad or Mr. Abernathy. Gone was just as good.

Could they exile Rafe? How? Where?

Ram barked and growled for a minute while Ian's thoughts ran on.

"I am not a coward," Gil said in Fae, "and the prince is better than you. I'm sorry you don't think even one more day is worth living without the lords in power."

Prince? What prince? Different from the lords? Ian had never seen anybody who looked like a prince.

"You're a piece of scum," Shaun told Ram, "but I value your mother and brother. Shift."

Rafe turned his back and lay down.

The officer checked his watch. "Time's up."

"Rafe," Gil begged.

Shaun took a deep breath and said, "Naram, shift."

Though he spoke quietly, the words felt like a shout. Those closest to the truck wobbled on their feet. Ian rubbed his ears, wincing. That was the second time Shaun's voice had done that, and it didn't feel any better this time. How did he do that?

Gil's eyes shot open. Rafe shivered like a tree in a storm, then shifted to boy-shape. He sat up and glared at both Gil and Shaun.

Cameras flashed, and half the crowd screamed, craning their necks and standing on tiptoe to peek inside the truck.

"The wolf is gone," someone shouted. "There's only a boy left."

"Werewolf," someone else screamed. Oh, great.

Alexandria swung herself into the truck bed with a pained grunt and raised her arms. "Everything is fine. Please don't panic. He won't hurt you."

The crowd paused for a long breath, then half of the people turned and stampeded down the street. The animal control officer bolted to his van and slammed the door before shouting into his radio.

"You might as well come down," Ian told his sister. "The secret is blown now, and I think we'd better get out of here before somebody comes back with silver bullets."

Nikos swung her down, and they all headed for the truck doors.

"Hold on," the officer said, facing them from the shield of his open van door. "Nobody's going anywhere."

"Too slow," Ian muttered. "We're busted."

Chapter 21

In Which Council is Held

June 3, 2023

From the back seat of Jin's car, Zak raised her head just enough to peek again at the disaster in front of her. The soldier who had tried to take Ram still watched the truck's passengers from behind his car door. The human strangers that hadn't run away entirely had retreated to a safe distance and were pointing their phones at the truck.

Jin reached for her car door. "I'll tell the rubber-neckers to leave."

"No," Zak said, not caring what the strange word meant. "Stay in the car. Let the others handle it."

"But—" Jin protested.

"Stay," Zak repeated without taking her focus from the truck.

It was bad enough Shar and the others were out there, and they couldn't face down the entire crowd. If they needed to escape in a hurry, Jin needed to be in the driving seat.

Alex calmly removed her white jacket and dropped it over the edge of the truck into Ram's lap. "As you can see, officer," she said, smiling, "we don't have a wolf anymore, so you have no reason to hold us."

"But I saw—" He stopped. "What did I see?"

Shar held out his hand in the human gesture of greeting, smiling even more charmingly than Alex. "We do appreciate your concern for public safety, Officer..." He squinted at the black tag on the man's shirt. "Burnett."

Absently, the man took Shar's hand. The prince tightened his grip and looked deep into the man's eyes. "Officer Burnett, you saw nothing unusual. Everything is fine. Let us go, and tell your superiors you made a mistake."

Would that be enough of his name to make the magic work? Zak raised her head a little more to watch closely.

The man blinked. "I guess I made a mistake. Sorry about disturbing you. Go on home."

Zak blew out a relieved breath. It worked! Kirill looked at her inquiringly, and she shrugged.

"Magic," she whispered.

Alex's eyebrows shot up her forehead, and she narrowed her eyes at Shar, pursing her lips in intense concentration. Shar smiled again and dropped the man's hand. He jerked his head toward the truck, then walked calmly for the car. Gil hopped into the back of the truck and flattened his brother until neither showed above the sides. Alex's family hurried into the front, and Nikos pulled his truck back into traffic.

Yes, it was time to leave before something else happened. Lowering her head again, Zak braced herself for Jin's driving.

As Shar opened the car door and slipped in next to Zak, one of the humans crept closer and bent to peer inside. From their seats on that side of the car, Two and Kirill immediately stuck their hands in front of her face to block her view.

"Go," Shar said.

The woman tossed a small card through the open window. "If you want to tell your story," she shouted as they raced after the blue truck.

Kirill pushed the card off his lap with a disgusted noise. Curious, Zak picked it up and read, "Iris Rowland, Reporter." What was a reporter? She slipped the card into her pocket to ask Gaby later, then put her head back on her knees to avoid letting passing drivers see her green skin.

The ride back to the school seemed to take forever, though the sun was just sinking below the horizon when they parked. Jin had barely turned off her engine by the time the school doors opened and chaos boiled out. Taras and several of his warriors ran out first, splitting into two groups. One group hauled Ram from the truck, while the others yanked open the car door and angrily waited for Shar to exit.

"What were you thinking?" Taras hissed at him. "Running off *and* revealing us?"

Shar's guards, who had been left behind at Alex's event but were somehow here now, glared at the prince. Zak ducked her head, sure they could tell it was her fault the prince had been involved. Though truthfully, she hadn't thought he would abandon his Companions. If they had come in the back of the truck, there would have been more warriors to fight Ram.

Shar straightened his shoulders. "I did as I thought best."

The scales on Taras's face darkened, and he angrily motioned for the guards to surround Shar. As Zak edged out of the car, trying to avoid notice, Maia, Shalla, and Mak-swill caught up.

"Are we missing anyone else?" Mak-swill asked. "I collected everyone I saw at the competition."

"We're all here," Taras ground out between his teeth.

Maia threw her arms around her sons and wept. "Oh, Rafe, how could you?"

Ram lifted his chin and didn't reply.

"I prepared an office," Shalla said. "We should get out of sight quickly."

She glanced up at the bedroom windows that faced the parking lot. When Zak followed her gaze, she saw nobody. Hopefully, most of the students were dancing in the basement, with no idea of the catastrophe so narrowly averted.

"Move it," Taras barked.

With a shocking lack of respect, he grabbed the back of Shar's neck and marched him toward the front door. Ram was dragged after him with a guard on each arm and several before and after. Gil escorted his mother, who still wept. His face was dark gray instead of black, and his shoulders were tight. Zak and the rest of the humans followed as quickly as the crowd allowed.

Inside the school, Gaby and Miknon waited in the hallway. Miknon immediately flew to Gil's shoulder. The guards swept past them, dragging Ram into the office that had a light on. In the open doorway, Shar paused to watch the humans, Taras hovering behind him.

"I told the dance chaperones to keep everyone in the basement longer," Gaby said. "Was that right?"

Mak-swill patted her on the shoulder. "Good idea. Go back to the dance." She looked at Jin, Kirill, and Two. "You lot, too. Have fun, but don't say anything about what happened."

Jin frowned at her pink silk. "How will I explain the oil stains from Gil dropping my jacket on the ground?"

"We went for a walk outside and you fell down," Two suggested.

Jin rolled her eyes and bopped him lightly on the head with her flute case. "Great, I'll be a clumsy idiot. Come on, let's go have some fun."

She grabbed Two's hand and ran for the stairs with Gaby following. Kirill held out his hand to Zak.

"Zee must stay to witness," Shar said. "I regret the necessity."

Cringing, Zak turned toward the office. The last place she wanted to be right now was Ram's trial, but she couldn't leave Gil to be the only voice against his brother.

Kirill nodded, smile wry. "Duty calls. I understand."

Zak took his hand for a moment and smiled up at him. "You were a good date. Better than a month."

He flashed a smile. "Can we try again later?"

"Maybe. We'll see. Now go!"

After a nervous look at Taras, Kirill dashed for the stairs.

Taras turned to the Fitches and Mak-swill. "We will handle this ourselves," he said. "No humans. It is our responsibility, and so we will say to others if you get in trouble."

War Lady sucked in a breath and puffed out her cheeks. "Right. Okay. I'll go chaperone. Call me if you need me. Fitches, go home."

Alex folded her arms. "Gil and Miknon live with us. We're not abandoning them."

Zak winced. How sad that Gil's adopted siblings had more loyalty than his littermate.

"Then go study or something." Mak-swill pointed down the hall. "March!"

"Come on, Alex," Helen said. "Let's go find some ice and bandages for your wounds."

She guided U.N., and Nikos wrapped an arm around Alex and dragged her with him despite her protests. Mak-swill saluted Taras and disappeared down the stairs. Taras pushed Shar inside the room and beckoned for Gil's family and Zak to precede him.

Inside, Ram sat on a hard chair, surrounded by guards. Shar took the softest chair and folded his arms. Taras shut the door and lurked behind the prince, while Gil's family stood as close as they could get to Ram. Zak sidled into a corner and wished to disappear. Unfortunately, Shar only glanced at Gil before he focused on her.

"You came with the news," he said. "What do you know?"

Here, in the midst of people who all knew who he was, he was no longer pretending to be ordinary. Despite his shorter hair, Shar looked so much like his father in that moment that Zak nearly flinched.

"I got a message from Father," she said again, and then recited the whole tale, including how Ram discovered the news by mistake and ran to tell the warring fae. "So Gil went after Ram, and we went for help."

Gil continued the story, telling how he and Alex fought Ram until Shar arrived. "And you know it from there," he ended.

"I don't," Taras growled. "But I want to know before I execute him."

"I want to hear it all," Maia said quietly.

Tears still trickled from her eyes, and she kept her arms wrapped around herself. Shaking his head, Gil swallowed hard and looked at Shar. The prince said nothing, sitting as motionless as a stonegazer's victim. Taras glared at Zak and motioned for her to continue.

One reluctant word at a time, Zak told how Ram tried to kill Shar. Even more slowly, she told how Shar forced Ram to shift in public in order to save his life.

"With the fleet coming so soon," she argued, "Earth will know, anyway."

Cringing, she stared at the floor and waited for her punishment. This was all her fault for leaking the news. Now the secret was out and Ram would still die. Would it have been better to let the human take him to die in private?

Taras waited, but Shar still said nothing. "Ram, do you have a defense?" the naga finally asked. "Why shouldn't the human have executed you before you revealed our secret?" He cast a frustrated glance at Shar that clearly betrayed his opinion.

"Shar doesn't deserve to rule," Ram spat out. "It was better when everyone thought he was dead. Kishar is more experienced, wiser, and has a better vision for our future. All I needed was a little more time to rouse the fae to his support. He's not afraid to take what we need. Why should we cajole these *humans* when we are stronger! Besides stamina, humans have few personal war skills. I could kill them with one hand, unarmed."

"You didn't kill Alex," Gil retorted. Miknon yanked on his ear, but he ignored her.

"I would have soon," Ram snarled. "If Shar hadn't come, I would have killed all of you. Then, with the others, I would have presented this world to Kishar and taken my place as his chief Companion."

Maia burst into noisy tears and sank to the floor. Gil turned his back to his brother and knelt to embrace his mother.

Zak shuddered. By now, she wasn't surprised Ram cared so little for humans or for her, but if Gil's own brother didn't believe in his quest for peace, what chance did his plan have to succeed? Would they yet end up in a war with Earth?

"Kishar isn't even on this world yet," Taras said.

"But his followers are," Ram said, "and they would conquer instead of bowing to these humans. I almost had our students convinced to join us, too."

Without looking at his twin, Gil growled, a long, frustrated rumble.

"Humans wouldn't fight you unarmed," Zak squeaked. "They would use their tech."

Of all the fae, she had most studied their contrivances, and she feared their power if it was turned against the fae. After months of study, she knew only a tiny part of their capabilities, but it was enough to know they outstripped her knowledge even if she studied for a lifetime. She couldn't possibly offer the humans any technology they didn't have. The only advantage to her people she could offer was the warning to avoid such a battle.

"We have magic," Ram retorted. "We would triumph."

"Would we?" The voice was so quiet Zak almost didn't recognize it.

Shar rose to his feet. "We don't know who is stronger. Neither side has a clear advantage, and many would die trying to prove who was better and more powerful."

"It's worth trying," Ram said. "If we conquer, we need not bend to their terms."

But wouldn't combining their abilities benefit both sides? Zak dared not interrupt to ask.

"It is not worth the risk," Shar said. "We already lost nine of every ten fae in our exile. Must we lose those few we rescued?"

Ram opened his mouth.

"Silence," Shar commanded, his voice ringing with power. "I have heard enough, and I will hear no more of your venom. For your betrayal, you are outcast."

Taras, already reaching for the knife hidden under his tunic, paused. Maia pressed both hands to her mouth to smother her sobs. Miknon swept her wings forward to cover her face. Gil bowed his head, and his shoulders trembled. Zak crept forward enough to touch his shoulder.

"You may not own property," Shar continued, walking directly in front of Ram. The warriors tightened their grip on the prisoner. "You may not speak in court or council. You may not marry or sire children. You may not live among us except as a slave. You have no freedoms and no rights."

He reached out and pressed his thumb against Ram's forehead. "You are no longer one of the fae."

His voice echoed in the room, and when he removed his thumb, a glowing mark remained on Ram's skin. Taras grunted and let his hand fall to his side. A vindictive smirk revealed his snake fangs.

Zak winced, unsure whether this was mercy or torture. It was certainly a slower punishment than execution. Though Ram would live, no one would speak to him, or live with him, or eat with him. He would be invisible, inaudible. Utterly shunned. Nobody would admit to remembering his name for the rest of his life. As lonely as she had been on the ship and when they first landed, Ram would be even more isolated.

Shar touched Gil's unoccupied shoulder. "I'm sorry."

He left the room with several guards following.

Taras yanked Ram to his feet. "Let's take this scum to the apartments and lock him in solitary confinement. Once we have the treaty, we can dump him in the wilderness."

"Nikos is still here," Zak said. "He can drive you over."

"Acceptable," Taras said.

He dragged Ram into the hallway, and almost everyone followed. Shalla shut the door to the office, closing out the sight of Maia, Gil, and Miknon still on their knees, heads bowed and arms around each other.

At Taras's curt gesture, Zak took off, calling for Nikos. He emerged around the corner of the hallway and waved. His siblings popped out behind him. After she explained the request, Nikos dug out his keys and headed for the front door.

Zak joined Alex, U.N., and Helen in the closest math classroom, which had bandages and ointments spread out on the table. With both hands, Alex still held ice packs to her bruises.

"Nikos is driving them," Zak explained. "He will come back to get you."

"Is everything okay?" Helen asked.

"No." Zak sighed. The worst disaster was averted, but at a price she regretted. "But we did what we must."

"What did you do?" U.N. asked.

Alex elbowed him.

"What?" U.N. said. "Don't you want to know?"

"It's none of our business," Alex hissed.

"The culprit has been outcast," Zak said. "I should warn you not to speak his name anymore. We no longer recognize it or him."

"Ouch," Alex said. "That's harsh."

"At least nobody's dead," U.N. said.

Helen winced and looked toward the door. "I should go check on Meg and the kids."

"Not yet," Zak said. "Let them mourn first."

"Ra— He's not dead," U.N. repeated.

"He no longer exists to us," Zak said numbly. "Gil has no twin. Meg has only one son."

"Oh." U.N. flopped into a chair and shoved his bangs out of his face.

Helen sat beside him and put her arm around him.

"Before we talk to Gil," Alex said, "we have another problem." She dropped one ice pack and picked up her phone, which Mak-swill had retrieved with the other fae. "Someone caught the whole werewolf thing on video and posted it on the internet. Even though he was in the bed of the truck, it shows enough. The whole internet is going crazy, and this time we can't pass it off as a movie. We knew the secret might be revealed if he shifted in public, and it has. More and more people are starting to believe in werewolves after watching the video. What will we do now?"

Helen sighed. "Since we have to wait for Nikos, we might as well get started. I'll get Ms. Maxwell and let her call Mr. Compton. There are a few advantages to not being the one in charge. Alex, put the ice back on."

She walked out and Alex sat, rearranging the ice bags.

Zak winced. "I'll get the others. Their mourning will have to wait."

Chapter 22

Interviews

Alexandria shifted to a slightly less tender position. Thank goodness Rafe hadn't had a knife, because the rock and his hands and feet were bad enough. She hunched her shoulders, remembering yet again the crazy who had slashed her in his quest to murder Gil. How many more would hunt them now? Starting a war was exactly what they'd been trying to avoid.

And that wasn't including what the fae might do. Even without magic or full training, Rafe was terrifying. Not to mention that Gil shook in his sandals when he talked about fae magic in war.

Zee returned with Gil, Meg, and Miknon. Tear tracks ran down all three faces.

"Chantelle is getting the others," Zee said.

Alexandria threw her arms around her fae brother and patted Miknon on the back. "I'm sorry." She reached for Meg but stopped when Gil's mother shrank away. No touching, right. "I'm really sorry."

Ian pulled Gil into a seat beside him. Meg took a seat on the other side of Gil, and Alexandria reclaimed her chair, settling the ice back on her bruises.

From the basement, the bass of the dance music pounded softly. Alexandria's feet twitched. The rest of the students were having fun, and here she was in an old uniform and new bruises, trying to save the world instead of dancing. She rolled her eyes. Par for the course.

They all sat quietly until Chantelle brought less familiar fae to join the meeting and Nikos returned with Tom. After nearly an hour, Mom came back with Raquel.

"We've got a problem," the principal said crisply. "Mr. Compton and Mr. Farrell are out of the country, finalizing arrangements for the ambassadors. We have no way to contact the President and ask him to move up the announcement about the fae."

"It would have been easier to let the human execute the wolf and preserve the secret," Tom grumbled.

"Easier, certainly," Raquel said, "but I understand saving a life."

"Is one life worth it?" Tom asked. "Especially a traitor's?"

"Of course it is," Alexandria protested.

Gil shrugged. "We have to tell the rest of Earth, anyway. It's hard enough to hide a spaceship on the moon; we can't possibly hide a thousand ships in orbit. It's hard enough to house ten thousand; we can't integrate three hundred thousand in one place, with or without people noticing."

Alexandria nodded. "Plus, the dragons will stay on Earth once they finish bringing down the barges, and they are very noticeable!"

"Don't forget the giant," Ian said.

"So the deadline for revealing the fae was always when the fleet returns," Chantelle said. "And that is now almost here. It is our choice to reveal ourselves."

"What about the NDA?" Mom asked. "We promised to keep the secret."

"*We* didn't," Chantelle said. "Your agreement has no binding on us. Until now, we kept silent because it was best, but matters have changed."

Tom folded his arms and leaned back in his chair.

"Well, if that's your decision," Raquel said slowly. "The school is the closest we have to a fae embassy, and I have no authority over you except what you allow me. Fortunately, school will end in a week, and we've been prepping the ambassadors, so we can handle the deadline. We just need to decide how to handle the public finding out about werewolves like this."

Mom sighed. "It would have been nice to have more notice and less drama."

"Then let us make a plan now," Gil said, "because if we are not united when the fleet lands, Lord Kishar will take advantage of our disarray."

"Social media is going crazy," Alexandria repeated. "We could announce it there, but you'd need proof. The weirdos who already believe werewolves are real aren't voting for peaceful immigration." She opened her phone to a social media page so they could watch the comment numbers spin. "Whatever we do, we need to convince the public that the fae are friendly."

"I wish we could get the President to announce it on television with the fae present," Raquel said. "But we don't have access to him without Compton, and security would never let the fae near him, anyway."

"And no regular TV reporter will believe us," Ian said.

"What's a reporter?" Zee asked.

"One of the people who investigates news stories and talks about them," Alexandria explained.

Zee pulled a business card from her pocket and handed it to Alexandria. "Like her?"

"When did you get this?" Alexandria asked.

"She threw it into the car after the wolf shifted," Zee said.

"She was there?" Alexandria pursed her lips. "I'd say there's a good chance she'd believe us then, yeah? Should I call her now or wait until the morning?"

Raquel held out her hand. "I will call, if you please."

Alexandria handed over the card, and Raquel dialed. She held her finger to her lips, then touched the speaker button. The reporter's voicemail came on.

Raquel skipped straight to the drama. "You saw a werewolf today. I can tell you the whole story. Call me." She added her name and number and hung up. "Whenever she calls, I'll set an appointment. I think the dance is still going on, if you kids want to run down there."

Zee ran her hands nervously down her skirt and sidled from the room. Mom looked at Alexandria and her siblings, who all shook their heads.

"I guess we'll go home," Mom said. "We could use some quiet time."

Raquel's phone rang. She picked it up and put it on speaker.

"What do you know about the werewolf?" a breathless voice asked. Iris Rowland, presumably.

"Everything," Raquel promised. "And I can prove he's real on live TV, so nobody can say we used camera tricks."

"If you can get me an interview with the werewolf, I can get you on live TV," Ms. Rowland promised. "How soon?"

"The sooner the better," Raquel said, glancing at Tom and Chantelle, who both nodded.

"Tomorrow morning?" Ms. Rowland pressed.

"It's Sunday," Mom protested weakly.

Raquel raised her eyebrows, and Mom nodded. Raquel discussed time, place, and procedure with the reporter. Alexandria made notes on her phone, including ideas for who to take with them to impress Earth but not scare them.

As soon as Raquel hung up, Alexandria read her ideas aloud. Humans and fae debated and planned until they had a workable strategy. The music in the basement drifted to a stop, and everyone headed off to find the people they would need in the morning.

Imagine, they were going on live television — with the mythical fae! Alexandria grimaced at her dirty uniform. At least they had a few hours to prepare. *Only* a few hours, so she'd better move it!

EARLY SUNDAY MORNING, Alexandria and her family parked at the school and transferred to one of the buses. Raquel already had the fae and their military escorts loaded, so as soon as the Fitches slid into the empty seats reserved for them, the bus pulled out. On the way to the studio, Raquel reviewed the plan.

"Remember to keep it short," she said. "We don't want to give anyone time to intercept us."

Everyone nodded solemnly, and Alexandria sat on her hands to keep them from twitching. When they'd created this plan, she'd assumed one of the adults would be in charge, but the fae had voted for her and Ian to finish what they started.

An hour before show time, they walked through the front door in a group, hiding the fae in the middle as much as possible. Nate rode in a wagon with a box over him, and Tom kept a hat pulled low. Gil waved to everyone until Ian elbowed him, careful to miss the backpack slung across his chest, where Miknon was hiding.

A harried-looking man focused on Raquel, who was dressed in her military uniform today. "Are you all here? What a crowd. I need you to sign in. Names, contact info. Then we'll get you to makeup." He glanced at Zee. "Wasn't expecting green. Here we are." He handed a clipboard to Raquel. With another scan of the crowd, he grimaced. "Maybe you should sign in for everyone?"

"Sure thing," Raquel said. "Alex is in charge for this interview. She and her brother were first contact. What's next?"

"Makeup." The man pointed at the wagon and the pink backpack. "You can leave your packages here."

Nate pushed up the box enough to poke out one of his snake heads. "Not package," he said.

Miknon unzipped the backpack from the inside and peeked out. "No, thank you."

The man sucked in a breath. "Not packages." With an anxious look at the wagon, he opened the inner door and waved them through. "This way, please."

As he escorted them through the hall, he waved at other employees but sped up until he nearly ran into a nearby room. Ian pushed the box gently down as Nikos pulled the wagon. Miknon ducked back inside her refuge. With Raquel near the front, Alexandria dropped back to make sure everyone was following. Zee nervously smoothed down her pretty dress from the night before. Freya waved like the model she resembled, though she was dressed in a simple blouse and skirt like Alexandria's. All of the fae except Gil had dressed Earth-style to be less conspicuous.

Alexandria had chosen a high collar and long sleeves to hide as many of her bruises as possible. At least Ram's blows had usually missed her head, and she'd had only one blue mark on her jaw to hide under concealer.

The makeup artist had a mild heart attack when she got a good look at everyone. She refused to touch Tom, Miknon, Zee, or Nate, so Mom applied the no-shine powder to them herself, reminding Gil in Fae to keep his mouth shut so he wouldn't scare the poor lady more.

Freya complimented the makeup artist until she agreed to spend extra time on her look. When Chantelle was offered extra attention, she shook her head and ducked her eyes. Alexandria's jaw got a second look and an extra layer of makeup, along with a whispered suggestion to call the police.

The guards and Nikos, who were not going on screen, stood by the walls and provided peanut gallery commentary, which Alexandria matched quip for quip. Somebody had to lighten the mood!

"Next is the mics," their guide said. "I mean, microphones."

"Yeah, we know," Ian said. "And we explained it to them. It'll be okay."

He turned around so a mic could be attached. The process went smoothly until they reached Nate, who had no belt or waistband to use. The hydra stuck out several tongues and slithered from the wagon.

"If I sit by someone," he asked, "can I be heard?"

"Yes, but the sound won't be as good."

Alexandria waved her hand to brush off the problem. "It will be good enough."

A Black lady rushed into the makeup room. "I'm Iris Rowland. Are you ready?"

She was shorter than Mom and wore her box braids pulled back in a ponytail. Her dangling earrings were the same peacock blue as her glasses.

"We're ready," Alexandria said. "Do you like television reporting?" She smiled, trying to act like this was all normal. *We're friendly, so friendly.*

Ms. Rowland took a deep breath. "I love it, but I've got to admit, today is a new experience. Are you a werewolf, too? Or, um, what?"

"One hundred percent human." Alexandria held out her hand to shake.

"Eyes," Gil muttered in Fae.

"Not a stonegazer," Alexandria murmured back likewise.

Gil laughed, exposing his sharper-than-human teeth.

Ms. Rowland flinched at the sight. "Oh, I — expected English? Or can you interpret?"

"They all speak English," Ian said. "They're just teasing each other right now."

He rolled his eyes at Alexandria, who took revenge by ruffling his hair.

The reporter checked her watch. "It's almost time. Let's do a sound check."

Everyone passed except for Freya, whose mic had died. A new one was quickly attached, and Alexandria didn't mention the futility.

"Okay, guys," Alexandria said in Fae, "we want to persuade Earth to let you live here, so behave."

"Yes, Alex," they chorused, except for Ian.

"Yes, bossy," her brother said.

"Let's go," Ms. Rowland said.

After a worried glance at the lot of them, she forced a smile onto her face and led them into the studio. Tom carried Nate for simplicity, and Miknon retreated to her backpack. Alexandria swiped a potted plant on the way. Ms. Rowland sat on a padded armchair and indicated the red couch surrounded by extra chairs. There was nobody else in the room, though a camera was already pointed at them.

"Nikos and I will wait with Ms. Maxwell." Mom leaned against a wall out of the camera's view.

Nikos waved and took a similar stance, though Raquel remained almost at attention, as did the guards.

Pulling Ian and Gil down with her, Alexandria took the couch. Gil pulled his arms free of the backpack and settled it on his lap, unzipping but not opening it. Tom and Chantelle took chairs on one side, and Freya and Zee sat on the other side. Ms. Rowland gestured frantically for another chair, but Abe dropped to the floor in front of the couch and took Nate from Tom, hugging him like a large teddy bear. Alexandria leaned down and put the flower pot next to the red-headed boy.

The camera tilted downward, obviously by remote control. Ms. Rowland smiled at the imaginary audience.

"Some of you may have seen the videos circulating on the internet that seem to show a werewolf," she said. "A hoax, most of you are saying, or movie magic. In fact, it's all true, and some of his friends have agreed to a live interview."

The camera backed up, and Ms. Rowland turned to face Alexandria. "Good morning, Alex Fitch. You said you're human, but how did you meet the, um—"

"The fae," Alexandria supplied. She put her hand on Gil's arm. "This is Gil. He's a werewolf, like his brother on the internet video. Last summer, he and his adopted sister came to Earth as advance scouts for their people." Ran away was more accurate, but not the picture they wanted to paint. "We picked them up late at night in the middle of Kansas." She paused for dramatic effect, then pointed to Ian. "My brother always wanted a dog, you see."

Ms. Rowland chuckled, then sobered. "How did you protect yourself from a werewolf? Did you wear a cross or something? Wait, is that for vampires?"

Ian scowled. "Earth legends scrambled everything. Werewolves and vampires are perfectly safe."

"Anyway," Alexandria continued, ignoring Ian's exaggeration as she subtly rubbed a bruise on her thigh, "they asked for an alliance between Earth and the fae. To make a long story very short, the U.S. government agreed to open a language training school for humans and fae. Now the rest of the fleet has almost arrived, and it's time to introduce them to the public before they land around the world."

She didn't mention there were almost ten thousand fae already hidden in Pennsylvania.

"I have so many questions," Ms. Rowland said. "Let's start with where you came from."

"Far from here," Tom said, "the seven worlds of the fae rotate a red sun. But they were dying, so we left."

"How did you get here?" Ms. Rowland asked.

Tom looked at Zee, whose ears turned orange. Someone in the studio gasped. Alexandria grinned. *Yeah, not makeup, guys.*

"In a magic spaceship," Zee whispered, though her mic caught every word.

"Zee was one of the navigators," Alexandria said.

"Then you are the perfect one to answer my next question," Ms. Rowland said. "Why did you come *here*?"

"The map led here," Zee squeaked.

"What map? Can we see it?"

"It's painted on the wall of the spaceship." Zee shrank farther against her chair.

"Long ago," Chantelle said in her musical voice, and everyone fell silent to listen, "two lovers fled our worlds, taking all their household with them. In our direst circumstances, a young girl found a map the seer left behind, showing worlds around a yellow sun. We followed the constellations on the map until we reached here."

She stopped talking, but it took a minute for everyone to recover from the spell of her voice. Not that the sirin was using her magic, Alexandria knew, but her voice was compelling even without it.

"Since the map led here," Ian said, "and we have all those legends of the fae, like the sirens—" He nodded at Chantelle. "Well, we have to assume they made it here, long ago."

"What happened to them?" Ms. Rowland asked.

"Honestly, we have no idea," Alexandria said. "But that's a problem for another day. Right now, *these* fae need a place to live. Their worlds are gone, and they have nowhere else to go. In exchange for a home, they're willing to become our allies and trade their skills and magics."

"So magic is real?" Ms. Rowland asked. "Can you give me an example?"

"We did promise you proof we had a werewolf." Alexandria bumped her shoulder against Gil.

With a wink at their host, Gil shifted. He sat for a moment, a huge black wolf wearing a skirt and hanging out his tongue in a canine laugh. Ms. Rowland jumped up from her chair and took a rapid step backward. Gil shifted back, and Alexandria handed him a granola bar to replace some of the calories he had used.

"Sorry for startling you," Gil said. "We do have less alarming examples." He folded down the front of the backpack, revealing Miknon.

"Some magics are big," Miknon said, leaning toward Gil's mic on his collar, "but most are small. Pixies make light."

She began to glow blue, brighter and brighter, then faded back to normal. Ms. Rowland slowly took her seat again.

"As I introduce you to everyone else," Alexandria said, "please realize the Earth words are not always accurate. Tom is a naga. He can change to a snake or half-snake, but we'll spare you that."

Tom removed his hat, exposing his scaled skin and yellow eyes. He smiled with lips closed, and Alexandria made a mental note to congratulate him on not showing his fangs. Gil never did remember to keep his teeth hidden. Despite Tom's discretion, Ms. Rowland pulled back slightly.

"And you would call Freya an elf," Alexandria said.

Freya smiled and waved. "Hello, everyone," she crooned.

Her words were picked up from Zee's mic, but her own was silent. She reached behind and touched her mic, then pouted.

"Sorry," Ian said. "She tends to fry technology. And since she calls lightning, she won't demonstrate her magic now, either."

He shot a warning look at Freya, who stuck out her bottom lip farther.

"And Nate is a hydra," Alexandria said.

Nate, who had been motionless until then, moved all of his heads at once in a spiraling dance. Ms. Rowland put her hand on her chest.

"Sorry," Nate hissed.

"But we saved the best for last," Alexandria said. "In terms of trade, I mean. Abe is a dryad, and he can make plants grow anywhere."

With a shy smile, Abe put his free hand into the flower pot. The plant suddenly grew taller and sprouted more blossoms.

"That's amazing," Ms. Rowland said. "Think what you could do for agriculture."

"I like plants," Abe said.

A vine sprouted from his hair and crawled up Alexandria's knee. She gently brushed it off. By the wall, Raquel glanced at her phone, then beckoned urgently. Time to go. Ms. Rowland opened her mouth for another question, but Alexandria didn't give her the chance.

"The United States is already in peace talks with the fae." Alexandria smiled directly at the camera and hoped the others were remembering to do the same. "Ambassadors and translators will shortly leave for other countries. We call on people around Earth to give the fae a home and a chance to prove themselves. Thank you, Ms. Rowland, for allowing us to introduce the fae to Earth. That's all the time we have today."

That was Freya's cue. She pointed at the camera and winked. A spark shot from her finger, and the camera light went off.

Ms. Rowland hopped to her feet. "Oh, but I still have questions."

Raquel stepped forward. "Sorry, gotta go." She motioned sharply, and the guards rushed in to surround everyone.

"Can we talk later?" Ms. Rowland called as they double-timed it out of the studio.

"We'll call you," Alexandria shouted over her shoulder.

"Alex," Raquel chided.

"Hey, you never know," Alexandria said. "We might need the media again."

Raquel collected all their badges and signed them out while they hurried to the bus. As soon as she joined them, they drove home, splitting up in the parking lot. Most of the fae and guards entered the school, but the Fitches transferred to Nikos's truck and drove home.

"We could catch a later ward," Mom offered wearily, "since we missed our own church."

Ian covered his eyes. "I have a migraine. The studio lights were too bright."

"I'm hungry," Gil said.

Mom laughed. "Okay, lunch and a nap it is."

They settled for PBJ sandwiches and milk and were all asleep within twenty minutes.

When Alexandria awoke, she had an email waiting for her. She had to read it twice before she understood.

"AHHHH," she screamed.

Her family rushed into her room and stared at her.

"What's wrong?" Mom asked.

Alexandria sank onto her bed. "Remember how I didn't get into college?"

"Yeah," Ian said. "So? You'll get in next year."

She turned the phone to face them. "They changed their minds. They saw me on TV and want in on the fae knowledge. I'm invited to the summer session if I can make it, or fall semester otherwise."

Nikos squinted at her. "Is it a prank?"

She read from the email. "We'll send you a hard copy ASAP with all the information you'll need, but we didn't want you to accept another offer first." She dropped the phone onto the bed. "And they're giving me a scholarship."

CHAPTER 23

IN WHICH THE AMBASSADORS LEAVE

JUNE 9, 2023

GIL POKED his head into the fae administrative office. "What's the latest word?"

With a sigh of probable relief, Shalla put down the paper at which she had been squinting. "The fleet should reach orbit late today. I've been sending the updates to Ohrteez, and her math agrees with Zak's."

"Do we need to move up the landing?" Gil asked.

The sirin shook her head. "No, they still need to disconnect the ships and spread out around Earth before they descend. Tomorrow will be early enough. And they won't all land at once, anyway."

"Right," he said, "of course. Do you have the list of all the landing places?"

She tapped the paper on her desk. "Right here. We're all ready, and the President has made his speech."

Even though Alex and Ian had been the ones to break the news with the fae, official word had followed quickly.

"Then come say farewell to the ambassadors," Gil offered. "Everybody is packed, and the cars are starting to arrive. They have to leave soon to catch their planes."

After locking the paper in a drawer, Shalla rose and brushed off her dress.

Gil ran ahead, knocking on office doors. "It's time," he called. "Hurry."

Behind him, doors opened and closed, and hurried footsteps followed him. By the time he reached the parking lot, it was already chaos. Thirty cars were packed in, each with a sign taped to the window to designate the final destination of its passengers. Each had a political consultant and adult fae chosen to advise and support the teenage ambassadors. Once they reached their destination, more staff would be hired, including cooks, tech specialists, drivers, and more. Hopefully, every need had been anticipated.

Now they just needed the translators themselves.

Mak-swill's military stood guard and directed traffic, making sure everyone found the correct car and loaded their bags properly. Just as importantly, they checked that everyone who got in a car belonged there. No stowaways or spies were allowed.

Gil's ears ached at the noise. And once this lot was gone, they would have to do it all over again in the afternoon. Not only were the ambassadors leaving, but since the end of classes yesterday, the other graduates and the foreign exchange students had been trickling away. By evening, only a third of the students would remain for next year. Fewer, actually, since many human students were going home for the summer.

In the future, roommates would be reassigned only two to a room, and the rest of the empty rooms would be occupied by some of the fae landing tomorrow.

But that was tomorrow's problem. Right now, he had friends to see before they left.

All the students had come for the goodbyes. Those leaving now dragged heavy luggage behind them. Those leaving later or staying behind ran around giving hugs or back slaps.

By scent, he tracked Ian in the middle of the crowd, talking to a couple of the former students.

Ian flashed a grin and brushed his hair from his eyes. "Hey, Gil. Tell Jin she'll be fine, please."

"You'll be fine," Gil obediently said.

Jin rolled her eyes. "Thanks a lot."

"Really," Gil said. "You know Fae well. You've learned the most important customs. You get along with Freya, and that's probably the most difficult thing to learn."

Freya stopped admiring herself in a pocket mirror long enough to turn up her nose at Gil. "I am not difficult."

With a raised eyebrow and a faint nod, Jin conceded Gil's point.

"And we'll keep in touch," Ian assured her. "If you have a problem, just call. Or email, if that's easier from China."

"My parents are freaking out about the China thing," Jin admitted, pushing back a loose tendril of her brightly dyed hair. "They never want to go back, and they don't want me to go, either." She smirked. "I told them if they didn't want me to visit China, they shouldn't have insisted I learn Mandarin. It's their own fault."

Ian laughed. "I bet they loved that." He threw a glance over his shoulder, then lowered his voice even though Mom was out of hearing range. "Parents never like admitting to mistakes, even if they apologize."

"I think," Gil corrected, "they don't like to *make* mistakes, especially with their precious children."

His mother was still fretting over what she could have done differently with his brother, but he had made his own dumb choices.

Gil stomped his own sorrow deeper into his heart and focused on Jin's partner. "Are you ready, Freya?"

The highborn shut her mirror and smiled at him. "Of course I am. Why wouldn't I be?" She snapped her fingers at a passing soldier and shoved her towering stack of luggage at him. "Put it on the China car," she demanded. "China."

"Please," Jin added.

She grabbed her own two suitcases and followed the soldier. Freya trailed after, yet again looking into her mirror.

"Are you sure she's a good idea for an ambassador?" Ian whispered.

"She'll be fine," Gil said. "She knows English and Mandarin and won't kill random humans. For a highborn, she's doing very well, and she does like Jin."

Ian scrunched his nose. "If you say so. Who's next?"

"Have you seen Abe yet?" Gil asked.

The dryad was one of his oldest, closest friends, but Ashur had been so busy the last week that Gil had barely seen him.

"Nope, but the Japanese car is that way." Ian stood on his toes and pointed to the left.

Ian was too short to force his way through the crowd, so Gil towed him along, weaving between luggage and people alike. They passed Alexandria and Zak saying goodbye to Yuri and Kirill, who were returning to their countries as private citizens rather than ambassadors. If their war stopped, the fae would reconsider their status and the possibility of settling fae in the area. In the meantime, it would do no harm to have Fae language-speakers in place.

Considering the way Zak and Kirill were looking at each other, Gil expected plenty of correspondence to cross between them. Private friendship was also useful in the long run. He grinned, sure neither of them would notice. Zak still had a tiny tool kit in her pocket, the same place it had been ever since Kirill gave it to her for her birthday two days before.

A familiar red head appeared by a car, and Gil stretched his legs more. "Abe," he bellowed. "Wait!"

Ashur stopped and turned, waving when he spotted Gil and Ian. Touji's face appeared from the other side of the car, and both boys approached to say farewell. Gil had been just in time, because they were obviously ready to leave.

In a moment, Gil was close enough to wrap his old friend and his new one in hugs.

"I'm glad you made it," Ash said. "I thought you might be too busy to say goodbye."

"Never," Gil promised. "And I won't be too busy for your emails, either."

Ash grimaced and shrugged.

"Don't worry," Two said, "I'll help Abe with the computer. I'm pretty sure that falls under my duties, right?" He grinned and nudged Ash.

"Yes," Ash said emphatically. "You deal with the tech. I'll take care of the garden."

"Oh." Gil snapped his fingers as he remembered what Zak had told him. "When the fleet lands, I expect you'll probably get mostly ships that can crash in the ocean, since you'll have a lot of that nearby. The ships that must use dragons to unload by barge will go to inland positions. So make sure you arrange for water rescue as soon as you arrive."

Two pulled out his phone and tapped on the screen. "Got it. Water rescue, ASAP. You'll send us more details when you get them?"

"As soon as we hear," Ian promised.

The driver tapped the horn gently.

"Time to go," Two said. "Are you ready?"

Ash threw himself onto Gil for another hug. A vine tendril curled around Gil's shoulder, and the two friends held fast for a long minute.

"Okay," Gil said. "I'll talk to you later." He loosened the vine and returned it to Ash.

The dryad snapped off a leaf and handed it to Gil. "Sayonara."

"Sayonara," Gil whispered.

Email or no email, Japan was on the other side of the planet, and nobody knew when Ash would return. If ever, since the fae would disperse and settle across Earth. Ash wasn't the only friend who might end up living too far away to visit.

Ash and Touji hurried into the car, which started moving almost before they were seated. Gil and Ian jumped backward to get their feet out of range of the tires.

Gil twirled the leaf, then slid it carefully into his pocket. On the old world, he and Ash might never have been friends. On the ship, they had seen each other almost every day. When Gil had dreamed of the new world, he had naively thought that "bigger than the ship" meant a few miles between settlements and that he could arrange to live near all his friends. Of course, he also expected his grandsire and his twin to live with the family. Now Grandsire was dead, his twin was outcast, and most of his friends were leaving.

"Who's next?" Ian murmured, reaching up to pat Gil's shoulder.

The touch shook him out of his thoughts. He was not alone. He still had Miknon and Mother and a whole new family. And with the Earth technology available, he could talk to his friends every day. Their new world was beautiful and full of opportunities and equality. And on the old world, Gil and Ian would *definitely* not have been friends, much less brothers!

Gil took a deep breath. "Let's see who looks like they need an encouraging word. I haven't seen Okoro yet."

"Okay," Ian said. "You're taller; you find him."

Gil laughed and jumped into the air to scan the crowd.

HOURS LATER, the parking lot was empty, and the remaining students and staff gathered for lunch. After eating a large meal and returning his empty tray, Gil checked the clock on the wall. In another hour, it would be time to say goodbye to more friends. He cleared his throat, trying to swallow the lump choking him, but nothing helped.

He desperately needed a distraction. His family was still eating and talking, so he wandered down the hall to get another update from Shalla. But when he entered her office, it was Shar at the desk.

The prince was reading a stack of papers, probably all the plans and reports. He didn't squint like Shalla did, but he already knew how to read before coming to Earth, albeit in a different language.

"Greetings, Gil," Shar said without pausing in his work.

"We missed you at lunch," Gil said. "And in the parking lot."

Shar sighed. "You know I'm still anonymous. I did talk to Ashur privately."

"You don't need to stay hidden," Gil said. "Now is a great time to announce yourself."

Shar put down the paper and met Gil's eyes. "I told you from the start that I would surrender my crown if it would save my people. Your plan has succeeded without my presence. You don't need a king anymore, and I don't want to ruin your work. Besides, I thought you wanted equality for everyone. How does a king fit into that?"

Gil shrugged. "Equal rights, yes. I never planned to overthrow you. I don't imagine the lords will give up their rank, so who will keep them in line if you are gone? Above all, I wanted freedom and peace. I believe your rule would protect both, not ruin them."

"You have peace," Shar said. "You've accomplished your goal."

"Not quite yet." Gil crossed his fingers in the human gesture of hope.

"With Earth and the fae in peace talks already," Shar said, "the lords are defeated before they even land. Our ambassadors will succeed, and the lords will see that our way is best."

"I hope you're right," Gil said, "but what if you aren't?"

The treaty was now in the hands of the students, and it wasn't that he didn't trust them, but they were barely adults — or not, under fae standards.

"You still have my ring," Shar said. "Wave that around a little more."

"Oh, yes." Gil nodded solemnly. "The humans accept my authority and the lords will be just as convinced, certainly." He shook his head. "I'll be executed for picking the dead king's pockets before I get a chance to explain I'm not a thief. Very helpful, I'm sure."

Shar flashed a grin for the first time in weeks, perhaps months. "I'm not dead, Gil, just in disguise. I won't let them do that to you. Though I suspect the lords would contest my identity strenuously, since I'm supposed to be dead."

"You are obviously your father's son," Gil commented.

In fact, his resemblance to the old king was striking. Now that Shar was approaching adulthood, they could have been copies except for the prince's narrower nose and silver-blue eyes that matched portraits of the queen.

"They will say I am counterfeited by magic," Shar argued, "and I do not have Father's crown to prove my lineage."

"Did you leave it on the ship?" Gil asked. "That was foolish."

Shar raised his eyebrows and frowned at him. "It disappeared when Father died."

Gil flopped into a chair and stared in dismay. "You never mentioned that."

He could have had Miknon look for it. Though she probably would have refused on grounds that she was already putting herself in enough danger snooping around. And she was right, considering they had to flee the ship to save her life.

"No," Shar drawled. "I didn't think it mattered when I couldn't even leave Zak's quarters. Whoever took it couldn't go anywhere with it, so I bided my time. And I could hardly search for it in the middle of our escape. I did have Nik scour the ship before he left, but it was nowhere to be found."

"You might want to make that a higher priority now," Gil suggested. "What with Earth giving plenty of hiding places. If you don't hunt it down, you might never see it again."

"What a brilliant suggestion." Shar actually rolled his eyes, and Gil smothered a chuckle. Apparently the prince had picked up more from his human roommates than the language and hairstyles. "Nik knows about the problem," Shar continued. "We plan to ask our ambassadors to diplomatically search for it. And if anyone tries to use it, I will know. Now, do you need anything else, or may I return to work?"

Gil dragged a chair closer to the desk. "If you pass me some of those, I'll help. Unless you prefer to stay in here all day? I could send Shalla with some bread and water for you."

Shar pushed a stack of papers to him. "I suppose you could help, just so that I can get a proper meal."

Laughing, Gil bent over the first report.

Chapter 24

Duty

Ian stared at Ms. Maxwell in dismay. "What do you mean, I'm in charge of everything now?"

When the principal had called him to her office early Saturday morning, he'd expected a request for an update, not an inquisition with everyone staring at him, followed by a jail sentence. He had fixed the grades Mr. Abernathy ruined, and that was supposed to be the end of his responsibility, except for occasional translating.

The row of faces in front of him showed sympathy but no mercy. His head started to pound, and sparkles danced at the edges of his vision. With the help of Miles doing whatever magic he did, Ian's migraines had dropped to short and infrequent, but this news was enough stress to trigger a doozy.

"Not really everything," Mom said. "Just the language program and materials."

"That's still too much," Ian wailed. "We're adding lessons for the adult fae in a few weeks, and I don't know how to write a dictionary."

"We'll get you whatever help you need," Ms. Maxwell said. "Just let us know. But you're the best Fae speaker we have."

"That's Chantelle's magic," Ian said.

The sirin shook her head. "No, it's not. You worked hard and were already speaking well. I gave you a — what do you call it? A bust?"

With a grin, Alexandria pointed to the meaning of the wrong word.

"Boost." Ian giggled. "A little push."

Eyes crinkling, Chantelle chuckled. "Yes, a boost."

"More importantly," Mom said, "you like the fae and work well with them. We've already seen what can happen with the wrong person in charge."

Chantelle smiled. "The fae want you. We trust you."

Ms. Maxwell spread her hands in a "there you have it" gesture.

"But Nikos *and* Alex will be in college," Ian protested. "Mom will be busy with the history classes, and even with Miknon and Gil helping, I don't have time to teach that many hours."

Ms. Maxwell shook her head. "More people speak Fae and English to translate, so you don't have to teach all the classes yourself. There are fewer high school students, and everyone will be on a less intense lesson schedule. We just want you to supervise and plan."

She made it sound so easy, but there would still be fifty fae teenagers, and twice as many human students, plus dozens or hundreds of adult fae. And no textbooks, no actual curriculum, no resources beyond what he created himself.

"I'm only fourteen," Ian protested.

"We're judging you on merit, not age," Ms. Maxwell countered implacably, though she smiled kindly.

Ian argued more, but it did no good. Everyone was against him, and when they finally dismissed for dinner, his fate was sealed, though Miles did touch his head and magically dissolve his migraine. Too bad no human med could do that so easily.

On the way to the cafeteria, Alexandria threw her arm around Ian's shoulders. "We can do hard things. We've done them before."

"Maybe this is too hard," Ian grumbled.

"Like getting my black belt?" she asked. "I thought that would be easy, too. Look, my last bout of the season is tonight. If I get my black belt, will you believe we can do hard things and you can manage the language program?"

Ian rolled his eyes. "You almost got it already, so of course I believe you can do it."

"Well," Alexandria said, "I believe in *you*." She pushed him through the doorway and handed him a tray. "Pick two desserts. Maybe they'll help you feel better."

"They won't," Ian promised, but he still took a piece of cake and a cinnamon roll.

Alexandria sat beside him and kept talking. "I don't need my black belt anymore, thanks to my scholarship, but I want to finish what I started. Come on, make me a deal. If I can do it, you can do it."

Stuffing his mouth full of cake, Ian raised his eyebrows. Alexandria laughed and stopped talking to gobble her own dinner.

Now that the fae were no longer a secret, most of them came to watch Alexandria in her last competition, filling an entire bleacher with her fans. The humans in attendance spent almost as much time watching the fae as they did the competition. Some of the fae entertained themselves by waving and winking at the humans, but most kept their attention on Alexandria, cheering when Ian, Mom, and Nikos cheered.

Alexandria wasn't in every bout, of course. During the other competitor's turns, Tom and some of his friends whispered a steady stream of analysis that included words Ian didn't know how to translate. He made a mental note to ask later, even if they were using jargon that wouldn't matter to most people.

Though Alexandria didn't win every match, she was doing well, racking up points like her life depended on it. Not even her bruises seemed to be slowing her much, despite occasionally flinching at an opponent's move. Slowly, her name crept up the scoreboard.

Finally, it was time for her final bout, and if she won, she would have enough points for her black belt. Her opponent was six inches taller and noticeably wider. She looked like a child next to him, but she shook out her arms and legs and squared her shoulders. Both athletes bowed, and then they attacked. Alexandria was beauty in motion, smooth and graceful and fast. She countered every move and responded with an attack in almost the same motion.

In less time than Ian thought possible, she had won. After bowing to her opponent, she looked over her shoulder and winked at Ian.

He rolled his eyes. Sure, she could do it, but she was an amazing athlete who had been training for years, and he was completely out of his depth. No deal. With a sigh, he forced a smile on his face and ran to congratulate his amazing sister.

By the time the event ended, their entire contingent needed to hurry to the landing site. If all went well, the rest of the fleet would start landing today. And Ian still hadn't convinced anyone else to be in charge of the language program. Everyone seemed determined to dump it on his shoulders, which were caving under the weight.

"THERE!" Ian pointed upward.

In the empty blue sky above the river, small dots suddenly appeared. The mages had released the shields hiding the fleet, and now the humans could see the ring of ships surrounding Earth. On the phone screens of everyone in the crowd, a similar view showed from locations all around the planet. This was the hottest event in the world, and nobody wanted to miss a second of it.

Here, the military had set up a perimeter to keep out random bystanders, and the closest roads were closed. Even the river had barriers across it, though far enough in either direction to allow a landing strip for a dragon barge.

Inside a nearby truck, Mr. Farrell and Mr. Riggs sat in front of a row of laptops, monitoring the situation and communications from all the ambassadors and various governments. Runners relayed messages to the fae, and texts flew between human leaders.

Ms. Maxwell looked up from her phone. "We're ready. Tell them to go."

Chantelle nodded, and one of the pilots of *New Kunisu*, which was now empty on the moon, closed his eyes in concentration. Gil had explained that though the pilots' main magic was lifting things, they all needed at least enough mind-touching to receive or relay orders. He would send his thoughts to the pilots on the other ships, signaling the beginning of the landings.

Ian held his breath in a stomach-churning mix of excitement, hope, and worry. Thanks to Gil's encouragement, the fae had described the fleet and explained the planned descent in detail, to the particular fascination of Mrs. Ortiz and Ms. Maxwell. The alien technology would probably be discussed for years by the scientists, to say nothing of being disassembled and diagrammed if they could get their hands on any of it.

Every country that had agreed to immediately host the fae had a plan for the ships coming to their area. The new ambassadors were overseeing the process, prepared to translate as soon as the rest of the fae emerged from their ships.

So far, the public comments had been mostly favorable. It seemed Alexandria's idea to talk to the media had worked, though it was too early to guess what the end result would be.

If everyone was very lucky, the treaty would go through and fae and humans could live in peace.

"I believe we are starting now," Iris Rowland said into the camera.

She turned to look upward with everyone else. The reporter had been given first choice of locations, to thank her for the earlier broadcast. She had chosen the river, though she hadn't admitted if it was to stand loyally with Alex and Gil, for the chance to meet some of the fae lords when their dragon barge landed, or just because it was the most local and thus her home territory.

On the screens, the same picture played out in dozens of locations, with dozens of reporters speaking in dozens of languages. But all of them sounded equally excited.

Beside Ian, Gil bounced on his toes. "Come on," he muttered. "What's taking so long?"

He spoke in English, proof the language was becoming second nature to him. Ian now felt the same way about Fae, but that was at least in part because of Chantelle's magic. It normally took him longer than a year to feel truly at home in a new language. He was still getting used to ancient Greek.

"I'm sure they'd rather be careful than crash," Alexandria said.

Gil wrinkled his nose and gently slugged her shoulder. Instead of laughing, she sighed and slipped him a quick hug.

Ian kept his mouth shut, though he was just as worried. Unlike humans, who had gradually worked up to more and more complex vessels and missions, the fae had jumped from small interplanetary ships that only traveled the distance of Earth to the moon, without engines, to interstellar travel for light years, still without engines or any technology more advanced than radio. So mind-boggling!

But most of their fleet had been built in space and had never crossed an atmosphere. Only the smallest ships were built for re-entry and could be guided down by a dragon.

Slightly larger ones would have to crash-land in the ocean, with a magic impact shield lasting only until they hit. Depending whether a spaceship was full of water fae or others, the wrecked vehicle could either be left to sink while the passengers swam away, or would need rescuers before it filled with water and drowned everyone in it.

A few of the biggest spaceships must be unloaded in orbit, one dragon-barge at a time, like the ship on the moon had been. That part of the landing would take weeks, if not months, though no other ships were as large or populated as *New Kunisu*.

In theory, the ships actually landing would survive long enough to reach the surface. In theory. No matter how much they planned, accidents could still happen, and with three hundred ships in the fleet, there were a lot of opportunities for something to go wrong. The ships could crash, or burn up in re-entry, or sink too fast, or lose the shields too early, or get lost, or... Really, any disaster was possible, as NASA's history proved. Just because events *usually* worked out didn't mean they would this time. And the fae had never landed a fleet before.

Of course, Earth had never had real aliens before last year, either. Myths had only been stories, and near-light-speed travel was only in science fiction. Now all of that was true, more or less, and Earth might never be the same.

Ian was already changed.

He glanced at Gil and Miknon, who had changed even more. Just under a year ago, the werewolf had landed on Earth with only his sister. They had run from certain death, risking themselves on a strange world that might be toxic or full of enemies, on the slim chance they might find allies and a new home. Neither could speak a single word of any Earth language or even walk. A bit of bad luck could have put them in the hands of people with no hesitation about killing aliens. Like Dad.

Now they both spoke English, had numerous human friends, and worked with government officials. Gil had set up and guided an entire school of translators and ambassadors to reach his goals, *while* learning everything himself.

And Ian knew Gil was not important in his own society. He had no magic to affect anyone else, no rank or status. He had been a zookeeper and nothing more, in a culture where that meant he was nobody. And he had still managed to get Earth and the fae to within arms-length of a treaty.

That was much harder than a black belt, and he was only a couple of years older than Ian.

If Gil could manage that, couldn't Ian handle one little language program? Ms. Maxwell wasn't expecting him to do everything himself, after all.

Ian inhaled deeply and squared his shoulders. He had survived Dad *and* Mr. Abernathy. Compared to that, supervising people who actually wanted to help should be easy. Mostly easy? Sort of easy? Possible, anyway. Everyone he'd have to deal with wanted him to succeed. All he had to do was the planning and supervising and dictionary-writing. And if he needed help with the planning, well, Alexandria was a champion planner. He rolled his eyes. If he let Alexandria do the planning, they'd be buried in lists. Yeah, maybe he should try it himself before he asked her for help.

Besides, she wasn't as good at speaking Fae. Ms. Maxwell and Chantelle were right — he was the best speaker among the humans. Whether that was from his own hard work like Chantelle said or from her magic like he thought, he was still the best.

And the fae deserved the best.

He wrinkled his nose. Logic had disappointed him. But he would try.

Unexpected excitement rushed through his veins. If he was in charge, he could learn whatever he wanted. No more learning only what the teacher assigned.

A whole world of language lay before him, almost literally, and he could have it all.

Epilogue

In Which the Fleet Descends

June 10, 2023

Zak stared at the ships in the sky until her eyes burned. Father was up there somewhere, and the plan called for him to land here. If he survived the trip. She clasped her fingers together until the joints protested.

Gil elbowed Zak. "Breathe."

She sucked in air and let it out slowly. Father had been gone for nearly a year, and her chest ached with missing him. How long would it take until his turn to land?

He wouldn't be first, but no matter how long she had to wait by the river, she wouldn't go home until he was with her again.

The phone in her back pocket beeped. She jumped, then pulled it out. Kirill texted.

I'm watching. Which one is your dad's ship?

Too small to see, she texted back. His barge wouldn't be visible until it was much closer.

High above, one of the dots slipped out of line and began to fall. In a moment, a tail of fire surrounded it.

"The first ship has entered the atmosphere," Iris Rowland said breathlessly.

Not Father's ship. He wouldn't be first, and he might be last. Another ship fell, and another, and handfuls more. Zak bit her lip, and Gil clutched her elbow.

Iris maintained her patter as the ships plummeted on every phone screen. Less than ten minutes later, the first fae ships hit the ocean with a sizzle. Nearby, the small human boats surrounding their ships floated motionless. Zak bit her lip again. The water fae should be first, able to take care of themselves. But what if the wrong ships had landed? It wouldn't matter at the local shore, for the selkies and kelpies from *New Kunisu* had already been taken to the ocean. At the other locations, it might mean the passengers drowned before they could reach the surface.

As they waited to see what happened with the first ship, more fell into other oceans. Zak twisted her fingers and tried not to vomit. This was worse than her own descent to Earth. She glanced at Gil. It might be better than his, though, since he hadn't even known if the air was breathable on the planet. And he had traveled in a message capsule barely bigger than himself, with a dragon who had never traveled by itself before, to a world where he had no allies and possibly enemies at every turn.

"How could you stand to risk it?" she murmured, not expecting him to understand.

"It was the only hope we had," Gil said softly. "If it didn't work, we were no more dead than if we stayed." Apparently his memories had been running along the same lines.

At the first landing site, the water rippled, and heads suddenly popped above the surface. Arms waved before the fae dove below again. An audible sigh of relief echoed from the phones and television crews. Within moments, the same success was reported at every location.

The pilot closed his eyes again, and the line of ships turned into a shower of stars. With the early ships proving the plan could work, it was time for more to crash.

"Oooh," the crowd sighed.

Ten minutes later, the oceans splashed again. The boats headed for each landing site, but before humans could dive into the water, fae emerged and waved them off.

"We're waiting to see if the fae need help," Iris said, "or if — oh!"

She broke off as two heads popped above the surface. One gasped for breath as the other fae held them up, beckoning the closest human boat. The sailors rowed close enough to haul the first fae aboard, and all around, more fae surfaced in the arms or on the backs or shoulders of their water kin.

War Lady checked her phone, then gestured thumbs-up. Good, then all the landings were going well enough. Two steps down. The next round with the dragons would take longer, though as the smaller ships emptied, their dragons would be temporarily reassigned to help the larger ones.

"All right, folks," War Lady bellowed. "The sun will set in only an hour. If you don't know your job by now, find your supervisor and ask! Are the buses ready?"

Someone shouted, "Yes."

"Lights?" The lights, laid out in the rayed circles that were the fae symbol for a thousand, would guide the dragons down and mark the landing portion of the river.

"Yes!"

War Lady continued down the list, checking on food, blankets, trucks, and more. Finally, she shouted, "Translators?"

"Yes," Gil bellowed, and U.N. echoed him in a squeak.

All the remaining students raised their hands, Zak included.

And then she could do nothing but wait, and worry, and watch the other fae be pulled from oceans across the world.

The worry part was the easiest, and the wait was nearly impossible.

ONCE DARKNESS FELL, more trails of fire ran between the stars. Some marked descents to other locations, but one headed straight for the river.

Zak sucked in another breath and rubbed her sweaty hands on her jeans. Though both boys and girls commonly wore pants and her shirt was almost long enough to be a tunic, the shirt was in a feminine style and snug enough to show her figure. Miknon had done her hair in girl's braids. It would be the first time Father had ever seen her look like a girl. She *was* a girl. It was fine to be a girl. She wanted to be a girl — mostly.

Oh, what would Father say?

The fire died out, and now the crowd waited silently. Legs wobbly, Zak sat on the ground and put her head on her knees.

A hand touched her back, and warmth settled beside her. "You okay?" Gaby asked.

Without raising her head, Zak nodded.

"Not long now," her roommate said. No longer her roommate after Father arrived. Gaby wouldn't even be at the school during the summer, as soon as her parents came to get her.

Zak rolled her head side-to-side across her arms. Not long enough, and way too long.

"There it is," War Lady snapped. "Everyone to your positions."

With Gaby's help, Zak stumbled to her feet. A dragon was swooping low, almost to the river, and by the time the translators gathered together, the barge had splashed down. In another moment, the dragon and barge were on shore.

The dragon was unharnessed and led to its truck, and the door of the barge cracked open.

Gaby squeezed Zak's hand, then pressed her forward. Gil beckoned urgently, and the students made way for her to be in the front row next to him and U.N.

The door slid open wider. Unlike the evacuation barges that had been emptying *New Kunisu* for the past year, this one was set up for a long voyage, with places for meal preparation, sleeping, and work. Instead of triple-high bunks filling every square inch, it had beds only along one wall.

Two lords shared the lower bunk closest to the door, and the rest of the beds were occupied to maximum capacity for the landing. Zak craned her neck, but she couldn't see Father.

Gil stepped forward. "Welcome to Ki. Our allies, known as humans, are prepared to take you to accommodations, if you will allow them to carry you."

The lord with elaborate braids sniffed, but the one in blue silk nodded.

"You may proceed," Lord Kishar said.

Zak exchanged glances with Gil but said nothing as he waved the human volunteers forward. They took the lords first, then lifted the first of the commoners, who was the pilot.

The next fae was a short pukel, the king's secretary, Nik, so the barge had obviously made a stop at the moon. Shalla, who had refused to wait at the school, cried out and ran forward. She grabbed the pukel's hand and touched it to her cheek, then walked to the closest bus beside the soldier carrying him.

"Well, well," Gil said. "The pukel and the sirin? Who would have guessed."

Since Zak had seen their farewell on the ship, she had, but it was none of her business. And on Earth, with new rules and no need for old traditions, maybe the two of them would have a chance to be together. Maybe all of them had a chance for a new life.

"Zee." Gil grabbed her arm and pointed. "There he is."

Unable to see over the soldiers, she bent sideways to see around them. Father was just being scooped from an upper bunk. Zak stepped forward and beckoned the soldier. He obediently brought Father to her, but Father was still scanning the area. His gaze brushed across her and kept going.

"Father," Zak croaked.

With a start, he focused on her. "Zak?" he whispered. He examined her from head to toe and back again, eyes wide. "Is that you?"

"Welcome to Earth." Zak bit her lip and looked down. He wouldn't understand why she had betrayed his efforts to hide her.

But she didn't need to hide anymore. She was competent and brave, like a girl. She looked up and met his eyes. "Hello, Father."

He smiled through tears, holding his arms wide. With a sob, she threw herself into his embrace.

Well, dear author, that's a very nice happy ending!

Sure is. Glad you liked it.

Are you going to ruin it in the next book? *angry glare*

I'm sure nothing could possibly be ruined in a book called The War of the Fae. Right? Turn the page for a sneak peek!

THE WAR OF THE FAE

The Earth-Fae treaty is almost complete when rogue highborns halt negotiations.

In an effort to discover why cooperation failed, the ambassadors agree to spy. Before they can uncover the lords' plot, the ambassadors are imprisoned or disappear.

Determined to save the treaty, the prince finally comes out of hiding.

But his enemies already tried to assassinate him and will surely try again. Even if his allies can protect him, they first must rescue the ambassadors to prevent them from becoming hostages when he claims his throne.

But the lords declare him an imposter and command the fae to conquer Earth.

*In a brilliantly imagined blend of sci-fi, mythology, and character-driven adventure, teens fight to stop a war before monsters enslave Earth. The War of the Fae is the fourth book in the **Return of the Fae** series of clean YA contemporary fantasy with a dash of sci-fi & mythology, from the author of **Unexpected Heroes**, and is best read in order for the most enjoyment.*

Get it now! https://books2read.com/b/warofthefae

Still want more? Get free stories by joining my newsletter. Every two weeks, I chat about my current writing or my life & offer book news and deals. And did I mention free stories?

Sign up at MCLeeBooks.com.

Free story #1: Spotting the Fae

Zak is considered too young to navigate the spaceship, even though he's the best among the fae.

On Earth, Gaby loves math and helping her astronomer Mama with her data.

When Mama spots a new asteroid heading toward Earth...

Everything will change.

The author of **Unexpected Heroes** *returns with a startlingly plausible blend of sci-fi, mythology, and the modern world.* **Return of the Fae** *is a clean YA contemporary fantasy series where fae from space don't match Earth's legends.*

Free Story #2: The Cat's Fortune

On another world, so long ago that truth has faded into legend, a cat and a boy seek their fortune together. You think you know the story, but do you?

Orphaned and homeless, young Aktar travels to the city of Rapata for a better life.

But it seems the rumors of gold-paved streets are false. Can he find a home and a job before he starves? Maybe with the help of a foundling kitten.

A retelling of Puss in Boots and Dick Whittington, with timeless themes of belonging, courage, and self-discovery, set on the fantasy world of Kaiatan, home of the **Unexpected Heroes**.

Please leave an honest review on any retailer or reader site. Seriously, it would really help me. :)

If you found a typo, you're welcome to report it at mcleebooks.com/report-a-typo/

Character List

Humans
Mr. Abernathy: language teacher
James Anthony: Major General
Artur, Takis, & Vasil Antonakis: Nikos's cousins
Damianos Antonakis: Nikos's dad
Marina Antonakis: Nikos's mom
Nikolaos Antonakis: 18-year-old Greek student, semi-adopted by Fitches,
"Nikos" or "Nik"
Craig Beltran: tech teacher
Yuri Berezin: Russian exchange student
Officer Burnett: animal control
Jinyuan Chung: Chinese-American student, "Jin"
Emil Compton: U.S. State Dept
Okoro Dambe: Nigerian refugee student
Helen Ellison (Fitch): Alex & Ian's mother
Clyde Farrell: Office of International Affairs
Alexandria Fitch: 16-year-old student, "Alex"
Ian Fitch: 13-year-old student, "U.N."
Troy Fitch: Alexandria & Ian's father

Callie Hahn: science teacher
Touji Kihara: Japanese exchange student, "Two"
Kirill Kovalenko: Ukrainian exchange student
Marguerite: school security guard
Raquel Maxwell: military linguist & principal
Gabriela Ortiz: 14-year-old local student, "Gaby"
Therese Ortiz: astronomer & Gaby's mother
Allan Riggs: Compton's secretary
Iris Rowland: reporter
Tricia Stafford: refugee specialist

Fae
Arishaka: prior king of the fae
Ashur: dryad, Gil's friend, "Abe"
Azidaka: baby dragon
Dagan: prior chief guard, Gil's grandsire
"Freya": Zak's highborn roommate
Gil: 15-year-old wolf shifter
Izdu: gremlin, chief navigator, Zak's father, "Ike"
Kishar: fae lord, Arishaka's cousin
"Lili": gorgon security guard
Maia: wolf shifter, Gil's mother, "Meg"
Merodach: fae healer, "Miles"
Miknon: pixie, Gil's adopted sister
Nashuja: hydra, "Nate"
Nik: pukel, king's secretary
Ram: wolf shifter, Gil's twin brother, "Rafe"
Shalla: sirin, king's housekeeper, "Chantelle"
Sharrukin: 16-year-old fae prince, "Shar" or "Shaun"
Taras: naga, king's Companion (chief guard), "Tom"
"Wes": highborn student
"Vince": troll student
Zaidu: fae lord
Zak: 16-year-old gremlin, youngest navigator, "Zee"

Places

Ki: the intended new home of the Fae; Earth

Kunisu: the old home of the Fae

New Kunisu: the flagship of the Fae fleet

ACKNOWLEDGMENTS

Thanks to my critique group for their usual spot-on comments: Carol Malone, Donna Gonzales, Gail Porter.

Also thank you to my fabulous alpha and beta readers: Jessica Ecklund, Lea Carter, Molly Morrison, Ry, Vickie Grider, & Virginia Cummings.

Special thanks to Annette Hamm of CHCH for correcting my TV scene, to Robin Cranney for once again teaching me about the military, and to Hanna Mecham for adding Pennsylvania color. If there are still mistakes, they are my own.

About the Author

Marty C. Lee told stories for most of her life, but never took them seriously until her daughter asked her to write one for her. Between writing and spending time with her family, she reads, embroiders, paints-by-number, and gardens.

She has lived in five states (including Colorado), seven cities, and eleven houses so far. She knows bits of two extra languages, but some days can't even speak her native tongue fluently. She isn't any kind of athlete but does have sneaky ninja (or fairy) feet. Though not an extrovert, she does have friends besides her books. You are welcome to write to her as a new friend. :)

You can find her at MCLeeBooks.com and on Facebook and book sites.

www.ingramcontent.com/pod-product-compliance
Lightning Source LLC
Chambersburg PA
CBHW031226020726
47499CB00002B/657

9 781950 230426